The Cockatoo Called

Also By Rachael Rawlings

Dearly Departed

Dearly Remembered

Dearly Beloved

The Parrot Told Me

The Cockatoo Called

Rachael Rawlings

Hydra Publications

Copyright © 2015 by Rachael Rawlings
All rights reserved.

This book or any portion thereof
may not be reproduced or used in any manner whatsoever
without the express written permission of the publisher
except for the use of brief quotations in a book review.

Printed in the United States of America

ISBN-13: 978-1-942212-32-4

Hydra Publications
Goshen, KY 40026

www.hydrapublications.com

Dedication

This one is for you, Heather and Thad!
To my sister and brother and their wonderful families, it's a wonderful thing to say that I love my siblings and know that they would do anything for me, as I would for them.
Our little adventure have led me to many of my book's characters, all my quirky parrots and fuzzy companions.
Much love.

RACHAEL RAWLINGS

CHAPTER ONE

Ainsley turned off the water to the kitchen sink and wiped her hands on the towel. Another meal completed in solitude. She tried to ignore the feeling of aloneness. The dishes were done, her kitchen tidied up and ready for the morning, the coffee maker already filled and ready to greet her with that fantastic fragrance of fresh coffee. From her place at the sink, she could look out on her property, during the day a warm landscape of mature trees turning from green to gold to amber, flashes of scarlet and orange.

But tonight outside the window, the October night was picking up a chill. She looked out into her dim back yard as the leaves danced with the wind. A cold front was coming, bringing with it a chilly rain for the next day. She shivered a little even though it was warm inside. A dash of movement, a white flutter caught her attention, and she leaned closer to the glass. What was that? It wasn't paper, captured by a gust of wind, or tumbling trash. It was moving of its own accord, against the wind, a hopping fluttering motion. Then it had to be something alive, something with wings. A bird for sure. A chicken? It almost made her smile to imagine some wayward poultry whipped up by the wind and carried into her yard Wizard of Oz style. But then she thought of the chill and the threat of rain and frowned. If it was a lost animal, perhaps she should check on it. She had no pets of her own. Since the move from her apartment close to her parent's home to her first self-owned property in Louisville, she had spent most of her time trying to get used to her new home and new job as a secretary for the dentist's office. In her free time, she had taken hours to make her house more habitable with plenty of vibrant paint colors and throw rugs. She had no roommate to comment on her decorating; she liked living alone. She had fostered a cat for about a week, but then his forever home had become available, and she had reluctantly let them pick him up. She sighed now. She hadn't had time to fully furnish her new place, much less adopt an animal for

THE COCKATOO CALLED

companionship, but she was coming to realize that sometimes it wasn't good to live alone.

She hurried to her back door and swung it open, looking through the darkness to the lawn beyond. Her neighborhood was an old one, filled with mature trees that stretched long limbs across the lawn like a giant canopy of green in the summer. But in the autumn, with many of the leaves falling in multicolored heaps, the branches looked more like a cage shielding the earth from the moon's glow.

She opened the flimsy screen door and stepped out into the darkness, her feet landing first on the few steps of concrete and then sinking into the damp earth. As she grew closer, the shape continued to flutter in the wind. Definitely something alive, she thought to herself. The white figure gradually grew more distinct, and she realized that it was a bird. But not a chicken. It was a big white thing; its feather's puffing in the gusts, a great black beak thrust into the wind. When it caught sight of her, it cocked its head so that one round, dark eye appraised her from its place on the ground. She stopped and stared. This was no chicken, no duck, but some parrot. It was a tropical bird. Her mind shuffled through her limited knowledge of avian facts. A parrot, yes, an amazon? No, that wasn't it. A macaw was a bigger, colorful bird, and then there were the green ones. The little ones at the pet shop were parakeets, and their larger cousins with the tuft of feathers atop their heads, the gray or white ones were, her mind stuttered, cockatiels. Cockatoo! That was it. This bird was a...

"Cockatoo!" The plume of feathers on his head rose as she said the word aloud as though to assure her of the title. He turned his head to examine her with his other eye then started walking toward her in an odd waddling gait, his feathers fluffing in the wind.

She stood very still, uncertain as to what he was doing. He was coming toward her faster now, eyes going first to the ground, the damp grass and fallen leaves, and then up in her direction. She was afraid to move. She didn't know if birds attacked, but this thing had a huge beak, and she was pretty sure he could bite hard.

Once at her feet, he lifted one dark claw and placed it atop her tennis shoe. With the same hesitant move, he bolstered his body up and climbed until one sharp talon was planted in the leg of her jeans while the other tangled in her shoe laces. Moving as though familiar with the motion, he used his beak to grab the fabric of her jeans and climbed, beak to foot and beak again until he had reached her middle where her heavy sweatshirt draped almost to her hips.

"Um, okay, Birdie," she said, her voice soft and strained. "You can stop now. Stay. Birdie, stay." She couldn't believe she was ordering him around like a dog, but she was terrified to move. If she tried to shake him off, he might bite her. Or, worse, she might hurt him. If she ran, he could certainly chase her. He could fly, couldn't he? And what was his intention? If a bird did want to attack you, did it climb your clothes to do it?

She heard the bird give a soft, gravelly mumble as it began to climb her shirt. She felt the claws dig into the material, but they didn't graze her skin. Then he stopped climbing and ducked his head, the tuft of soft feathers just reaching her chin. His wings fluttered out slightly, and she felt him press up against her like a puppy would cuddle close.

"Bird?" she softly said. He was very still, but she thought she could feel his body trembling. She slowly raised a hand and placed it so gently against the creature's feathered back. She thought that he was shaking. After a moment of stillness, she realized that he was shivering. When she laid her hand more firmly on his back she could tell that under all of the soft fluffy feathers, his body felt fragile and light.

"You're cold!" she exclaimed. Parrots were tropical birds, weren't they? They certainly weren't from Kentucky where the temperature could go from a balmy seventy something degrees to the forties in a few hours. "Okay, we'll go inside," she mumbled and slowly turned back toward the house.

The bird clung to her as she opened the back door and then closed it behind her, shutting out the wind and the dark. In the kitchen, it was cozy and warm, and she sighed now from relief. The bird shifted a little but still stayed planted in her heavy shirt.

"What do we do now?" she asked.

The bird did not reply. She hadn't expected that he would. So now her problem had changed. What did one do with a lost parrot? If she had found a dog or a cat she might have called the veterinarian or the Humane Society. But would there be any open at this late hour? And frankly, who else could she call? She slowly and gingerly walked to the table and picked up her cell phone. The brightened screen seemed to catch the parrot's eye, and he turned to look at it more closely. As she held it in her hand, he began to stretch away from her and towards the phone, leading with that impressive beak, his black claws still buried in the material of her shirt. She put the phone on the table in front of her before he could touch it.

"Okay, now Bird," she admonished, "you can't have my phone." She carefully bent over the table and the bird, to her surprise, flopped onto the table, using feet and wings to stand upright. He headed quickly

THE COCKATOO CALLED

toward her phone in a scrambling hop step, and she snatched it up and backed away from the table a few steps. He stood on the edge of the table; bright eye directed her way, watching her with interest.

"Distraction," she said. "I need to distract you now, Bird." She looked at her cabinets as though appraising their contents through the wooden doors. "What do parrots eat?" She thought of the many "Polly want a cracker" jokes and opened one door. Inside was an assortment of crackers she had bought from the organic foods aisle of the grocery. Low salt, less flavor, they had seemed like a good idea at the time.

"Whole wheat," she muttered and tore the package open. The bird was watching her every move. She smiled. "Okay, so let's see what you think." She held the cracker out carefully and watched as the bird waddled over and took it gingerly in its beak. Using its foot to hold the treat, it proceeded to demolish the cracker into fine crumbs spread out on the table.

"You like that, huh?" she asked and took out a second one. "You might be getting thirsty," she said as she put the cracker on the table while she went to get a bowl. She chose a plastic bowl, yellow and blue polka dotted, and filled it with water. The bird dropped his half eaten cracker and rushed to the bowl, first eagerly leaning over it to dip in his beak, then lifting his foot and in a quick motion, attempting to stand. But the bowl, even with the water, wasn't heavy enough to keep him steady and the bowl flipped, splashing bird and table with the contents. He skittered back from the mini-flood and looked at her reproachfully.

"I didn't know you would stand on it!" she exclaimed. Then she laughed at herself. She grabbed a towel to mop up the mess but soon realized that the bird had other ideas. Like a puppy with a pull toy, he caught the side of the rag in his beak and tried to tug it from her grasp. Flipping with wings and funny hops, he played with the towel until most of the water had been sopped up.

"You are a mess," she said holding in a smile. She pulled out a heavy crockery bowl to put water in and then got out some all-natural cereal and spilled it out on the table with a few more crackers. While he ate, she pulled out her phone again. Technology like this was her friend. With ease built on practice, she pulled up the voice recognition program and told it to search for veterinary hospitals closest to her location. The list was short. She carefully scanned through the listings, finally finding one local vet that was open 24 hours, and hit the icon to dial the number.

The voice on the other end of the line was rather strained as she gave a quick greeting.

"Hi," Ainsley began, keeping a watchful eye on her new visitor.

"Um, I live about a block away from your office, and I have found a parrot on my lawn. I think he's lost. I mean, I know he's lost," she felt flustered.

"A parrot? Are you sure it's not a native bird?" The woman sounded like she had had a few too many cups of coffee and not enough sleep.

"I'm sure. He's a cockatoo, I think."

"Hold on just a second," the woman said absently. Ainsley could hear her cover the mouthpiece with her palm and call out to someone else, her voice muffled. "Just put him there!" she yelled and returned to the phone. "You said it's a cockatoo?" she asked.

"It's white and it has funny feathers on its head." Ainsley was studying the bird as he spread more crumbs over the tabletop.

"Is it large or small?"

"Big," she exclaimed. "It's as big as a small cat."

The woman paused. "Okay, sorry, that sounds about right. If you can give me a moment, I'll ask if anyone has reported a missing bird." The wait felt like hours. Ainsley was looking at the bird as he dipped one of the crackers into the water bowl when the woman came back on the line. "I've got no reports here," she said. "But it has been a crazy day. We don't have any reports from today or yesterday. I can continue to check around."

"Should I put up signs? Put it in the paper or on Craigslist?"

"Oh, no," the woman responded quickly. "There are people out there that would take him just because exotic birds are worth money. Let me look into it. Can I call you back tomorrow? By then I'll know if he's been reported missing with anyone else."

Ainsley frowned. "Sure, yes, that would be fine. I'll give you my number."

The woman on the other end of the line repeated back the number that Ainsley gave her and then hesitated. "I'll be in around four since my shift starts late, but I'll leave a note for the day staff. I'm sure that the owner will be looking, and we should hear something by then."

Ainsley heard a disruption in the background of the vet clinic, and the woman muttered an exclamation. With a breathless voice, she quickly said goodbye, leaving Ainsley standing with the phone in her hand. She stared at the blank screen, watching as the red phone symbol flickered away, replaced by the clock and background. It looked like she was on her own for now.

The cockatoo had completely demolished his crackers and was busy chewing on the edge of the table, leaving huge gouges in the wood

THE COCKATOO CALLED

when she looked up.

"Hey, stop that!" Ainsley cried out.

He stopped his gnawing and headed back toward her. She stuffed her phone in her pocket and went to the kitchen cabinet.

"You can play with these," she said and dropped a plastic set of measuring cups on the table. She didn't know what birds liked to play with, but if a puppy would play with them, then maybe he would too. He eagerly hopped close to the new brightly colored cups and studied them with the funny sideways look that he practiced. Then he caught one up in his beak, bobbing up and down, making a clatter whenever the cup hit the table. While he was busy with his new 'toy', Ainsley pulled her phone out again and pulled up the search function. She started by asking what a cockatoo might eat. The device responded with a list of websites, and she chose one of the most promising. She found some informational passages and highlighted the text, letting her phone read the facts aloud as she watched the bird play. She soon became overwhelmed with the descriptions. It seemed that parrots ate a whole lot of different foods, from fruits and nuts to some mysterious 'birdy bread' that owners made.

"Okay, well, we'll have to settle for this tonight," she told him, passing him a few more crackers. It was getting late. She didn't have to be at the office until late in the morning, but she had worked an especially long day today and was getting sleepy. What to do with her new friend? She probably would only have him for the night, so she just needed a way to keep him contained. However, he did seem to be fairly destructive, if the gouges from her table and the dents in the plastic were any indications.

Slowly she stood and walked to the basement door, swinging it open and stepping down the bare wooden treads. Only parts of the basement were finished, a carpeted area with a desk and computer, and a tiled space with an abandoned treadmill and outdated television. The rest of the room was storage. She flipped on the light and looked over the wooden shelves, skipping over stacks of old towels, pots and pans dusty and abandoned, some well-worn books with cracked spines, finally seeing the cat carrier. She had used it for the month that she had fostered the cat and then cleaned it out and put it down in storage. She had hoped to get another pet eventually and thought that she might be able to use the cage. Now she studied it critically. It wasn't beautiful, but the combination of heavy plastic and wire would be safe for the bird. She picked up the carrier by the plastic handle and carried it up the stairs, emerging into the little hall next to the kitchen. The bird hadn't moved. He perched in the middle of the cracker crumbs, the wadded towel tossed to one side while he worked on the plastic rims of the measuring cups, chewing them until they were ragged.

She used paper towels to wipe the dust out of the cat carrier and then lined the floor with paper. She had seen that much when she had visited the pet shops. She picked up the heavy crock, dumped out the water with cracker crumbs floating on the surface, and added new water. She put it in the carrier as well. Next she took a small stack of crackers and put them in the carrier.

"What else would you like?" she asked the bird.

He responded by looking at her with one bright eye.

"Okay," she put the carrier down on the table next to him. "Go on in, birdy."

He looked into the cat carrier but didn't move toward it.

Ainsley felt a flash of concern. She hadn't thought this far ahead. This might just be a problem. "Now how do I get you in?" Pushing him might make him mad or scared. But she couldn't just let him stay there. She looked behind her at the cabinet top. She kept a bowl of fruit sitting out, and among the choices were a few bananas and apples. She went to grab an apple and used a knife to cut off a slice, bright red peel like a slash of lipstick. She held it out to the bird. "What do you think?"

He looked more interested, giving a little skip hop toward her and the carrier. She brought the apple slice a little closer to the crate and waited. With slow suspicion, he crept a few steps. She let him nibble a bit off the flesh of the apple and waited until he came for more before she tucked it inside the crate. His body language conveyed that he was unsure about the crate. She could almost see him considering his options. To go in it to get the treat? To risk the possible dangers in that strange place? In the end, his stomach won, and he scurried into the carrier. As he was feasting on the apple, she closed the wire door slowly so she wouldn't startle him. She would have sworn the look he gave her was accusatory.

"Sorry, but I have to go to bed!" she exclaimed. She considered him in the crate. Now what? If she left him in here, she wouldn't hear him if he got in trouble. For now, he seemed to be a quiet bird. She didn't know if that was going to last because she had learned in her research that parrots, especially large ones, were notoriously loud.

Still thinking about her options, she went to the door back door and engaged the lock. Slowly, she went around the house, extinguishing lights and locking doors, checking on everything as was her habit. When she returned to the kitchen, she could hear the bird crunching on crackers again. She carefully picked up the carrier and took it into her bedroom,

THE COCKATOO CALLED

settling it on the floor where she could have a clear view from her place on the bed. She would have a quick shower, and they would go to sleep. At least she hoped that he would cooperate. And tomorrow she would find his owners, his home, and her life would go back to normal.

CHAPTER TWO

Morning dawned warm and soft. So soft. Something tickled her nose, and Ainsley brought a hand up to her face, hearing a soft rumble. Her eyes blinked open and she looked up at the ceiling. It was still early, but she wasn't going into work, at least not yet because…

She turned her head quickly catching her breath. Tucked up against her pillow like a ball of feathers, the bird turned and cocked his head at her, his round eye studying her quizzically.

"Oh, my," she breathed. "Well, there you are. How in the world?" She sat up and looked toward the closet where the carrier had rested. The wire door wasn't opened. Not at all. Instead, the bird must have found some weakness in the heavy plastic and started chewing his way out of his confinement. Crumbles of plastic littered the floor and were scattered across the small braided rug next to her bed. A plop of bird poop was on the wooden floor by the bed, another amid the mess from the carrier. Cracker crumbs mixed with torn newspaper decorated the floor as well.

The hole in the carrier was big enough to allow a softball to fit through, and this was obviously the exit that he had taken.

She sat up in bed and muttered an expletive that her mother wouldn't appreciate. Then she sighed. "Okay, so now what?" She asked the bird. Hearing her voice, he responded by strutting over to her and snuggling against her side.

"So maybe some breakfast," she said conversationally. The bird remained tucked under her arm like a feathered puppy. "So how to get you from here to there?"

She slowly slid her legs over until her feet brushed the floor. Keeping the blanket still wound in a nest with the bird tucked within, she stood. When he felt her move, the bird tumbled out from under the blankets and stood, his neck stretching in a completely silly way.

"Do you want me to pick you up?" she asked. She had no idea

how to do that, but she bent over, offering her arm. As though he had done it hundreds of times, the bird caught her sleeve with his foot, and using his beak as an extra grip, climbed until he perched on her forearm.

"Okay," she said straightening. "Now how do I keep you from falling off?" With one nervous hand, she cupped her fingers over his silky back, feeling the slight weight of him. As soon as she started to move, though, he did as well, swiftly climbing from her arm toward her shoulder. She stopped at the doorway as she felt him grab her sleeve and pull himself up to her shoulder. Now that was not going to work! She couldn't have this animal that she barely knew sitting that close to her vulnerable face. And besides that, she had seen what he could do with his beak. She certainly wasn't going to risk a bite.

"Um, down Bird," she said, trying to sound firm. She felt a flutter of feathers as he shuffled and preened. She couldn't see him well unless she turned her head, and it wasn't good to be that close up anyway. She started walking down the short hall, thinking that perhaps if she made it into the kitchen, she could lure him off of her shoulder with a bribe.

She heard him making comfortable little mumbling sounds and felt the warmth of his head and the hard curve of his beak as he nibbled at a strand of her hair.

"You don't have to fix my hair for me," she said, her voice a little breathless. She walked to the cabinet and plucked an apple from the bowl. He liked those, she knew. She opened the drawer, all the while, feeling the little nibbles on her neck and thinking of that huge beak.

She cut the apple into four slices and then held up one slice. From her shoulder, there was a shift and movement. Then a growly voice told her, "good bird." With a sigh, she felt the bird climb back down her arm, docilely perching on her wrist while he took the piece of apple in one clawed foot. "Good bird," he told her again, and she decided that that was what she was in his book, a good bird.

*****

Breakfast was a messy affair. After she had managed to transfer the bird onto the table using the apple as persuasion, she glanced at her cabinets. After a little contemplation, she chose to make oatmeal after seeing online that it was an appropriate birdy choice, and placed a bowl on the table, unsweetened, for the bird to try. She made a second bowl for herself, adding milk and sugar, and sat down at the end of the table.

As soon as she picked up her spoon, he left his food and scurried over to her place. Before she could think of what he was doing, he had dipped his beak into her bowl and taken a large bite of her breakfast.

"Hey!" she protested. "You have your own!" He scooted closer to her bowl, and she picked it up from the table before he could have seconds. "No, bird," she said, trying to sound firm. "Mine!" But she had to laugh. He looked so silly with oatmeal spread on his black beak; his head cocked so that he could eye her from his place on the table.

She stood and took her bowl to the counter. There, she ate around the part that he had sampled; leaving a glop in the middle that might have 'bird germs'. She wasn't sure what a bird might be carrying, germ wise, but she wasn't willing to take that risk.

After breakfast, she went back into her room to survey the damage. She needed to go out, if, for nothing else, she needed to get supplies for her new temporary roommate. And now she had no way to take him anywhere. The cat carrier was toast.

"How can I fix this?" she asked the perching bird. He viewed her from his place on the chair back in the kitchen. She plopped the carrier on the table and studied it. There would be no fixing it. But she couldn't let him run rampant in the apartment.

In the end, she cut a large square out of a cardboard box and fitted it onto the outside of the crate. Next she used duct tape to strap the cardboard in place. She stepped back and looked at her work. It was fine. Okay, it was a mess, but it would hold him. It might hold him, she mentally amended. She flicked the cardboard experimentally. If she left him in the cat carrier and headed out, how long would it take him to nibble his way out? Without her watching, she imagined he would be out in a few minutes, and that was being generous. The rest of his time would be spent sculpting her woodwork into something new and different, and painting her hardwood floor with poop stains.

"Guess what," she announced. "You and I are going out!"

She quickly dressed and started to comb out her hair. The blond curls seemed to have a mind of their own, so she pulled it back tightly in a ponytail at the nape of her neck. She was brushing her teeth when she noticed motion out of the corner of her eye. The cockatoo came strutting in, stopping to look at her as though questioning what was taking her so long.

"How did you find me?" she asked. No, her house wasn't that big, but it seemed amazing that he had tracked her down. "You didn't want to wait anymore?" she asked him.

He didn't respond, but kept looking at her, then waddled into the bathroom. When he looked like he might chew on the cabinet, she bent down. She put her hand out, hesitantly, and watched with amazement as he climbed onto her outstretched fingers. She slowly stood as though she thought he might flutter off, but found that he didn't seem inclined to do that at all. She walked gingerly into her room and slipped on her shoes. When she brought her hand closer to her chest, he leaned against her, and she smiled slightly. This was not how she would have ever dreamed a parrot would behave, but she figured she had a lot to learn.

Once back to the kitchen, she looked appraisingly at the crate. How to get him in? It had worked by baiting him the first time she had attempted it, so she would try that again. She went to the refrigerator and opened the door. She and the bird peered inside.

"Hmm, so anything look good?" He didn't comment so she reached in and took out an apple. It had worked before, she figured that it might work again. She carried it to the counter and pulled a knife out of the drawer, working one handed. Gently she pried the bird off of her shirt and put him on the table, almost laughing as he skittered around on the slick surface. Quickly she cut the apple in half and then carved off a slice. She took the piece and showed it to the bird, watching with interest as he eyed the treat and then moved purposefully toward her as though he knew exactly what it was. She took the apple and tossed it into the rear of the crate and grinned as he followed. She quickly closed the door and listened as he clucked and chattered as he sampled the apple.

Outside, she hurriedly locked her front door one handed and rushed to the car. The rain from the night before had cooled the air, but the clouds were gradually giving way to a pale blue sky. She set the crate on the passenger seat of the car and turned it so that she could look through the wire door. The bird was peering out at her, still clutching the remnants of the apple.

"We're going to the pet store. Maybe they can give us the right kind of food for you," she informed him, feeling a little silly for talking to him. But parrots talked, didn't they? And they were smart. Obviously he was. So okay, she might look a little strange holding a full conversation with him, but then again, people talked to their dogs and cats all the time.

Feeders Supply was a locally owned pet store that featured a few small animals for sale, some rescue dogs for adoption, and lots of pet food. She carried the crate toward the cash registers and put it on the counter.

"Can I help you?" If the girl was out of high school, she hadn't been out long. Ainsley frowned and glanced around.

"Do you have anyone who specializes in birds?" she asked,

gesturing to the bird peering through the crate.

"Oh, how beautiful!" the girl exclaimed. "Is that your bird?"

"Um, sort of," Ainsley responded, feeling awkward. She remembered the warning from the woman at the vet hospital. She didn't want it spread around that she was looking for the owner, but she also wanted to find the bird's home.

"Well let me go get Patti," the girl said grinning. "She's our bird expert."

She left Ainsley staring into the crate while the cockatoo eyed her and made soft grinding sounds. When the girl returned, talking animatedly with gestures and punctuated by giggles, she had a lady in tow. Patti was slightly older, falling gently into middle age with warm blue eyes and a soft smile. As soon as she saw the crate, her eyes lit up with delight.

"Look at you, you beautiful bird!" she exclaimed. "Can he come out?"

"Sure," Ainsley said, shrugging.

This woman seemed very sure of herself, however, and she opened the wire door without hesitation and called to the bird. "Come on out, baby!"

The bird quickly tumbled out.

"Do you want some skritches?" Patti asked.

Ainsley raised her eyebrows at this question, thinking that she knew what she thought the term meant, but hadn't heard it before. However, the bird seemed to know exactly what she meant, and he bent his head as Patti gently stroked the feathers around his neck and his cheeks.

"So is it a male or female?" Patti asked, glancing at Ainsley.

"Actually," Ainsley said honestly, "I don't know."

"Haven't had him sexed yet?"

Ainsley looked at her blankly. "Not exactly." Another customer came in, and the young cashier went over to help them. Left by herself with the more knowledgeable Patti, Ainsley decided to explain. "I actually found him, or her. He was in my backyard last night."

"Really?" Patti said with shock. "Outside, in this weather?"

"He came right up to me and climbed up my leg. I decided to take him in because it was so cold. Now I need to find his owners, but a lady at the veterinary hospital is trying to look for me. She suggested that I not advertise too much in case someone tries to take advantage of the situation."

"Well, poor guy," Pattie said. She gently pulled at one of the

THE COCKATOO CALLED

bird's wings, spreading the feathers to reveal lovely yellow feathering beneath. His wings also looked a little odd to Ainsley. "He's had his wings clipped, so he didn't fly far," she said conversationally. The bird let her gently examine him, rubbing his face against her hand in a friendly way. "But they can fly some with clipped wings. He's not too old either," she said.

"How can you tell?"

"His beak and feet. As they get older, their feet get more rough and scaly. But age on a bird like this can vary a whole lot. They can live to be 80."

"80 years old!" Ainsley exclaimed.

"They can." Patti gently fluffed up the bird's crest. "He's in good shape. Probably wasn't out on his own too long. But he is lucky. Birds like this can be caught by dogs, cats, some wild animals, hit by cars, they just don't know how to take care of themselves." She looked at the cat carrier and smiled. "So you did a little interior decorating?" she asked.

"He got out this morning and came to bed with me," Ainsley admitted.

"Really?" Patti still looked amused. "So is that what you're keeping him in?"

"I did for last night, but I don't think it's going to hold him." Ainsley gently stroked the bird at his neck, feeling the silky feathers.

"So you're planning on keeping him until you can find his owner?"

Ainsley hadn't considered what she would do from this point. She knew that she didn't want to take him to the pound or the Humane Society. She would hold onto him and keep him at her home rather than doing that. "I guess I will. I figure that his owner should be found pretty quickly. I mean, how many people around here would have one of these?"

"Not that many," Patti agreed. "But I don't think you can keep him in here anymore." She gestured pointedly to the wrecked carrier.

"I think you're right," Ainsley agreed.

Patti looked thoughtful. "You know, I have a cage at home that you could use until you find his home," she said. "It's not beautiful, but it's safe, and he shouldn't be able to escape."

Ainsley hadn't thought very far ahead, but suddenly the idea had real promise. She was enjoying her new roommate, but knew it wasn't going to last. She didn't want to invest a ton of money to get him settled in just for the limited time he would be with her. But she didn't want to give him up just yet. "That would be wonderful!" she exclaimed.

"Then you can come by my house this evening when I'm off work," Patti said. "I'll get the cage cleaned up, and you can take it with you. In the meantime, do you have any other supplies?"

Ainsley realized very quickly that she had a lot to learn. Birds did not eat seeds, or at least, not exclusively. There were recipes that you could make for your feathered friend, but for a beginner, there were pellets that made a good base for their diet. Chocolate and caffeine were a no-no. As were most junk food. Although Patti admitted that some parrots she knew had a particular weakness for pizza or French fries. A cart was brought out, and they started to add what were the basics for bird ownership. The bird himself was being completely spoiled by a trio of store employees who were passing him around for skritches, apparently what you called petting the bird.

"And you'll need toys for him," Patti said, gesturing to the long rack of dangling objects with shiny bells and sprouting wooden sticks and what looked like straw. "These are on clearance," she pronounced, pulling down three. The toys consisted of a chain with a hook on the top to hang from the cage. Blocks of wood and some stuff that looked suspiciously like colored rawhide that you might give to a dog was strung on the chain. At the bottom of two was a metal bell, on the third a pom pom of dried grassy bits. "Make sure if he has a bell that the clacker can't be taken out. He'll like chewing on the wood," Patti assured her. "Toys can get expensive, so you can give him other things to chew on like untreated wood with no chemicals and pieces of clean cardboard."

"Okay," Ainsley said, taking the toys carefully. "And I just hang these?"

"Sure!" Patti was smiling, watching as the other employees played with the big white bird. "Let's see, and one very important thing, their respiratory system is very fragile. Never cook with nonstick Teflon. The burning pan puts off fumes that would kill him. And try to avoid scented things like candles and air fresheners. If you want something to smell nice, you can warm cinnamon and cloves on low heat on the stove." She stopped as though considering any other warnings. "And this bird is tropical. You don't want him to get too cold. And especially avoid drafts. Leaky windows or air vents can make them sick. And when a bird gets sick, it will do everything in its power to not let on. In the wild, it's for survival. Often times, by the time we realize they are sick, it's too late for treatment."

"Oh," Ainsley said, surprised. "I would have never thought of that."

"Birds are different than other pets. They have very specialized needs. They are complicated, and a lot of work, but they can be great." She hesitated, "for the right family, of course."

"Well, I have your number to call if I have any other questions." Ainsley checked her watch. "I guess I should get going. I had no idea how late it's gotten!" she said frowning. "I have a few more stops to make."

"Sure, and you can come by my house after six." They walked back up to the counter where Patti found a piece of paper and quickly wrote out her address. "I'll have the cage out and hosed off," she assured Ainsley.

"This is great," Ainsley said gratefully. "I don't know what I would have done without all of your help."

"Not a problem. Birds are one of my favorite pets." Patti pulled out her smart phone and showed Ainsley a picture on the screen. "This is Milton, my Moluccan Cockatoo. He's a big baby, and I've had him for over ten years now."

"Oh, he's gorgeous!" Ainsley said, admiring the extravagantly feathered, light peach bird. "How big is he?"

"Bigger than this guy," Patti said gesturing to the cockatoo sitting contentedly on the counter. "Moluccan's are wonderful. Messy, but wonderful."

Ainsley smiled. "I can imagine. This guy has already taken some chunks out of my furniture, redecorated my bedroom, and left crumbs pretty much everywhere he goes."

Patti grinned. "The joys of being a bird owner." She put her hand in front of the cockatoo and said firmly, "step up." To Ainsley's surprise, the bird immediately stepped onto her outstretched hand. "Okay, in the cage you go," Patti said, and smoothly slid the bird into the crate, tilted her hand until he stepped off, and pulled her hand out to close the door.

"Wow. That was easy," Ainsley said, impressed.

"You have to be sure of yourself. They are smart and need to know that you're the boss. There are lots of ways that you can train them too, like using treats as reinforcement for good behaviors. You can't punish these guys. They don't understand that kind of treatment. Beyond that, you have to remember that these are still wild animals. Dogs have been tamed and domesticated to live with us for centuries. These guys are one generation from the jungle. Keep that in mind." Patti began unloading the cart. "And now we get to pay to live with these wild things."

*****

RACHAEL RAWLINGS

Two employees helped Ainsley load her car with all of the supplies that the bird needed to have for his temporary stay. She placed the crate on the front seat again, and after she had gotten in and closed the door, she pulled out her cell phone. She was due to head into work in a few hours, but she was hoping for a reprieve. She had only had her job at the dentist's office for a little under a month. So far, it had been a very good job. She liked her co-workers and felt secure that she could work contentedly there. She didn't want to put her position in any kind of jeopardy.

She called the office as she sat in her car.

"You said you found a bird?" Nan repeated, her voice distracted.

"Yes, I found a parrot in my yard last night. I had to take him to someone for advice, but I'm keeping him until the owner shows up."

"A parrot?" Nan's voice was even more perplexed. "Ainsley, honey, people don't just find parrots in their yard."

"I know that," Ainsley replied, glancing at her companion in the seat next to hers. "I figure he must have escaped someone's home. They're probably looking for him now. I just need to babysit him until someone claims him."

"Well, we've had a few cancelations if you need the time," Nan said. "But I'd like to see this. Can you bring him by?"

Ainsley agreed after promising to stop by to show her curious co-workers her new friend, the bird. She couldn't work with him, so her stop would be a short one. And if they were okay for her to take the day off because it was going to be a slow day, it would be helpful. It wasn't like this was going to be a regular thing. She sighed in relief. For now, it would have to be a day at a time since she wasn't sure what the next day would bring.

She turned up the heater a little, thinking of Patti's warnings about temperature. She couldn't let the bird get too cold. She sighed. The bird was such an impersonal name. She didn't know his real name, and didn't know if he was like a dog that was familiar with his moniker. Then again, it might be hard to let him go if she had named him like he was her real pet.

"I'll call you Bird for now," she said looking over to the crate where he eyed her from within. "We'll just have to go with that!"

She stopped at a burger place to grab some lunch and ended up giving a piece of the bun and a French fry to her new companion. She ate with the car running to maintain the heat, and the radio switched on to give a little background noise. Bird seemed to like the music because he would occasionally break into a funny bobbing dance and cackle along.

THE COCKATOO CALLED

After she was finished, she dropped the garbage in the can by the parking lot and drove out to her office. It was close. She didn't like to drive, so she had chosen her job in part because of its proximity to home, shopping, and restaurants.

At the office, she bundled the carrier under her arm and hurried through the door into welcome warmth. Four patients sat in chairs in the waiting room, eyes glazed as they looked at their phones or paged through months' old magazines. When she rushed in with the carrier, they looked up with interest. It wasn't something that you saw all the time, someone with an animal carrier bursting into a dental office.

Theresa was a tall, dark-haired beauty with a gorgeous set of teeth that set off a fabulous smile. She had decided on becoming a dental hygienist as a child entranced by the character on 'Rudolph the Red Nosed Reindeer' Christmas specials on the television. Since then, she had won a few local beauty pageants and laid waste to scads of young men's hearts on her way to adulthood. Her current beau was a bodybuilder with tight abs and buns and a slight overbite that she considered adorable. She was leaning over the desk, one ear to the phone while she busily pecked in some information on the computer.

Nan was as short as Theresa was tall, and curvy in all the right places. She was married, a newlywed with stars in her eyes and a sharp sense of humor. She had worn braces for three years in high school, and after that had firmly believed that she had found her calling. She was bustling in from the back room and was ready to take another patient back to the chair when Ainsley arrived with Bird.

"Oh my gosh," Nan gasped, hurrying around the counter and out the side door into the waiting area so she could look in the carrier. "That thing is almost as big as my Louie!" Louie was Nan's first and treasured baby, a Shih Tzu with more sass and personality than any ten big dogs.

"He's an umbrella cockatoo," Ainsley said tilting the crate up so her friend could look inside.

"What happened to the cage?" Nan asked, peering between the wire bars.

"He ate his way out," Ainsley said grinning.

Theresa was hanging up the phone, and Ainsley walked a little closer to the counter.

"He ate his way out?" Nan said disbelievingly.

"What?" Theresa interrupted. "This is the bird you found in your yard?"

"Yep," Ainsley responded. "This is Bird. He's my temporary roommate until I can find his owner."

One of the patients, a middle-aged man with a steadily rising hairline stood and came to the counter as well, watching as Ainsley put the crate on the top and turned it to face the group.

"My Uncle had one of those when I was young," he said peering in. "It pulled its feathers out until it looked like a naked chicken."

Ainsley felt slightly offended for her companion. She saw on the internet how some of the birds had plucked feathers until they were quite the awkward creature, but their faces were sweet and the people who lived with them obviously cared very deeply for them.

"Bird doesn't do that," she said quickly, "although, if he did, I wouldn't care." She was surprised at her sense of loyalty.

The man shrugged. "They scream a whole lot too, ya know," he said as he slumped back into his seat. Theresa and Nan exchanged a funny little look and smiled.

"So how are you going to find his owners?" Nan asked.

"I have people at the vet's office working on it, and at Feeder's Supply."

"Can you let him out?" Nan asked, bravely poking her fingers in the cage. But Bird must have liked the attention, because he turned his head so that she could fluff the feathers at his neck.

"I'm not staying that long," Ainsley replied smiling.

"Shouldn't have that thing in here anyway," the balding man grumbled. "Against health code or something."

"He's not close to the patient care area," Theresa snapped.

He grunted but continued to glare at them.

"Ainsley," Deborah came from the inner patient rooms and peered around the corner. "I heard your voice."

"Hi, Dr. Blandford," Ainsley replied, seeing the dentist. As usual, she felt a flood of warmth for the woman, a gratefulness that surpassed someone's ordinary feelings for their employers. But Deborah Blandford was much more than a boss to Ainsley. In a way, she was a role model. Dr. Blandford was a great dentist who had struggled to get through dental school, fighting a poor family life and borderline poverty. Once she had graduated with her degree, she had worked hard to build up her practice. Daily, she specialized in cases that were nervous at the idea of dentistry, and was very good at keeping everyone, if not happy, then more soothed in the precarious setting. But on certain weekends she also donated her time and talent to help families who couldn't afford expensive dental work. She was just a good person, and Ainsley admired her for that. But beyond that, she had taken a chance and hired Ainsley, despite the honest truths that Ainsley had presented. And Ainsley was

THE COCKATOO CALLED

grateful for the faith that the older woman had shown her.

Now that there were several people waiting, she knew it was her cue to leave. Ainsley knew that Deborah and the other assistants were ready for more appointments, and Bird was causing a commotion.

"I'd better get going," Ainsley said quickly. "I have to get him home. But I'll see you all tomorrow."

Theresa huffed out a sigh. "Okay, see you then," she said. She leaned close to the cage and said, "we'll be seeing you again soon too," she assured him.

CHAPTER THREE

Patti's house was a comfortable brick ranch on one of the many side streets in Middletown. The driveway was a little incline down to the flat parking area where the concrete widened to an oval pad. It held one car, a late model sedan, and a large cage still glittering with water droplets from the running hose.

Ainsley checked Bird in the carrier, making sure that he hadn't loosened any of the tape holding the cardboard in place or made any holes. It appeared that he was content for his short rides, spending much of the time chewing on newspaper shreds and clinging to the cage door.

She grabbed the carrier by the handle and went to the front door, switching him to the other hand so that she could ring the bell. Patti answered almost immediately.

"I've got some towels to dry this, and then it'll be ready to go," she said cheerfully. "Do you want to put him inside here while we finish? It's a little too chilly out here for him anyway."

Ainsley nodded and handed Patti the carrier. She disappeared inside and quickly emerged with two handfuls of old rags.

"He'll hold for a little bit, but I don't trust those 'toos. They like to chew pretty much anything, and it's their favorite pastime."

"I've noticed," Ainsley agreed as they began drying the cage. The cage was really big, so after it was dried, they had to wedge it into the trunk of Ainsley's car and then tie the thing inside. After a few firm yanks to make sure that the cage was secured, Patti stepped back.

"That should do for the ride home. Do you think you can get it out by yourself?"

"Yes, I don't have many steps," Ainsley agreed still a little overwhelmed by the size of the cage. "And you said I just put paper down on the tray?"

"Yep, some newspaper and then you add in the perches." She

THE COCKATOO CALLED

pointed to a few rough pieces of wood that were anchored with a screw, washer, and wing nut set. "Put in a few toys and add the food and water. The dishes are in this bag," Pattie handed Ainsley a bag filled to the top with other items. "There's an old swing in there that he might like, and some nuts that my guy doesn't like. Walnuts. And the bowls."

"Thanks you so much for all of your help," Ainsley said looking in the bag.

"Well these are things we're not using now, so they might as well be of some use to someone," Patti said. "Now let's go get him."

Two things immediately struck Ainsley as they stepped inside Patti's house. In the corner of the room was a truly mammoth cage with a giant cockatoo tucked inside. It was larger than Bird, and it looked like it had been dipped, ever so quickly, in peach watercolors. Its eyes were as dark as Bird's, and it cocked its head and eyed them with the same inquisitive gaze that Bird had perfected.

Patti saw what had caught Ainsley's attention and grinned. "This is Milton," she said by way of introduction. "He's my baby." She was looking fondly at the creature in the cage. "He is one amazing bird."

"He's beautiful," Ainsley agreed. "Does he talk?"

"Oh yes," Patti said making a little face. "Milton has a knack for saying things exactly at the right time. His speech is very good for a 'too, but besides that, his understanding is excellent."

"Hi, Milton," Ainsley said, approaching the cage. Milton still eyed her. Ainsley noticed that there were rolled up socks at the bottom of the cage. "You give him socks to play with?" she asked curiously.

"Um, no," Patti said making a face. "He kind of took those on his own. As I was folding laundry this morning, Milty came over to keep me company and was sitting on the hamper watching. As I was rolling up a pair of matching socks, he was watching me carefully and saw where I put them." She laughed a little. "He said, 'I want,' but I told him, 'you can't have them, Milty.'" She shrugged, "so he hopped off the hamper, grabbed the pair of rolled up socks, and ran back to his cage. He can be pretty fast when he wants, but the socks were slowing him down some. He tried to climb to his perch, but he couldn't handle the socks while climbing, so they got left there. When I tried to get them, he started acting up, and with that look in his eye, I knew he wasn't going to let me get them." She sighed. "Whenever I get close to his cage, he yells, 'no, no, no'!"

"What are you going to do? Let him have them?"

"No, he'll get tired of them, and then I'll grab them when he's distracted," she said this in an undertone as though she thought he might be listening.

"You are quite the smart birdie," Ainsley said, looking at his lovely eyes.

"He is, and he's spoiled rotten," Patti said. "I can't help it, I still love him like crazy."

Ainsley was distracted from the fabulous Milton by a strange shuffling sound from the back room and a sudden increase in noise. Somewhere in the back of the house was a cacophony of tweets and trills that carried into the living room like a natural soundtrack of a rainforest.

"What is that?" Ainsley asked wonderingly.

"Those are my 'tiels," Patti replied. "I breed a few pairs of cockatiels."

"Really?"

"They're an easy bird to start with," Patti said. "Really sweet. Just a great little bird." She glanced back to the hallway. "Do you want to see one of my babies?"

"Yes," Ainsley said excitedly. She was quickly becoming fascinated with this new world of birds.

Pattie disappeared for a moment, and Ainsley could hear the increased chattering of the little birds as they greeted Patti. A minute later, she emerged. Cuddled in her hands was a sweet ball of fluff, gray and white, with a tint of orange on its birdy cheeks.

"This one will be ready to go in a few weeks," Pattie said. "You have to wait until they're done hand feeding."

"Hand feeding?" Ainsley looked puzzled.

"In the wild, the mama birds feed the babies until they're ready to take care of themselves. I let the mama's do it for a time, but then I pull them from the nest. I want them to get used to having a human flock. That way, when they find their home, they think of people as their family." She held the bird up for Ainsley to see. "Do you want to hold her?"

"Her?"

"I'm not sure at this age, but I'm betting this is a little hen." Patti took the bird and placed it in Ainsley's cradled hands. "There now," she said smiling.

The bird felt warm and incredibly soft in Ainsley's hand. "And these are related to cockatoos?" she asked.

"They are related. In fact, some recent studies have shown that cockatiels are not only in the cockatoo family, but they are most closely related to the black cockatoos. Something to do with the males and females looking different."

THE COCKATOO CALLED

"But cockatoos don't look different? The girls and the boys?" Ainsley asked.

"Not umbrellas like yours," Patti said. "At least not in any definitive way. But tiels definitely have different coloring, male to female, if you look at the normal grays. The fancier mutations aren't as clear, but with the normal grays, their cheek patches are brighter if they are a male."

"Oh, like wild cardinals. The males are bright red and the females are much duller."

"Like that," Patti agreed. As she spoke, her giant peach bird let out a squawk that could have broken glass. The bird was at the wall of the cage, feathers fluffed, bobbing. "Now you hush," Patti admonished the bird. "He gets very jealous when I don't give him enough attention."

"Wow is he loud."

"Your umbrella can be as loud," Patti said grinning. "Just wait."

"Do they talk too?" Ainsley asked, glancing toward the big bird and thinking back to her limited knowledge of birds.

"They can, and some do a whole lot. And some sing, and some just make noises. It all seems to depend on the bird itself in the cockatoo's case." She shrugged. "Most people hear about African gray parrots when it comes to talking because that is what they have become known for, but many different birds talk. The best talker recorded was a little budgie, a parakeet."

"Really?"

Patti smiled. "You'll learn a whole lot about birds once you start looking." She came over and held her hand out for the baby bird. "I'd better get their feeding started, or they're going to start crying," she said, gently cuddling the cockatiel.

"And I'd better get Bird back home and in his cage," Ainsley said, watching Patti with the baby.

"Call me if you have any questions at all," Patti said firmly. "They can be a challenge, but I think you'll have fun with him until you find his owner."

"Thanks for everything," Ainsley replied. "When I find something out, I'll call you. Then I can bring your things back."

"No hurry," Patti said, and watched as Ainsley scooped up the carrier and peered in at bird. He was working hard at chewing up some wooden sticks that Patti must have given him. Ainsley let herself out, knowing that Patti was still holding the smaller bird. She picked her way across the wet concrete and carried the bird in his carrier to the passenger side of the car to set it on the seat. She checked the security of his makeshift door and then went to the driver's side and climbed in. She had a feeling that he was very ready to get out and stretch his wings.

*****

An hour later, the cage was set in place, the oversized door hanging open. She had put the pet carrier, the cardboard still taped in place, on the little coffee table and opened the door. Bird had hustled out in that funny duck walk he had, skittering a little on the slick surface of her table and looking at her with a question in his eyes. How he could have so much expression when his face was all feathers and beak, Ainsley wasn't sure, but she could see his thoughts in every line of his body. She bent over and cooed to him.

"How do you like it, Buddy? Such a nice cage." She bent and put her arm down close to him and was pleased when he willingly stepped up. She was getting good at this! She took him close to the cage and let him look at it. After a moment, she put her arm close to the open door, and was surprised when he climbed on the door top before she could angle him into the cage itself. She frowned at him, thinking how skillfully he had outsmarted her with that move.

Ainsley had added in the rough-hewn perches, the shiny silver bowls, one filled with water and the other with the newly bought pellets, and a trio of toys. Now Bird was not even a little interested in going in to visit his new home. He continued to perch on the open door of the cage, glaring inside like he was sure that something truly evil lived within. Ainsley stepped back and looked at him, hands on her hips.

"This is where you're going to stay," she said sternly. "You can't sleep in my bed."

Bird cocked his head to look at her.

"I know that it might not look as comfortable, but Patti let us borrow it, and it was very nice of her. Now you need to use it."

Bird didn't look impressed. Nor did it appear that he was going to go into the cage willingly.

"Okay, so what do you think you would like that would get you in there?" She left him on the cage door in the living room and wandered into the kitchen. She stood at the refrigerator and looked in the harshly lit box. What did one feed a reluctant cockatoo? She heard a flurry of movement and looked down. Standing at her feet with his head cocked to look at her was Bird. She sighed.

Bird made one of his particular sounds, something like a squeak and a grumble. Ainsley leaned down and put out her hand, and Bird

THE COCKATOO CALLED

stepped up. She brought him closer to her body and cuddled him for a moment, stroking his back while she looked in the cabinets. She finally settled on some dry cereal that he looked interested in. She took him out to the cage and let him step off onto the door again. Then she poured a handful of the cereal into her palm and reached in and dropped it in the shiny bowl. Last, she took a single little piece and let Bird try it.

"Go on! There's a lot more inside. You'll like it," she assured him.

He ruffled his feathers as though irritated with her. He knew he was being tricked, but the treat was irresistible. He leaned over and swung himself, beak over feet, into the cage. While his head was in the bowl, she closed the door and latched it.

"Okay," she said smiling. "Just try it for a little while. I'll bring you another treat in a little while."

He was watching her as she left the room.

*****

Ainsley was surprised at how easily Bird fit into her life. Mornings were a cup of coffee, cereal for her and Bird, and a little shared toast. He made a mess, but he was so soft to cuddle, and he made the cutest noises. At least, when he wasn't mad.

And he did get mad. And when he did, it was a sight to see. He would bob, the cluster of feathers lifted high on his head like a crown, and start a ruckus like nothing that she had ever heard. His screams could wake the dead, no doubt. The first time he did that, she had backed off and hovered in the doorway, waiting for him to settle down. He hadn't very quickly, and she found that talking to him didn't help. When she turned her back on him but stayed in the same room, he eventually did quiet.

This behavior, however, was mercifully infrequent. His other fun was avoiding doing what she wanted him to do. When she asked him to stay on his cage, he chased after her and trailed her into the other room. When she wanted him to eat quickly, he played with his food. When she wanted him to be quiet, he yelled. When she laid out the toys for him to play with, he chose instead to chew her mail, to try for her phone, and to go after anything that had been left on the table accidently. But he was funny and charming. She enjoyed having him around.

On mornings, he would accompany her to the bathroom and watch critically while she applied the spare makeup. She would comb her blond curls and then let him nibble on his comb that she had gotten from the dollar store while she finished. He liked plastic barrettes, but she had to take away the ponytail holders so he wouldn't hurt himself with them. He had his clean plastic cup to nibble, and would slide into the sink at times, spending a few panicked moments before his flapping wings propelled him out of the sink. Finally, they would return to the living room. With bribery, he was back in his cage by the time she needed to head to work. She latched the cage, checked his water and food, and called out a goodbye.

Cheerful whistles and hoots started the evening as she walked in the back door. Bird liked to help with dinner preparation, standing on the back of one of her kitchen chairs and watching her. He got a sample of whatever seemed bird safe. Some things he liked, others he dissected, and still others thrown to the floor in avian disgust.

By the weekend, she was ready to take him out again.

On Saturday morning, she decided to go shopping again. She didn't need any supplies for Bird, but it seemed to be one safe place she could take him. She decided to go by Feeders Supply again, and then maybe catch some lunch at a little hometown restaurant that her uncle managed. She could take Bird there without any trouble, although, she suspected she would get plenty of attention.

At Feeders, there were a few of the same people that she had seen before, but Patti wasn't there. She opened the crate door and watched as Bird waddled out, ready to be adored. He seemed to love the skritches, and closed his dark eyes with pleasure. Ainsley left Bird with his audience and went down the avian aisle looking for toys or treats. She found a few discounted toys and collected them.

When she came back, Bird was cuddled up against an older man in a suit and tie, contentedly chewing on his tie.

"Oh, I'm sorry!" she said, quickening her step. "He'll ruin your suit."

"I'm not worried," he said smiling. "He's quite the friendly guy."

"He is," she replied.

"Young," he said, "I'm guessing. How old is he?"

"I don't know," Ainsley said, but then felt strangely protective. "I'm bird sitting him."

The man's cool eyes skimmed her. "Well, that's very generous of you."

She smiled politely. "And I guess we're going to head out," She said, holding out her hand for the bird.

The man seemed to release him reluctantly. Bird came to Ainsley willingly, perching on her hand and making funny little grinding

THE COCKATOO CALLED

sounds. She turned away from the man and toward the crate, praying that the bird would not embarrass her. She hadn't done this enough. She didn't know if he would cooperate with her. She tried to move with confidence, and to her utter relief, Bird allowed himself to be slipped into the crate. She quickly closed the door. When she looked up, the store workers were still circled around her, but the man was gone.

Back in her car, she tried to shake the strange feelings from the encounter. She drove slowly to her uncle's restaurant, Frisco's, and parked out front. It was a basic burger and rib place with a rustic bar at the front of the room. There were only a hand full of patrons, and she recognized a few. If anyone thought there was anything strange about her carrying the crate up to the bar, they weren't going to comment. Her uncle was a first generation Irish whose red hair was a true indicator of his temper. He was her mother's big brother, and in her mother's absence, had taken a strong parental role. Ainsley knew that he enjoyed it. He had no daughters of his own, just two mostly grown sons that would one day take over the restaurant, but for now, were enjoying college life. Maybe even having too much fun if her Uncle's complaints were to be believed. She set the crate on the bar and grinned at the bartender. Frank had been with her uncle since the beginning of the business, and he fixed her regular drink, a Shirley Temple with kick, without her ever asking. With a wink, he grabbed up a clean glass and scooped out ice as her Uncle came to greet her.

"So what's in the box, Babe?" her uncle asked. He called every woman babe, no matter her age. In this age of equal rights, Ainsley would wince when he said it to one of the young waitresses, but she needn't have worried. It didn't take most very long to understand that it was just a term of endearment, nothing meant by it but a greeting, and most seem to adopt her Uncle as an honorary family member anyway.

"Meet Bird," she said, turning the cage so that he could see the creature inside.

"What the hell is that?" he asked, humor lacing his voice.

"I told you. This is Bird. He's my temporary roommate."

"He looks more like a feather duster. Does he bite?" He leaned over closer to the cage. "Do you bite?" he asked the inhabitant. "You look like you could."

"He doesn't," Ainsley declared stubbornly. "At least he hasn't bitten me yet. Or anyone else we've been to visit."

"And what does your Mama have to say about this?" he asked, rusty eyebrows rising nearly to his equally red hair.

"I haven't discussed this with her," Ainsley explained. "It's no big deal. I'm only watching him until his owner shows up." She felt a little defensive and wasn't sure why. She felt like a child that hid a hamster, one of the neighbor's unexpected additions, for almost a week before her parents had found him.

"So this isn't like that mutt that you dragged home when you were twelve. You were only going to watch him for a night? You kept him for, what, nearly ten years? Isn't he still with your Mama?"

Ainsley flinched, reluctantly agreeing that perhaps her uncle was right. Or, maybe, slightly right, because this was not the same thing at all. "A bird like this is totally different than a stray dog. People don't just lose parrots like that. These birds are worth hundreds, or even thousands of dollars. Someone is missing him; they'll show up soon." Ainsley bent close to the cage and opened the door. "Your family will find you soon enough," she cooed to the bird.

Bird emerged from the crate with a silly tumble. Her Uncle took a little step back from the bar.

"He won't hurt you," Ainsley said quickly. "Just give him a pretzel."

Her uncle took a pretzel from the bowl on the bar and held it close enough for the bird to take.

"See, not so bad," Ainsley said smiling.

"I suppose not," her uncle replied. "Frank, come here and see this bird Ainsley has brought in here!" he called over his shoulder.

Frank approached, his head of silver hair catching the yellow of the lights above, holding her glass with the pale pink liquid. "And what's that crazy thing?" he asked, his rough voice sounding skeptical.

"Frank, meet Bird. Bird, this is Frank." She smiled at the older man's expression. "He's just staying with me for a little bit. He accidently flew into my backyard."

"And you kept him? What if he was mean? Look at that beak on that bird!" Frank was shaking his head, but placed the drink on the bar, sitting it a few feet away from where Bird was standing. Bird saw the glass and decided that it, like everything else that Ainsley had, was meant for him. He started across the wooden top in his funny strut, and Ainsley snatched the glass up.

"Oh no you don't," she scolded the bird, but she was smiling.

Bird's antics attracted people, much like walking a cute puppy in the park. Diners crowded to watch the bird as he strutted down the bar, sampling chips and pretzels. He ended up with his own snack plate of goodies, but was not quite content until he had snatched a few of Ainsley's fries as well.

THE COCKATOO CALLED

She stayed to finish her quick lunch. When she finished, she chatted with her uncle. Bird perched on the bar next to her arm, watching with interest as patrons came in, skirting the bar with curious glances. He sampled several things that other diner's offered, and Frank even brought him a drink of his own, water with a cherry floating at the top. Bird spent a few hilarious minutes trying to bob for the treat.

When it was time to leave, Frank and her Uncle had grown brave enough to pet Bird on his head as long as Ainsley held his beak down.

"We'll be back in next week," Ainsley said as she headed out. Then, when she strolled toward her car, her smile melted. There wasn't a great likelihood that the bird would ever return. By next week, he would be home.

CHAPTER FOUR

Time had led to comfort with the status quo and Ainsley was beginning to wonder if Bird's owners were ever going to claim him. Bird was quite accustomed to their life together, and Ainsley was almost sure that he was learning some words from her. Some mornings she thought she could hear him mumbling, "Time to eat, Bird."

On Saturday, Ainsley spent the day running errands and had popped a frozen dinner into the microwave. She was ready to settle down, maybe read a good book. She had just put Bird in his cage when she heard the knock on the door. She froze in place. She didn't expect anyone. She had no plans for the evening. So who was this? She peered out the peephole, noticing a shadow pacing on the front porch. It occurred to her that she could just ignore the sound. No one knew she was at home. She could just sit back down, maybe pour a glass of wine. That was a great idea. She didn't get to drink wine when Bird was out. He seemed to feel that he could sample anything that she had out on the table, so wine was a definite no-no. But he was in his cage. His grinding beak, a contented sound, was the only sign that he was still awake. Then the knock came again, and she knew that she couldn't ignore it. She opened the door a crack and peered through. The man turned, and she saw his face clearly in the yellow glow of the porch light.

He was attractive in an artsy geeky kind of way. He had a sharp jawline darkened with stubble, and his nose was a blade over a somber mouth. His hair was styled a little long and careless, but swept back from his face so that it was easy to see his eyes, a clear hazel, now greenish behind dark-rimmed glasses. He towered over her, but he held himself with slightly stooped shoulders the way tall people do when they are trying to be less conspicuous.

"Yes?"

"Ainsley Maddock?"

THE COCKATOO CALLED

"Yes," she said, her voice low, the door still standing before her like a shield.

"I'm Gabe. Gabe Donavan. I spoke with Patti at Feeder's Supply. We were talking about parrots. She told me that you had found a parrot. She said that you might have my cockatoo."

Her heart plummeted. She had wanted to find Bird's home, his worried owners. But now the idea of losing her little buddy was entirely too painful. She stood holding the door open, wordless and slightly shocked.

"I didn't think I would see her again," he said hurriedly, seeing her expression. "Dolly was taken from my home. Someone broke into my apartment and wrecked the place. I thought she was killed." His face reflected his pain at the thought, his fine brows creased over dark eyes. "But I didn't want to give up on her. I had hopes that whoever got her, stole her, well," he glanced down at his feet and then quickly back up, "that they would know she was worth money and maybe try to sell her."

"I didn't buy him," Ainsley said hastily, and then realized that she had just agreed that she had his bird. "In fact, I found the bird outside standing at back in my yard."

His face fell and he looked distressed again, shoulders slumping in slightly. "Oh, Dolly couldn't fly well. Her wings were clipped. I don't see any way that she could have made it out here."

She saw the anguish clearly in his eyes. He had cared for his pet, and someone had ripped her from him. It seemed incredible that someone would break into an apartment just to take the bird, but she supposed that stranger things had happened.

"I'm not sure how far Bird flew," she admitted. "His wings are clipped."

He shook his head. "Dolly is a terrible flyer. She never learned how, and she is still young. Almost a baby." He tucked his hands in his pocket. "She spent most of her time on a stand in my office. I work at home as an architect, and she always wanted to hang around me. I wanted her to stay close, but I had to keep her away from my computer. She would pluck the keys off the keyboard." He smiled at the memory, a sad little smile. "I would tell her to stop and she would say 'bad, bad bird.'" He smiled at the memory. "I would say, 'cut it out!'"

"Bad, bad bird!" the voice was the same gravely sound that Ainsley had heard so often, but the words were plain and easy to understand. Bird was talking back to his, no, her owner.

*****

She stepped back and let him into the house. It felt like everything had changed in that moment, and it made her feel incredibly bereft. Ainsley pasted a smile on her face and said, "I guess you were right! Bird must be yours."

"Oh, Man, I can't tell you how happy this makes me! Dolly is a wonderful bird. Really fun. But I guess you know that." He was grinning, an expression that turned his face from just attractive to gorgeous. He seemed totally unaware of this.

At the cage, Bird had plastered herself to the cage wall, black claws wrapped around the bars. Her head turned; one piercing eye watching them as they approached.

"Hey Dolly!" Gabe leaned closer. "Damn, it's good to see you."

Ainsley reached over and unlatched the cage and watched as Bird reached out one claw to grab the door and swing with it. She climbed to the top of the door and perched there. As soon as Gabe put out his hand, Bird stepped onto his fist. Gabe brought her to his chest, and Bird tucked her head under Gabe's chin. They had done this before. It was sweet, beautiful, and very sad for Ainsley.

"So you're Dolly," she said. The bird peered at her. "And a girl."

Gabe was smiling. "To be honest, I'm just assuming that she's a female." He saw Ainsley's confused expression. "I inherited Dolly from my uncle. I never even met Dolly while he was around. He was my great-uncle, actually. I hadn't been to his house for quite a while. We always met at his 'club'." He made a gesture in the air, indicating that the title was a quote from his uncle. "He told me one day that he had gotten a parrot and named it Dolly. I never got the details. And then out of the blue, she was dropped off, cage and all, at my apartment." He shook his head. "I had just heard that my uncle had passed, so I was pretty surprised to get that visitor. And the lawyer sent a note along with the bird and supplies saying that she was six months old and named Dolly. And that my uncle wanted me to have her. That's it, really."

"Oh, so you inherited him, um, her."

"Yeah," he smoothed his hand over the bird's head, stroking the soft white feathers. "My uncle was a unique type of guy. I didn't get to see him that often recently. More when I was younger. But lately, well, I should have taken more time." He sighed softly. "I felt so bad when I heard he was gone. He was a great old guy. Strange, but great."

"You said someone broke into your home?"

"Two and a half weeks ago. I came home and found that the door had been cracked and my apartment turned upside down. I mean, seriously destroyed. I couldn't tell if they were looking for something or were just that vindictive."

"Is your neighborhood, um, rough?" Ainsley asked, not wanting to offend him.

"No, not at all. I live off Shelbyville Road, out by the Mall. My apartment isn't that impressive, so I'm not sure why anyone would think to target me." He was frowning now, his mouth in a thin line. "I've gone over and over it in my mind. What did I have that was worth anything? My computer is the only expensive equipment I have, and it wasn't touched. So I just don't know." He gently smoothed the bird's feathers again. "I sometimes wonder if it had anything to do with my uncle. I mean, he was loaded, and maybe someone thought that if I inherited the bird, I might have gotten more of his stuff." He held the bird out a little and looked her over, then shook his head dismissively. "But the will isn't even out yet. Tied up with lawyers. They just delivered Dolly to me because she's alive. Couldn't very well stay in the house by herself."

"That's terrible," Ainsley said. "I can't believe that someone would break in just in case you had gotten anything from a will."

"You know, it was horrible." His eyes quickly skimmed her little living room. "I hadn't thought about how a break in would make someone feel. Like how you know that your space has been invaded. It has freaked me out in a way," he admitted, glancing at Ainsley.

Ainsley felt herself shiver a little. The idea of someone coming in your home, going through your things, touching everything, made her feel a little creepy. "I don't blame you for being bothered by it," she said earnestly.

He sighed and ran his long fingers through his hair in silent frustration. "This is the first time that I've felt like I can't control a situation. I keep thinking that something has been moved in my apartment, like I'm not alone. In fact, I've wondered if someone has been there again." He pushed his hair back with one hand, looking sheepish. "I sound like an idiot, I know. But it's weird how you can have this sense about a place. And even though I feel like I'm paranoid," he paused a second, his eyes drifting over the room as though someone might be listening in, "I'm almost sure that someone has been in since the robbery."

"Again? You think they've come back? Why?"

"Little things. I swear it's true. There are things out of place, doors open, they shifted some of my tools, papers scattered. And that's after I had everything taken care of. I had reorganized after the break in so I knew where I had replaced everything. And I'm a visual guy. I'm usually pretty good about remembering where I leave my things."

"Oh," Ainsley murmured feeling a nervous shiver, thinking of

Bird, no Dolly, she corrected herself, alone in the apartment when the thieves came back. The last time, they had apparently taken her and then let her loose. This time? "Who would do something like that? And why?" She looked at the bird cuddled up to Gabe's chest, leaving a pale shadow against the dark fabric.

"You know," he was talking fast. "I know that this is a whole lot to ask, but I'm almost afraid to take her home. Do you think she could stay here for a little while longer? Until I can figure out what's going on?"

Ainsley looked at the bird's expressive eyes. She couldn't say no, and she didn't want to. "Um, Sure. Of course." In the back of her mind, she knew that it was crazy, the idea that someone was breaking into his apartment, not just once, but repeatedly. But she felt like she couldn't refuse. She had fallen for the parrot.

He sighed in relief. "I can't thank you enough. And I can pay you," he started.

"Don't be silly. I borrowed the cage. It's no problem."

"I'll reimburse you for food then," he insisted.

"I bought the first bag, you can buy the rest," she said.

"If you're sure," he said, but the smile was coming back, his shoulders relaxing visibly.

"It'll be fine." Ainsley felt a strange little happiness. Bird, no, Dolly, wasn't going anywhere yet. And she had so many places that she wanted to take her new companion. She had promised the girls at the dental office that she would bring the bird for a lunchtime visit. She was going to take her back to her uncle's restaurant so that Frank's two girls could come by and meet the parrot. And she wanted to take some pictures for her parents to see. They hadn't believed her when she said that the bird had followed her into her bedroom and climbed in the bed with her.

Gabe was still holding Dolly close, and Ainsley felt guilty letting them just hang there. "Would you like a cup of coffee and a cookie," she asked, seeing his reluctance to leave.

His eyes lit up. "That would be great," he responded immediately. She led him into the tidy little kitchen and motioned to a chair.

"I'll get the coffee on. We'll have to find something for Dolly, or she'll be after everything we have."

"She's bad about that," he nodded. "We argued every morning about who got toast until she agreed to eat her own and not both of ours."

Ainsley laughed out loud and gestured toward the table. The man and the bird followed her direction. Dolly was chattering contentedly.

THE COCKATOO CALLED

Ainsley pulled out a kitchen chair. "Have a seat. And this is where Dolly usually perches." She smiled as he transferred the parrot to the back of the chair, already marked with little dents where Dolly had tasted the wood. "Is coffee okay?"

"Sure," he agreed and ruffled Dolly's feathers on the top of her head. "Is she okay here?"

"She's fine. I can generally catch her before she has an accident." She motioned to the nearby garbage can.

"Yeah, she was almost potty trained when I got her. She was like a dog. As soon as I figured out the trigger word, she would just wiggle and do her business."

Ainsley looked over her shoulder as he played with the bird. She could see the familiarity, the bond between them. "How long have you had her?"

"Only a couple months," he answered. "My great uncle only had her for a few months himself. His lawyer sent a note explaining just a little of their history." He was smiling. "They had an unusual relationship too, my uncle and his attorney. I think they got together monthly for drinks and for my great uncle to change his will." He gave a rueful smile. "So I was pretty floored when he called and told me that Uncle Topper had died."

"Uncle Topper?"

"His name was Horace Topper. He chose to go by Topper. So for all of us kids, he was just Topper."

"Did he have kids?" Ainsley finished fixing the grounds in the coffee pot and started it brewing.

"Nope. Never married. He had three brothers and three sisters. He said that was enough family for anyone."

"How many nieces and nephews did he end up with?"

"There are fifteen nieces and nephews and twice that many greats. But some are out of town, so there are only about ten of us that get together regularly. We're scattered from coast to coast, if you count Joe slumming in LA."

"Are you close?"

"Some of us are. I'm close to my two sisters; didn't have a choice about that one. Mary Grace wouldn't allow it to be any other way."

"I'm an only child," Ainsley said ruefully putting a mug at each of their places. She added a bowl of water with some floating ice cubes for Dolly to mess with, and then brought out the sugar and cream for the coffee. On a plate, she set out a few homemade chocolate cookies and some of the wheat crackers that she had kept for the bird.

"I had days that I wished I was," Gabe replied. He added a little cream to his cup and sipped. "Good coffee."

"Thanks," Ainsley slipped into her chair and offered a cracker to Dolly. "So you're an architect?"

"Yep," he took a cookie. "I was at a big firm downtown, but I'm working with a partner now in a small business. We do some commercial, some residential."

"That sounds great." Ainsley took a cookie and gently steered Dolly away from snatching one. "I work as a receptionist at a dentist office." She made a little face. "I just haven't found anything that suits me." She made no claim to any education. It was a hard won degree and a rather touchy subject.

"Do you like your job?" He had taken another cookie and was distracting Dolly with a cracker.

"You know," she paused with the thought, "I do."

"And you make money."

Ainsley smiled. "A little."

"Then your job suits you." He pulled Dolly to him and gently stroked her feathers. "So tell me more about how you found this crazy thing."

*****

It was a week later, and Ainsley was trying to wrestle a rag from Dolly's beak when Gabe called. "I have a kind of strange request," he began.

She hadn't heard from him much except for a few texts asking how things were going with Dolly, so she was curious. "Oh?" she said.

"One of my great uncle's best friends, Jack, found my number and called me. Turns out that he was the one that located Dolly for my uncle. He has a parrot himself. I think he might have given Uncle Topper the idea in the first place." He chuckled a little at the memory of the conversation. "He's another of my uncle's unique friends. But anyway, he was saying that he'd like to meet up with me, and with Dolly."

Ainsley was surprised. He wanted to meet up with a bird? "Well, okay," she said doubtfully.

"I told him that I would bring Dolly and a date. You're the date." He paused for a second. "I mean," he amended quickly, "I'm not saying we're dating. But you're my date, like, you're coming with me, not just Dolly." He took a deep breath. "I'm not explaining this well. I didn't want to go into why Dolly wasn't living with me while I was talking to

THE COCKATOO CALLED

Jack, so I thought I'd give him another reason for you coming along."

"That's fine," Ainsley said, feeling slightly sorry for him. "And yes, Dolly and I would be happy to go."

"Great!" he responded, sounding immensely relieved. "We planned to meet on Saturday at 12. Will that work out? I can pick you up at 11:30."

"Sure," Ainsley said, then grinning she added, "it's a date!"

*****

Ainsley was nervous about where they would choose to eat. It wasn't like every restaurant was bird friendly. But she had underestimated Jack, Uncle Topper's friend. He knew exactly the place to go since he was a regular patron with his macaw, Hemingway.

Hemingway was a huge green-winged macaw. The name didn't mean much to Ainsley; she only knew the macaws that she had seen in picture books, but Hemingway seemed to be a particularly singular example of the species. The name was interesting as well, and a little puzzling since he seemed to be mostly red in color. Dominating the room, he perched on an actual bird stand situated in the corner next to a window. When he stretched his wings languidly, his rich colors stood out like a flag against the rough wood of the unpainted walls. He had a large red head with white patches of skin around his eyes. Tiny white lines of feathers crossed the scarlet patches. His eyes were a strange light green, with a pin prick black pupil. The inner surface of his wings was as red as his body, but the other feathers varied beautifully from a dusky green to an almost turquoise blue melting to a darker blue. Fastened around his body was a strange harness like contraption. The bird appeared to be totally unaware of it. Unlike Dolly, his feathers were slightly tattered, his large beak mildly chipped, his eyes sharp. When the door closed, he yelled with a boisterous croak, "They're here!" His voice was loud enough to be heard quite clearly outside the restaurant as well.

"Holy cow, will you look at that!" Ainsley said, staring at the bird.

"I'm guessing that's Hemingway." Gabe grinned and approached the bird, holding Dolly's crate so she could peer through the wire. "How about that, Dolly?"

Dolly made no sound but clung to the bars studying the larger bird.

"Gabe, my boy, it's been years!"

If they hadn't been in Kentucky, maybe living on the beach in southern Florida, she would have said the man before her was a pirate. His beard was long and full, his cheeks rosy, his clothes a creative combination of a long sleeved shirt, a leather vest, and a stocking cap that covered just the top of his head.

"Jack," Gabe said, and passed the crate to Ainsley so that he could shake the other man's hand.

"See you met Hemingway. He's a great old boy." Jack raised a glass to toast to the giant parrot.

"How old is he?" Ainsley asked.

Jack eyed her and smiled again. "So you're young Gabe's friend. And you like our bird here. My macaw is nigh 25 years old and will outlive me yet. He's been with me since he was just a chick. A big bumbling baby."

"He is awesome." Ainsley couldn't help but admire the bird, his colorful feathers, his huge beak, light on top with a dark lower beak, his pale eyes studying everything, looking for all the world like he owned the place. Regal was a word that came to mind.

"She's got good taste," Jack said, winking at Gabe. "Grab a table and I'll order for us. They only serve one good thing. Not worth trying anything else." Jack turned back toward the bar and Ainsley looked around the dining room. It had been built cheaply with wood siding and rough-hewn posts. The chairs and tables were a dark wood, stained by age and finish. There was one man behind the bar taking drink orders, and one middle-aged woman, thin and spry, taking care of the few customers there.

"So I did mention that Jack is a bit of a character, didn't I?" Gabe asked Ainsley in an undertone.

"I believe you did. Is he from around here?"

"Oh, Lord knows where Jack has been. I don't know where he's from, and I know for sure that he's traveled at least as much as Uncle Topper. He might not have had the same kind of money, but he always seems to be getting along just fine."

"If he has money, it's probably gold doubloons," Ainsley said wryly.

"Oh, yeah, the pirate thing. He has always said that he has an ancestor that was a real pirate. Lived on some island off the Florida coast when it wasn't such a tourist attraction." Gabe chuckled. "Don't ask him about his life unless you're ready for quite a story."

"Is he married? Does he have kids?" Ainsley asked as she watched Jack flirt with the waitress.

"He's got one daughter. I've never seen her."

THE COCKATOO CALLED

Jack stomped back to the table. Ainsley noticed with amusement that he was wearing heavy boots, rough and scuffed, something between what might be worn while riding a Harley or building a skyscraper.

"She's bringing over the tea in a minute. Sweet tea for all of us. You can't be on one of those healthy granola diets if you come in here."

The tea was sweet, but it was a blend of lemonade and tea and tasted rather good. They served fried fish sandwiches with creamy coleslaw, reinforcing Ainsley's idea that Jack was a misplaced pirate.

They had chosen a table close to the bird stand, but not within snatching distance, although, the macaw was trying hard to get his beak on some of their food. Jack would occasionally reward him with a bit of fish, and the waitress came by and handed him a cracker on the fly.

After they had eaten most of their meal, Jack grabbed up the crate and popped open the door. "Good God, man, where did you get this box?" he asked Gabe. "Looks like a shark got to the side of it."

"The bird got to the side," Ainsley said shaking her head. "She chewed her way through. Dolly has quite the determination when she doesn't want to stay."

"Wait, Dolly?" The older man interrupted.

Gabe looked confused. "That's what we were told," he said. "Isn't that right? She was always called Dolly."

Jack laughed, a loud, boisterous sound that Hemingway echoed. "Not that it matters that much, but the correct pronunciation is 'Dali'. As in 'Salvador Dali'. The painter."

"Really?" Gabe looked amazed. "I always wondered why Uncle Topper would have picked that name." He watched as the bird strutted out of the crate. "But why Dali?" Gabe asked, trying to get over his initial surprise.

"You hadn't heard?" Jack asked, humor still lighting his eyes. "That was one of his best stories, how he found a Dali, purchased the painting for a song. The find of the century. A real Dali. And no one knew about it."

"He owned a Salvador Dali original?" Gabe asked, disbelief plain on his face. "I mean, I knew he had money, but he was never an art fan. That wouldn't have been his style."

"He liked a lot of different stuff," Jack corrected. "He liked to collect things that are rare, better if they were one of a kind. Why not a painting?"

Gabe continued to look puzzled. "So he named his new pet Dali after the artist or the painting?"

"Who knows why he did what he did," Jack said dismissively.

"But the painting, the Dali, how come I never heard of it?"

Jack shrugged. "You all were too young when the story hit the press. You wouldn't have been interested in any case."

"To the press? You mean it was in the news?"

"It was a scandal of magnificent proportions," Jack assured them. "But the past is in the past, where it should stay." Jack held up the cockatoo and looked it over carefully. "And this baby is all that's left of that story, I guess. Maybe you should call him Sal so people won't be confused again."

"So he's a he?" Ainsley asked.

"Yep, breeder told me that this one is a male. Had him checked as a baby."

"Dali," Gabe said shrugging. "Who would have guessed? Uncle Topper had a lot of good stories."

"So you have had Hemingway for a long time?" Ainsley asked, giving the macaw a piece of bread from her plate, a little nervous about her fingers.

"Me and Hemingway, we go way back. He's been to many countries with me. He's ridden boats and planes and trains. He's a tough old guy. This one's got stories to tell."

"Does he talk much?" Ainsley asked curious.

"Ah, only when I don't want him to. Picks up the damndest things. That's how they are, though, you know. They'll pick what they want to say, not what you want them to." He looked between Gabe and Ainsley, eyebrows raised. "Did you hear about the parrot in Lexington? Helped solve a murder!"

"I hadn't heard," Gabe said looking very interested.

"It was one of those African Grays. The lady that owned him was killed, and so he went to her neighbor. He kept telling them that his owner was murdered, kept replaying the scene, out loud. Damn amazing!"

"Did they catch the guy that did it?"

"Sure did. The bird caught her, and it wasn't no guy. It was the old lady that owned the building they lived in. She was smuggling drugs into the country in dolls' parts, their heads and such. Her brother was a higher up in a drug ring, and she wanted to get in on the family business. No one suspected a thing, an old lady like that. But she had paid off her building, and banked a pretty penny."

"Why did she kill her tenant?" Gabe asked.

"Seems that one of the shipments went to the wrong apartment. The lady with the bird figured out something was going on. I don't know if she was going to the police or just blackmailing the old lady, but it

THE COCKATOO CALLED

didn't last. You can't tangle with dirty like that."

"And the old lady killed her?" Ainsley's voice was horrified.

"Electrocuted her in the tub. The parrot heard the whole thing. That's how they knew it wasn't an accident. The parrot kept repeating what he heard." Jack gave a shrug. "The old lady came to get the next owner of the parrot, and probably would have killed someone else, but the bird attacked!"

"What do you mean, attacked?" Ainsley asked, looking at the long claws and hooked beak of the bird next to her.

"He came at the old lady, clawed her good, bit her too, and hurt her enough that someone else could come in and stop the crazy lady."

"So did the bird bite everyone? Her owner? Or was that a special situation?"

"Nah," Jack said. "They aren't usually like that. A bird will bite, don't get me wrong, but to attack like that, you don't hear of that every day." He handed Dali to Gabe and reached out to let the big macaw perch on his hand. "Now take my friend Hemingway here. Gentle as a lamb. Now I wouldn't push him, not that stupid, but I can read him pretty good. He'll tell me before he bites."

"That's good," Ainsley said cautiously.

"Here, you hold him," Jack said, holding out the bird. Ainsley hesitated. She hadn't encountered many birds before she had met Dali. She was just getting used to the experience. This beast was another thing altogether. He was taller, sleeker, his beak seeming twice the size. His golden eye, surrounded by chalk white skin, assessed her.

"Hi, Hemingway," she said slowly. She lifted her hand and was surprised when he brought one foot up as though to transfer his grasp.

"That's a boy," Jack encouraged. "He does like the ladies."

Hemingway climbed onto Ainsley's closed hand and started to climb her sleeve in that particular beak over claw way that the parrots had.

"Just put your hand out flat, the other one, to block him from going to your shoulder. He knows better. He might like to taste your earrings, he's a bad boy about that. Likes glittery things."

Ainsley followed the instructions and put her hand up as a block. The bird understood the gesture and stopped his gradual climb. She sighed in relief.

The door opened, and a roar of an engine sounded. The bird responded by letting out an ear-splitting squawk and flapping his massive wings, causing Ainsley's hair to flutter. The bird yelled, "take a seat, ya old bugger!" Ainsley had to laugh. The bird then yelled out, "they're here!" and the waitress came out from the back kitchen.

"I heard you the first time, you overgrown chicken," she said, pulling out her pad and pencil.

The newcomers were laughing as they took their seats.

THE COCKATOO CALLED

CHAPTER FIVE

Back at Ainsley's house, she tucked a tired Dali into his cage and looked at Gabe.

"Thanks for coming with me," he said. "I know Jack is a little much, but he is a nice guy. Kinda like part of the family too."

"I could tell," Ainsley said. "And he did seem to be a nice man. I had a good time."

"Not every day that you get to meet a real live pirate."

"True." Ainsley looked at Dali where he had settled on his perch. "It sounds like your uncle was an interesting guy. I wish I had gotten to meet him."

"He had his good days. He could seem a little crazy sometimes, but it always seemed harmless. Just an old fashioned adventurer."

"And the story about Dali and the painting."

Gabe shrugged. "I wouldn't put it past him. I honestly don't know a whole lot about that." He brightened, "but I guess I can do some research."

Ainsley felt herself flinch slightly at the idea of research. When she was a student, just the idea of having to tackle writing a paper was enough to have her breaking out in hives. And to be sat in a room with a bunch of books, thinking that she was supposed to be able to wade through all of that material, she shook her head. School had been a nightmare for many years, and it had taken some very special teachers to help her overcome that. "Maybe I'll look up some of the paintings online. I know I've heard of him, but I can't remember what Dali painted."

"Its interesting stuff," Gabe said. "Impressionism, I think."

"It sounds like your uncle collected a lot of things."

"Oh, yeah," Gabe agreed. "Uncle Topper's collection was fascinating, especially for us kids, but a painting like that would be a unique piece." Gabe checked his watch. "And I'd better get going. I've kept you too long as it is."

"I had a nice time," Ainsley said, her voice a little wistful.

"Me too," Gabe said. He smiled at her as he headed for the door. "If I find out anything more about my apartment, I'll let you know." He stopped by and bid Dali goodbye as he walked past. "And thanks again," he said as he opened the front door.

"No problem," Ainsley said giving an awkward wave. She watched as he pulled the door closed behind himself, and she hesitated, staring at the wooden panel, lost in thought.

*****

Dali went to work with Ainsley on Tuesday as promised. She brought the carrier, but he spent most of his time strutting along the desk. He delighted the girls with his funny walk, his awkward clucking, and his general easy manner, letting himself be the center of attention for the hour and a half that he stayed. By the time she had left to take him back home, he had met almost all of the people working in the building, all of the patients waiting to be seen in the dentist office, and a few strangers coming into the lobby of the building. Best yet, he hadn't yet met anyone who he didn't like.

Gabe had called twice, asking if she needed anything or if he should bring some food for the bird. She had answered 'no' to both of the questions automatically, and then regretted not accepting his company. It would be nice to see him again. The third time he asked if she needed anything, she did. Dali was a buzz saw when it came to the wooden toys she had given him, and she had run out of the pellets she used for the staple in his diet. He ate everything, there wasn't a morsel of food on her table that he wouldn't try, but she didn't want him to become dependent on junk food. She had spent evenings using her tablet computer to input searches and listen to the advice of other avian professionals. There was a whole lot of information regarding the diet he needed to be on, as well as things that were safe for him to play with.

Gabe came to pick them up at her house in a sporty little car with good gas mileage and an excellent sound system. It was a funny kind of date, the bird in his makeshift crate sitting on Ainsley's lap because she didn't want to leave him in the back seat by himself, their very own feathered chaperone. They had decided that a travel crate was one of the other necessities that they would look for. Dali had taken to nibbling on the cardboard, and once he found that he could rip off strips from the inside, he was making it his mission to peel the wall away. He had

THE COCKATOO CALLED

almost broken through when they got to Feeders.

Patti was by the register, and her eyes lit up when she saw them. "So you're back!" she exclaimed, holding out her hands for the crate. "Let me see that guy!"

Ainsley set the carrier on the counter, and Patti opened the door. Dali immediately came strutting out, looking very happy with himself.

"So what happened?" Patti asked, looking from Gabe to Ainsley. "Was this the right bird?"

"Oh, yeah," Gabe said, smiling attractively, one dark curl falling over his forehead. "I was so lucky that Ainsley found him."

Patti's eyebrows rose. "Is it a him or her? I thought the name was Dolly."

Gabe looked a little embarrassed. "We spoke to one of my uncle's friends. It turns out, that the name is Dali, as in the artist, Salvador Dali. And he's a he. My uncle's friend got Dali for him from a breeder."

"Well good." Patti gently lifted the bird and cuddled him in her arms. "It's good that we've learned his story, and he's found his home again."

"But Dali is still staying with me," Ainsley explained. "So we're still using your cage, if that's okay with you."

"Oh, I don't need it right now," Patti said. "And I'm just glad that you both are taking such good care of this baby."

Ainsley smiled. "Well, I'm learning a whole lot about taking care of him, that's for sure. We need to get more toys; he goes through them so fast, and as you can see, we still need another carrier."

"No problem," Patti began, heading out from behind the register with the bird. "Come on this way." She went down one of the aisles and stopped at a stack of animal carriers. "I know I've learned a whole lot from Milty. You know, Milton, my Moluccan?"

"You should see him," Ainsley said to Gabe. "He's a lot bigger bird than Dali, and so pretty. Pink and peach, a little orange almost."

"And rotten," Patti agreed. "Yesterday, he had me going, laughing so hard. I was putting on my jacket to come to work, and he said, 'Whatcha doin?' I told him that I was putting on my jacket to go to work. He said, 'Wanna go', just like he understood me. So I told him that I had to go to the grocery after work, and that they don't allow him to go to the grocery. I told him they sell people food in the grocery. I do take him here to work sometimes, so he does know that he can come to work." She chuckled. "Then he said, 'hungry, wanna eat' because I had told them they sold food! He had already eaten his oatmeal and some cheerios, so he wasn't hungry, but he jumped off the cage and ran down the hall yelling, 'eat a birdy, wanna eat a birdy'". She shook her head. "The poor tiels were completely in an uproar with Milty climbing the cage stand to get up to them and saying 'yum' the whole time. I had to catch him before he could scare them anymore. It took me a while just to get everything settled back down. And then as I was leaving, I could hear Milty in the back room calling bye, bye as I left."

"Now that is one smart bird," Gabe exclaimed, shaking his head in disbelief.

"You would be surprised what they understand," Patti replied.

*****

When they left the store, Dali was in his new crate, contentedly nibbling on some treats that Patti had slipped him. Gabe carried the extra-large sized bag of pellets, cheaper if you bought the big bag, and Ainsley had a little bag with a few new toys. They also had lots of ideas of toys that they could make at home that would eventually save them some serious money.

At the house, Gabe helped unload and carry in our purchases and Dali chattered contentedly.

"Well, I think that was a successful trip," Ainsley said, putting the crate down and opening the door.

"Yeah, pretty good." Gabe looked distracted, his eyes skimming to the window that opened onto the expanse of the lawn.

"What's wrong?"

"I don't want you to think that I'm crazy," Gabe began, "but I think someone came into my apartment yesterday while I was out on a job site."

"Really," Ainsley felt a tingle of fear for him slide down her back. "What happened?"

"Nothing really," he responded. "It's just, when I came home, I noticed the doorknob felt loose, and I could see some gouges in the wood like it had been forced. When I went into the apartment, I started looking at things. And it was like it had been before. Subtle things. Books moved to the other side of the coffee table, a drawer was left open just a little, my junk drawer looked like someone had rummaged through it, strange stuff like that."

"So do you think they came back? Do you think someone is still trying to get something from your apartment?"

He sighed and ran his hand through his hair. "I don't know. I don't have any proof of anything, but I just have this sensation," he made a face, his eyes narrowed.

"But why? If they didn't get what they wanted last time, why would they come back? What do they want? What do you have?"

"That I don't know," he said frowning. "I haven't gotten anything new that would be that valuable. My computer equipment is my most expensive thing, and it still wasn't touched. And I'm not expecting any deliveries. So unless someone knows something I don't, like I'm going to be the next multimillionaire, I have no idea what they could be after."

"Could it be related to your uncle like you thought?" Ainsley scooped up Dali and smoothed his feathers.

"You mean his will? It's still in limbo."

"Do you suppose they know that?"

"It's not a secret, if that's what you mean, but only the family and close friends would know how much it's been held up."

"So if they thought that you had gotten something from your uncle and were keeping it in your apartment, maybe they would have broken in." Ainsley looked at the bird. "Maybe because of Dali, they know you're due to inherit something."

"If they want my uncle's things, I don't know why they wouldn't just go to his house to get it," Gabe said sounding frustrated.

"Who lives there?"

"No one, as far as I know. He lived there alone with some help coming in now and then to clean and cook for him. The place is huge. Most of it is closed up now. But if there was anything valuable, well, that's where it would be." He crossed his arms over his chest and looked up at the ceiling, thinking. "Damn it, I guess I should go out there and check on things. If they've come out to my apartment to get something of his, then surely they've been out at the house." He glanced Ainsley's way. "I hope that you don't think I'm losing it."

"No," Ainsley replied quickly. "Of course not. Where did your Uncle live?"

"In one of those back streets off River Road," he said. "He wanted to be close to town, but not in downtown Louisville. His house was built a long time ago. He bought it at a good price, but hasn't done much to keep it updated." He smiled. "It's sort of like my uncle was. Colorful, full of stuff, very interesting."

"Can I come along? When you go visit the house, can I come too?" Ainsley said it before she thought it out, but realized that she did want to go. She was a little embarrassed that she had invited herself, but still, Gabe's uncle sounded intriguing. His house sounded equally fascinating. In all, she felt like it would be a nice little adventure. And besides that, it would give her an excuse to go somewhere with Gabe, and that was a plus all on its own.

"Do you want to?" he asked.

"Sure!" She smiled at his expression. "Your uncle's best friend is a pirate without the ocean. His house is a collection of a lifetime's worth of travel, his pet is an exotic bird, and you keep saying he was a great old guy. I'd like to see where he lived. I just wish I had been able to meet him."

Gabe's eyes softened. "Me too. He would have liked you."

Ainsley smiled with pleasure. "So when do you want to go?"

"Tomorrow, I guess. If someone has broken into his place, the sooner the better."

"How are you going to get in?" Ainsley asked, suddenly realizing that the abandoned place would be utterly empty.

"I have a key. I've had one for a long time."

"Will anyone care that you've gone in?" Ainsley had a sudden image of them being led off in handcuffs by the police for breaking and entering.

"Nah, everyone knows me. I'm the only local nephew that came to visit regularly. They've seen me around often enough." He paused. "Will tomorrow be okay? That is, if you still want to go?"

"I want to go," Ainsley said quickly. "And tomorrow is just fine."

"Great, what time?" he asked.

"It doesn't matter to me," Ainsley said.

"I'll pick you up at one then."

THE COCKATOO CALLED

CHAPTER SIX

The morning had dawned cold and blustery. A heavy mantle of clouds hung low in the sky. The sun had been dulled to a dusty glow. The wind whipped at the trees, and the few leaves that had withstood the worst of the autumn were now shaken loose and drifting to the ground like great, brown birds.

    Ainsley got up early and fed herself and the bird. She had toast and jelly. He had toast and jelly. They both were a little sticky afterwards. After they had cleaned up, he chased the napkin, caught it, and shredded it all over the table. Ainsley took him into her bedroom where he perched on the dresser and pushed a box of jewelry around on the slick surface, finally managing to drop it off the side where he turned his head and peered over the edge.

    After Ainsley was ready, she put Dali back in his cage and cleaned up a little. Having a bird as a companion ramped up her need for cleaning more than she had ever thought imaginable. Everything he ate, he crushed into fine grains that he then spread out on the floor around the cage with a furious flapping of wings. He continually shed, mostly little white feathers that floated in the air as though weightless, and landed on furniture in little snowflake like puffs. But worse, he had a powdery substance on his feathers. Patti had explained that it was to help them keep clean, but to Ainsley, it was one of the greatest challenges to keeping her home clean. It scattered like a film of chalk dust on every surface. Ainsley was just glad that she didn't have bad allergies, because this substance was sure to be an aggravation to those more sensitive.

    At one o'clock exactly, Ainsley heard a motor outside. She went to find her purse and keys, dropping her phone into her bag and checking the room. It looked nice. Homey. The honey gold walls were set off warmly by red accents. The old floors were still a little rough, but she thought had character. The rug rolled out in the middle of the living room was an old oriental one that her parents had used, but the colors were right and it was gentler on her bare feet.

When the bell rang she jumped a little, so lost in thought. She pulled open the door and stepped aside for Gabe to come in. It hadn't even been a question as to whether he would want to come in. She knew he would have to speak to Dali, check on the silly bird.

"Hey fluff," Gabe said.

"Thanks for the greeting," Ainsley quipped from behind him. He had the grace to redden, which made his narrow face that much more charming.

"Sorry. Hi."

She grinned and went up to the cage. "We spent some time cleaning up this morning," she said, sticking her finger between the bars and stroking the white feathers that the bird had pushed through the side of the cage. Dali was leaning against the cage wall; head cocked so that they could reach his cheek.

"I am sure you were a lot of help," Gabe said, looking at the bird.

"He is a great supervisor. And mess maker. I think that's in his contract."

Gabe grinned. "I've done my fair share of cleaning up after this guy. He can make an amazing mess."

"Okay, Buddy," Ainsley said to the bird. "We've got to go, so you be good."

The bird peered out at them as Ainsley tugged on her coat. As she closed the door after them, she heard the bird say in his gravelly voice, "be good."

The drive to Uncle Topper's home would be a beautiful one on a pretty day. When they got off the interstate onto River Road, the trees closed around them like a canopy of bare limbs, a premonition of the winter coming to claim them. Each turn off from the main road was crowded with shadows. The driveway snaked back from the road again, past a clump of mature evergreens that effectively shrouded most of the house, and then into a circular driveway. The house rose in front of them, a massive stone structure in the shelter of even larger trees, the surrounding gardens full of dead and dying plants. It was cruel what the fall and winter was doing to the old house, sucking it into mourning.

"Big," Ainsley muttered as they stopped the car. Gabe climbed out first, pulling his thin coat more closely around himself. Against the pewter sky, he had the illusion of a scarecrow as his black coat flapped around him, and his dark hair caught in the wind. But then he hesitated and turned to look at Ainsley, flashing that smile. She climbed out of the

THE COCKATOO CALLED

warmth of the car, and the chill caught her breath. Gabe held out a hand, and she caught it, feeling the strength of his fingers as they wrapped around hers. She let him lead her up the steps and into the shelter of the porch. They stopped there while he pulled out a huge ring of keys and shuffled through them, looking for the right one. He finally settled on a shiny silver key, modern looking for the antique lock, and the door eased open. Catching her elbow, he guided her inside the house, and the door slammed behind them, forced by the pressure of the wind.

The silence was deafening. The house was cool inside, and Ainsley wondered if they had turned off the heat, or just turned it down low. As it was, she could almost see her breath in the enveloping darkness. She feared for a moment that they might have turned out the electricity as well. But Gabe reached behind him and in a snap, the room was filled with light.

The house had been built in a time that a formal entrance was a sign of grandeur and sophistication, and this room might have once been a prime example of cultured taste, but Uncle Topper had put an end to that notion. Shoved in one corner was a stuffed lion, its mane matted against its head and noticeably missing a few of its front teeth. He appeared as though he had been in some very rough fights and had lost each and every one. Next to him, and similarly stuffed, was a monkey whose expression looked just plain surprised. His eyes were wide, his mouth pursed as though shocked out of a deep contemplation. Next to these poor creatures was a squat table made from a tree stump, still with knarled bark and a thrust of a branch that had been hacked free and then covered in a thick coating of shellac that looked like honey poured and frozen in place. On the table lay a set of keys, some loose envelopes, and a pair of sunglasses. It gave Ainsley a small stab of sadness. Life had ended quickly for Uncle Topper, and she wondered if he had seen death come knocking.

"Welcome to Uncle Topper's collection of the strange and unusual," Gabe said grandly spreading his arms wide.

"Wow," Ainsley said smiling. "Just wow."

"Yeah, I know. Sometimes I forget what eccentric means, and then I come in here and think, oh yeah, now I've got it!"

"Different, but cool," Ainsley replied. "Show me more!"

They walked on, passing through rooms with towering bookcases, oversized glass cabinets, and tables topped with what may have once been a collection of fossils.

"We'll start in the kitchen. I think that's where his address book might be."

"His address book?"

"The way I figure it, someone had to know him pretty well to come after me. I can't figure out any other reason why they would be coming into my apartment. And more than once! So maybe Uncle Topper knew them. Or maybe someone, like one of his good friends, would have an idea."

"Are you going to ask Jack?"

"I've thought about that, and I think I'm going to have to." He caught Ainsley's look. "And before you start to worry, I know for sure that Jack wasn't involved. He was out of the country when the first break in occurred. I tried to get in touch with him, and he was down in Mexico."

"But do you think that he would have known who broke into your apartment?"

"I have no idea, but I also would like to see if any of the names ring a bell. If I have Uncle Topper's address book, then I have somewhere to start." He glanced at her thoughtfully. "Uncle Topper had the book where ever he went." He walked down the hall. "We'll look for the book first. Then we can look around for things that might be missing or misplaced."

"Missing? How would you know? This place is so full of…" words failed her.

"Full of his collections. And I don't know that I'll recognize if something is gone. But maybe it will be obvious. Or maybe I'll be lucky and find that nothing has been taken."

"Okay, then I guess we can start. Kitchen it is," she agreed, thinking of his original destination.

The kitchen was another throwback, but this time much closer to the 1920s. It was charming. And it was fully stocked. Ainsley could see the cabinets packed with food, even months after the old man's death. The house had effectively been frozen in time.

"It looks like he just stepped out yesterday. Why hasn't anyone been here?" Ainsley asked.

Gabe sighed sadly. "The family is all over the place, scattered across the country, and to be honest, his immediate family, or what's left of them, are either in no shape to travel, or don't want to try. Uncle Topper was one of the youngest of the gang in his generation. Two of his brothers and one of his sisters had already passed away. My grandfather died when I was just ten. Uncle Topper kind of stepped in then. As far as the other nieces and nephews, well, Mom and Dad came in for the funeral, and so did most of the other family, but they didn't stay too long. And then some of the other family members weren't close at all."

"So were they all just waiting for the reading of the will?" Ainsley felt the stab of sympathy again. It seemed like a lonely life.

"It's not as bad as that. After the funeral, we agreed that the people who had been helping Uncle Topper before would continue looking after the house." Gabe wandered over to a cabinet and opened it. "They probably didn't want to disturb anything." He went over to the refrigerator, a small version, somewhat updated but still a good twenty years old, and opened the door. Inside was scrubbed clean, and although it was still running, it was empty. "They cleaned out the things that would spoil. We should have told them that they could take the food. Better if someone would eat it than let it go to waste."

"Who's in charge of that?"

"The executor of the estate is my Uncle George. He's up in Washington D.C. Government type. He has signed off on some papers for us to take care of the little things. When it's time to disburse all of Uncle Topper's holdings, I imagine he'll have to come down. Until then, we just call him and get his okay." Gabe pushed his hair back and closed the refrigerator. "I'll call him about this. If nothing else, the food that the caretakers don't want should go to a food bank or something."

"Caviar?" Ainsley asked, looking into the cabinet.

"Probably not the finest kind. It's not even refrigerated. Some of this will have to go straight into the garbage, and some of the more particular stuff won't be popular anyway."

Ainsley enjoyed poking through the cabinets a little longer. The choice of foods was amazing. There was Spam stored next to the caviar, some rice cakes with foreign writing placed on the shelf next to good old soda crackers, and an array of dried beans of every color, shape and size in plastic bags stacked one of top of the other. There were boxes and boxes of ingredients that Ainsley hadn't ever seen in her life, and she wondered if these were things that Uncle Topper had liked, or if he had collected interesting groceries along with everything else.

He had a little desk over in the corner of the kitchen, and the top was completely covered with papers, pens and pencils, envelopes, and an old phone, still plugged into the wall and receiver connected with a cord.

"Are you looking for the address book?" Ainsley asked, and walked over to where Gabe was standing.

"I'm not seeing it. I think he used to keep it here on top. I was hoping I might find some of his other friends to talk to. I guess I'll have to see if Jack knows anyone else that I can contact."

"What do you think they can tell you?"

"I'm not sure. I just want to know if the rumor about the Dali is true. Or if there are any other valuables that I should know about."

"Look around this place!" Ainsley exclaimed. "There has to be thousands of dollars of stuff in here!"

"Yeah, but I feel like whatever this guy was after, and that's assuming that I'm not losing my mind, is very special."

Ainsley nodded. "Well, if it's not here, where else could it be?"

Gabe looked up and his eyebrow arched, a speculative look. "That, my dear, is the question."

They left the kitchen, and Gabe led them into a small study in the front of the house. It looked like the place that some old guy might have snuggled up in his armchair and smoked a pipe. There were a few more very small stuffed creatures, a strange looking rabbit with a top hat and monocle, and a beaver that had been dressed in a velvet smoking jacket, posed regally with his nose in the air, one paw wrapped around a metal tipped cane.

"Funny," Ainsley said gesturing to the figures. "His sense of humor?"

"Yep," Gabe agreed. "And these guys are new since I was here last. He did have some birds, but maybe when he got Dali, he decided that it wasn't a good idea to keep them."

"Makes sense," Ainsley agreed. "Although I can't say that any of this," she gestured to the frozen animals, "taxidermy, is my favorite."

"Yeah, I prefer photos," Gabe agreed. He strolled over to the desk, a massive carved monstrosity with claw feet and a roll top that was closed. He tugged on the little knob, trying to pull up the roll top, but it didn't move. "Locked," he said. "He should have the key around here somewhere." He tugged on the drawers, but they were all locked as well. "Damn," he muttered.

"Where should I look?" Ainsley asked.

"Check out that cabinet," Gabe replied, gesturing to the big piece of furniture with the double doors.

Ainsley went over to the piece and tugged on the doors. To her surprise, they fell open easily. She jumped back as something large and furry fell out, dropping in a heap at her feet. She hadn't realized that she had screamed until Gabe grabbed her shoulder.

"What?!"

"Sorry, sorry," she breathed, her palm flat against her racing heart. "When that thing fell out, I thought it was something alive!"

He gently nudged the bundle with the toe of his tennis shoe. "Some kind of fur. Really old." He grimaced. "I don't get his fascination with this stuff." He pulled the doors open a little wider and peered in.

THE COCKATOO CALLED

"Nothing else looks like it's coming for us," he joked.

"Funny," Ainsley said, and nudged him aside.

The cabinet was stuffed. There were stacks of magazines, little bottles with faded labels, bird feathers of all colors, bits of straw and dried grasses, tiny cellophane bags with mysterious powders and splinters of substances, and a myriad of other specimens of the exotic and mundane.

"Whoa," Ainsley breathed. "He did collect everything."

"Yeah, here's his collection of insects," Gabe said, scanning over one of the bookshelves and pointing to a flat framed object. "At least, a few of them."

"Ick, well at least we know they're not alive and crawling," Ainsley said shivering.

"Or stinging. Check out this guy." He held up a small plaque and pinned to it was the biggest wasp type bug that Ainsley had ever seen.

"That is horrible. Or horrifying, I'm not sure," she said. "But as much stuff as is in here, I don't see any keys."

Gabe turned from the bookshelves. "I don't see any here either. He might have kept them with his other keys." He scanned the room. "They might be upstairs in his bedroom."

Ainsley felt a little uncomfortable going up into the dead man's bedroom, but Gabe started out the door. "Are you sure we should be hunting around in there?" she asked.

"It's fine. He kept some of his favorite stuff up there, so my cousins and I used to go up on our own to check it out all the time when we were kids. It's not like we'll be going through his skivvies."

Ainsley laughed at the term. "Why would he keep that stuff up where no one would see it?" she asked.

"He wasn't worried about what everyone else was doing. He wanted it to be somewhere that he could see it whenever he wanted to. Hence, leaving up in his bedroom." He grinned. "Wait until you see this place. It tops most of the other rooms."

"No more dead animals, I hope."

"None that I recall, but it has been years since I went up here." Gabe climbed the steps with great loping strides. His height made it easy for him to cover territory quickly, and Ainsley could tell that he had forgotten that she wasn't moving as fast. When he reached the upper hallway, he turned back towards her, and seeing her lagging behind, waited there.

At the top of the stairs, the hallway stretched out in both directions, with massive doors just in front of them. "Wow," Ainsley said, seeing the huge portal.

"Yeah, Uncle Topper had this area renovated so that he could fit the doors. He wanted to use them in the house. He said he got them in Germany when he was overseas twenty years ago."

"Wow," Ainsley said again and smiled.

The doors were painted a deep, blood red, but the surface was heavily chipped. It was difficult to assess the age, but you could tell that the descriptor old didn't cover it. The thing was closer to ancient. The carvings started at the top, and in a pictorial display, stretched down the door like a series of slides representing some long lost story. It would be difficult to tell if the thing was worth money. It wasn't in great condition, some of the smaller pieces of the façade had been chipped off, and the paint had certainly seen better days, but since she didn't know how old the paint was either, it was hard to assess any kind of value.

"Did he know the story behind this?" she asked.

"He always said that they were the doors from a castle. But he never said from where, other than he got them from Germany. He enjoyed telling the story of shipping it home. Apparently they didn't even consider a plane. So they chose to go over water and take their time getting back home. He was with it on board the boat, he and Jack. They wanted to travel back with it, even though the ship was not made for passenger comfort. They ended up running across a ship full of what might be called modern day pirates. But Uncle Topper had something that they must have liked, because they let them go on after some sort of exchange. It sounded damn crazy, but it was an adventure story like a lot of the others that I had heard. I imagine Jack would have his own version of the event." Gabe seemed lost in thought, his look slightly pensive. "Now I wish I had listened a little bit closer, so I could remember his stories. They were always so," he shook his head, searching for the word. "I don't know. He was a wonderful storyteller."

Ainsley put her hand on his arm. "I feel that way about my grandparents. I heard stories about what it was like for them as they grew up, but I wasn't listening close enough, and a lot of what they said got lost."

He nodded, and then moved to push open the door. The panels swung inward with a dramatic squeal of the hinges, but the lights within were off, and the room looked dusty and gray.

"Hang on," Gabe said quickly, "let me get the lights."

If Ainsley had thought that the bedroom was going to be a private affair, she was very wrong. The bed seemed like an afterthought. It was low, covered with simple blankets, made neatly with a single

THE COCKATOO CALLED

pillow. It occupied the far corner of the room, which was pretty funny in itself because the room had obviously been designed around a central area meant for a large and elaborate bed frame. The ceiling was recessed and painted with some type of intricate mural, which wasn't immediately discernible in the dim lighting. There was a large window to the side that opened out onto the front lawn, and at a distance, Ainsley could see the tops of the evergreens that they had passed on their way up the drive.

On one of the other inner walls was a massive fireplace, no doubt meant to warm the foot of the bed, had the bed been in place. Instead, there was a big recliner chair in front of the fireplace, real leather that was scuffed and worn with use, with a table at its side. The table held a decanter of some gold liquid, a pipe in an ashtray, a pair of glasses, presumably for reading, and a folded newspaper.

In place of the bed in the center of the room was a pool table. It was a beautiful old thing, the felt a little threadbare on the top, but still in workable shape. The pool cues were racked up in a mount on the wall, and the balls were unseen, presumably in the pockets of the table.

Every other wall surface was covered. The photographs were every shape and size, some in color, some black and white, some yellowed with age, all in plain wooden frames.

Gabe drew close to a large print on the wall and pointed. "Uncle Topper and Jack," he said, and Ainsley followed his gaze.

Jack was easily recognizable with the full beard, his hair long and strangely braided into tiny ropes. This picture had obviously been taken when Jack actually had hair. But even if you hadn't seen his face, the bird perched on his shoulder would have surely given him away. Hemingway sat erect, his ruby breast thrown out as though posing, wings close to his body. He looked younger, as did Jack. It might have been five years ago, it might have been more or less, but Jack looked happy.

Uncle Topper was at Jack's side, one hand on his nearer shoulder. And in his face, Ainsley could see a shadow of an older Gabe. He had the same narrow bones and sharp planes, his generous smile, the same light eyes and darker hair, although he had some streaks of gray that fanned from his temples in a rather dashing way. His nose was a sharp blade, and a narrow scar split one eyebrow in a rakish manner.

"That was taken while they were traveling in the Caribbean," Gabe explained. "Uncle Topper brought me back a huge shell. Said it come out of a shark's stomach." He grinned at the memory. "He said that when the shark came after him, he shoved it down his throat and he was so busy trying to puke it up that he couldn't eat Uncle Topper. Good story. Total bull, but I knew that."

His tone was warm with the memory, and Ainsley examined the picture a little more closely. "And that is Hemingway?"

"Yeah, he had already traveled quite a bit with the two of them." He chuckled. "He can be a grumpy old cuss, but I think Uncle Topper liked him almost as much as Jack did."

"Jack acted like Hemingway was a sweetheart," Ainsley said thoughtfully.

"And Jack might be just a little biased."

There were many other pictures of the trio. The settings changed, and the hairstyles, the fashion, and the amount of creases that lined the faces. There were group shots with scores of people in all state of dress and some with undress, a few looking like Las Vegas showgirls. Ainsley wondered if any of them were famous. She saw a few pictures with faces that looked suspiciously like some of the rock stars from the 70s. Hemingway was in at least half of the ones featuring the men, and there were a few without Jack that just showed Uncle Topper and Hemingway, often enough sharing a drink.

"That bird doesn't drink alcohol!" Ainsley exclaimed, horrified.

"Nah, they like the old buzzard too much for that."

Some of the pictures where the bird wasn't evident were taken in colder climates. It looked from some of them that mountain climbing might have been one of Uncle Topper's many hobbies. There were a few that showed figures so muffled in snow gear that it was difficult to tell who they were. Had it not been for Topper's sharp blade of a nose and Jack's ice encrusted beard, they could have been photos of anyone.

Ainsley walked the room, this time examining the photographs as well as the furnishings. The pictures were stacked, one on top of the other, starting at waist height, although on Topper, a tall man, it would have been considerably lower.

On closer examination, she noticed that there was an unintentional order to the pictures. The ones at eye level were younger shots, mostly of Uncle Topper in his midlife, a few with Jack, many more with a collection of kids.

"That's us," Gabe exclaimed. "Here are my sisters and my cousins from Canada, and me." The cluster of youngsters was sitting around a table, red popsicles staining fingers and face. Uncle Topper was in the center, his face stained as well. He was grinning. "These are my other cousins. He would visit all over, so he got to see most of us pretty often." He was scanning the other pictures with enjoyment. "I got to see him the most because he lived here, but with all his traveling, we all were able to see him."

THE COCKATOO CALLED

Ainsley looked at the lineup of pictures reflecting the kids growing, the chubby children, the gangly teenage years, the handsome young men and women.

"Sorry," Gabe said from behind her. "I think I've gotten distracted. Let's keep looking for the key."

"I don't mind," Ainsley said. "I like looking at the pictures."

"We'll come back to look at them," Gabe said firmly. "I'll make sure we can. But for now, I need to find that address book. And that might mean I need to find the key."

"Or the book might just be sitting out here," Ainsley said hopefully.

"It could," Gabe agreed.

But the search ended up not revealing anything. They combed the room, looking at the dresser top, the shelves, and laughing as they saw the fully working pinball machine, the collection of comic books, and the shelf proudly displaying a set of African masks and some horrible little balls that Ainsley was afraid were shrunken heads. There was a door to an adjoining room, and they were surprised to see a cage there.

"I guess maybe he kept Dali in here at night. The bigger cage, the one I have, must have been downstairs."

"So Dali had two cages?" Ainsley asked.

"The lawyer said something about that, but I figured I wouldn't worry about it. One cage is plenty big in my apartment." Gabe stood in the center of the room, arms crossed over his chest. "I just wonder what happened to those keys!"

"Could he have kept them on the keychain with the rest of his keys?"

Gabe seemed to freeze. "Well," he said slowly, "I'm embarrassed that I didn't think about it before. But it would make sense."

"Do you know where the rest are?"

"His keys? I know there are some downstairs, but I think the lawyer might have the rest of them. I'll have to see if I can run by and pick them up."

"Do you think that he'll just let you have them?"

"I'll borrow them," Gabe said casually. "I have before. I brought Uncle Topper's car back here for safe keeping about a month ago. Jack had been using it."

"Then we can look around here for anything out of place, and come back another time to see if you have the keys to his desk." Ainsley glanced around the room.

"You'll come back with me?" Gabe asked.

"Sure," Ainsley said, realizing that she had been having a good time.

"Okay!" Gabe turned and glanced out the door into the hallway. "Then before you leave, let me show you the living room."

They spent nearly an hour poking around the living room, Gabe pointing out some of the most unusual pieces of his uncle's collection. And he had been correct when he had said that his uncle had a little bit of everything. It would have taken many more hours just to explore the rest of the first floor.

"The basement is a set of cellars, and we weren't allowed to go down there when we were younger." Gabe checked his watch. "We'll have to come back to check out the rest on another day."

"That makes sense," Ainsley agreed. "So when do you plan on coming back?"

"I'll see about getting the keys this week," Gabe said, "and then I can call you."

Ainsley was grinning when she said, "it's a date then!"

THE COCKATOO CALLED

CHAPTER SEVEN

The day was crawling by. They had scheduled back-to-back patients; Mr. Baker had lost a crown and needed to be fit in the schedule, and then the root canal for Ms. Nancy Casey, not to be confused with her neighbor Ms. Denise Casey, had gone on too long. With the hours all jammed with paperwork and taking care of impatient people, Ainsley had thought that the day would whip along. She was wrong. The minutes dragged like a bad movie. And then the headache, aggravated by struggling to read and fill out forms, started around lunchtime. By the time she was done with work and was ducking her way into her car, protected only by a thin sweater, a cold drizzle had started.

"Please stop, please stop," she chanted as she shoved her key in the door lock and opened the door. She hated this cold rain, and to make matters worse, the next day was Halloween. She had hoped for good weather. It would be her first Halloween in the neighborhood, but she had heard that they generally had a decent number of trick-or-treaters that would come by begging for sweets. And she loved Halloween. Mostly because it brought back warm family memories of rushing home with a pillow case full of treats, her cousin insisted that it made a better container than paper bags that would tear under the weight of so much candy. And then they had dumped out their booty and dug through it, trading and complaining when her parents grabbed at a couple of pieces.

To have Halloween at her house seemed like a rite of passage. It made the place seem homier. She had gone out and purchased orange lights to string on the bushes outside as well as plenty of fake cobwebs to garner her door. There were candles, artificial of course, and garlands of fall leaves that hung over her curtains in her living room. She had loaded up on candy and placed it, still in the bags, in a giant mixing bowl by the door. She was excited for the holiday, but to make things better, Gabe had called and told her that he had gotten the keys from the lawyer.

"We can go back out there whenever you want," he had said, "but I don't want you to feel like you have to give up all your time for this."

She didn't feel that way but was straining to remain cool. She wanted to spend her time with Gabe, and besides that, it satisfied her deep need for something to keep her mind active. She was curious: about the bird, about Gabe's uncle, about the mysterious painting or the possibility of other treasures. And that wasn't to say that she didn't enjoy their outings. Gabe was a wonderful guy. He was smart, thoughtful, handsome, and had a great sense of humor. She also felt that he liked being with her as much as she enjoyed his company. She wasn't going to say that he was the love of her life, she was far too practical for that, but she knew that she was developing a healthy crush on him and was looking forward to seeing him again. When she mentioned that she planned to be at home on Halloween in hopes of meeting some of her neighbors, he had seemed a little down.

"The apartment doesn't have any arrangements for Halloween," he said glumly. "There aren't many kids here. I think one of the guys on the floor above mine is planning on having a get together, but I think it's just an excuse to party."

"I know the kind," she said sympathetically. She thought for a moment, and then burst out, "If you don't have any other plans, you're welcome to come visit Dali and I."

As soon as she said it she felt stupid. What young man would choose to go to someone's house in hopes of seeing costumed children when they might be able to go to a real adult party with all of the accompanying adult fun?

But his response was quick, "I'd love to come over," he said enthusiastically. "I can bring pizza. Dali likes pizza too."

It was funny how their plans now included the whims of a parrot, but in a way it was nice to have that interest in common.

"Okay, I'll fix something for dessert."

"Great," he had responded, and their plans were made.

Now she was just wishing the workday away. In front of her was a hand written note left by the last patient. She needed to enter the content of the note into the appropriate section of the record for the treatment in the computer. But the task was proving to be more challenging. The handwriting was in print, but the lines were thin and wavy, the penmanship of an older woman whose hands trembled. When Ainsley was tired, the letters jumped on the page like scattering insects, and she rubbed her eyes. Her vision didn't clear. On a typed note, she would use a scanner to enter the text into the computer and use symbol recognition to transfer it into a Word Document. From there, she could copy whatever she needed into the treatment notes. But this, this was handwritten and she was tired. She muttered a curse softly; making sure no one could hear her. Her co-workers knew of her disability, but she didn't want them to have to come in and rescue her.

She blew out a sigh and put the note off to the side. It would do no good to struggle over it now. She would have to do it later when she was less tense. She carefully laid it up with the other pending work. Organization was her saving grace. She had triumphed in hard won struggles through keeping everything very specifically filed, color coded, and electronic when she could. Hard work and preplanning, for her, paid off consistently.

She only had an hour before it would be time for her to head home. Dinner tonight would be cold cereal because she didn't feel up to cooking. And she would need the morning to work on her house. Dali's mess was still significant. It would take some time before the house would be presentable for visitors.

The final patient came out of the back room, smiling crookedly after having a tooth filled.

"Do you need a follow up appointment?" Ainsley asked.

"No, I'll call later," the woman mumbled.

"Okay," Ainsley said, and walked her to the door. She locked the deadbolt after her and watched as Theresa came out of the room, drying her hands on a paper towel after washing them in the little sink.

"Hey," Theresa said. "Friday night! You got any big plans?"

"Not for tonight. I'm just staying in and cleaning. Tomorrow Gabe's coming over."

"Gabe," Theresa said grinning. "When do we get to meet this guy?"

Ainsley felt herself blush a little. She was feeling better, her headache easing slightly now that she had backed away from her desk. "I imagine that you'll run into him at some point. He's just coming out to meet with Dali."

"Of course," Theresa said, her eyebrows raised. "He wants to meet with the bird."

Ainsley's smile was a little self-satisfied. "The bird and maybe me," she said.

"So when is he taking Dali back home?"

Ainsley's smile melted. "I don't know," she replied. "He's having some problems at his apartment. He needs to get that settled before he can take the bird there."

Theresa read her friend's face. "You're going to miss that crazy bird."

"I will," Ainsley agreed. She sighed. "I know it sounds silly. But Dali is more than just a parrot. I mean, I always thought keeping a bird would be like keeping a fish, pretty to look at, but not very interactive. But he's not like that at all. He's a real pet like a dog or cat. He's a lot of company since I live alone." She looked at Theresa. "I can't see myself being able to replace him when he leaves. You know how it is when you fall for something." She bit her lip, her eyes sad. "Do I sound crazy?"

"Well, yes," Theresa, "but no more than any other animal lover. Just because Dali isn't a common pet doesn't mean he isn't a pet." She put her hand on Ainsley's shoulder. "I had a dog when I was a kid. He slept with me every night, and I had a picture of him in my locker at school. He was my best friend. When he died, I cried for a week. I still think of him and feel that love. He was a true friend to me." Theresa smiled gently. "Dali is your friend."

Ainsley smiled shakily. "That's right, he is."

"And don't you think that Gabe will let you stay in touch after he moves home?"

"I'm sure he would," Ainsley said. She felt a little better, but still a little sad.

"Okay, so what are you and bird man going to do tomorrow night?"

"Have pizza, see some trick-or-treaters. Play with Dali. I'm not sure what exactly, but I have to admit that I am looking forward to seeing him."

"Hmmm, maybe I need to stop by and borrow a cup of sugar," Theresa kidded her.

"Why do you need sugar?" Nan asked coming from the back. "You don't cook, and what you do eat is all natural or organic."

"I'm just thinking of a good reason why I might need to visit Ainsley while Gabe is over. I'm dying to get a chance to meet this guy."

"Oh, me too!" Nan exclaimed.

"Okay, just no. That is not going to work. I don't need you all to come spying on me!"

Theresa and Nan shared a look and broke down laughing.

"But sometime soon," Theresa promised.

*****

THE COCKATOO CALLED

The morning was gorgeous. The rain had cleared, the sun had come out, and the temperature had settled into a pleasant mid 60s. Although the leaves had mostly drifted to the earth, some still held their color making the ground look like a mosaic of torn paper.

Ainsley finished her coffee sitting at her kitchen table, laughing as Dali snatched her toast. She had cleaned the cage completely and was moving on to the floor as soon as she was done eating. On the center of the table was a pumpkin. She had plans to carve it but hadn't started yet.

She tucked her ear buds in and switched on her cell phone. She had found the joy of audiobooks when she was in high school, and had devoured them ever since. She had broken down and bought a subscription for a service so that she could download the books directly to her phone. She also was able to find books at the public library's website and download some of theirs as well. Now she was 'reading' two books at once, a Nora Roberts for evenings, and a scary Dean Koontz story for the daytime. It seemed a good time to listen to a horror novel, so she settled in with the new Koontz track as she cleaned.

She was through a good fourth of the book when she finished cleaning the house. She had grabbed a quick peanut butter sandwich standing by the sink for lunch, guzzling water from her water bottle when she passed the counter. Now that it was midafternoon, she and Dali shared an apple as she opened a social media app on her phone. She checked up on notes that her friends had placed, pleased when she saw a picture of one of her hometown friends snuggled up with her new baby boy, now costumed as a chubby cheeked lion.

Thinking of her family, she got up and snapped a few photos of her house with the new decorations. She took several shots that included Dali before tucking him back in his cage. Then she went outside and checked on the lights out there. The sun was slowly waning, but it would be light for a few hours yet. The temperature had dipped a little, but it still would be a great night for the kids. She grabbed a few more pictures of the outside of her house and sent a variety of the ones she had taken to her mother. She stood out by her mailbox for a few more minutes, studying the house. Cute, she decided, comfortable. It was missing one thing though.

She went inside and closed the door behind her, stopping to study the pumpkin on the table. She looked at Dali as he snuggled up to the side of the cage, waiting for attention.

"Should I make it a happy jack-o-lantern, or a scary one?" she asked the bird.

Dali muttered a funny little noise and studied her with one bright eye. "Happy," he said in his gravelly little voice.

Ainsley was shocked. He didn't talk very much. When he did, it was usually calling his own name, Dali or Bird. Sometimes he would say hello. Other times his mumbled mutterings were totally unintelligible. But on occasion, something he said would be so clear, so perfect, that Ainsley would start to think again about what he understood.

"Okay, then, Bird," she said smiling. "Happy it is."

She had gotten out bowls and spoons and spread newspaper out on the table for the pumpkin carving when the doorbell chimed. She ran to the front door and threw it open.

"Whoa," Gabe exclaimed, seeing her knife. "I'm sorry. Whatever it is that I've done, I'm officially sorry."

"Ha, funny," she responded. "Come on in."

"You didn't need the knife to convince me to come in," he said, still grinning. She looked at his face, his hair windblown and flopping over his forehead, his eyes alight with mischief. The man was beautiful when he smiled.

"I was going to carve the pumpkin, so I could have it out on the porch before the goblins came."

"Nickname for the neighbors?" he quipped.

"If you like," she responded. "I haven't sketched out a face yet, but Dali wants it to be something happy."

"He does, does he?" he asked, one brow arched.

"Yes, he said so. I swear, I asked him if he wanted a happy or scary face and he said happy."

"So he's talking more?"

"Not a whole lot. He does once in a while, usually calling for me when I'm not in the room. But that time he seemed like he knew exactly what he wanted to say."

"He does that sometimes," Gabe agreed. "So you were going to draw a face?"

"It's going to be triangle eyes and nose if it's up to me. I can't draw worth a lick. I've never been much of an artist. I'm pretty good with a stick figure though."

"I'll draw it if you want. Did you have an idea of what kind of face you had planned?'

"Not really," Ainsley replied, and went to the little desk tucked next to the side of the cabinet and pulled out a notebook and pencil. "Will this be good enough?' she asked.

"That's fine," he said, and looked thoughtfully at her. When he started to sketch, his hand moved with quick sure strokes, but she stayed

THE COCKATOO CALLED

at her place until he was finished, savoring the anticipation a little. She could tell by the way that his hands moved that he hadn't drawn any gap toothed jack-o-lantern smile. When he held up the paper, she gasped in pleasure. It was the silhouette of a cockatoo, wings slightly extended, crest prominent on the top of his head. Since it was just an outline, there were no details that led her to believe that he had drawn a picture of Dali, but she knew anyway. There was just something in the way the bird held his body, cocked his head, that seemed familiar.

"Nice!" she said excitedly. "This is good! Do you draw a lot?"

"At work I do. I do a lot of sketches for ideas, then we transfer them to Sketch-Up. It's a program on the computer. I come up with concepts first by hand. It's easier for me to envision it that way."

"I wondered if architects still did drawings by hand."

"For creative things we do. It's a better way to get concepts on paper. Then we can flesh it out using computer programs."

She looked at the drawing of the bird and smiled. "This does look like Dali," she said. "Do you think we can carve it?"

"Do you have a little sharp knife? Like a paring knife?"

"Sure," she said, and stood to rummage through the drawer. She found a few more knives that she laid out on the newspaper and then a bowl to hold the innards of the pumpkin.

"Will those do?" she asked.

"That should work," he agreed quickly, and started to trace the shape on the skin of the pumpkin. After he had cut open the top, she assisted in taking out the guts of the giant gourd. While she separated and washed the pumpkin seeds to toast up in her oven, he finished whittling out the bird shape. "Will you use a candle in here?" he asked.

"Oh, yes," she agreed. "I always like to do it the old fashioned way. I kind of like the smell of the candle burning inside of the pumpkin. It must be something from my childhood." She went back in her bedroom and came back holding a little votive candle in a clear glass cup. "Here's one. It should fit fine."

"Okay, with a little cleaning out, it should be ready," he said stepping back to look at the carved picture.

"It looks great!" She watched as he went over to the sink with several knives, deftly washing them, drying them, and putting them back in the respective drawers. She tried to place the candle in the bottom of the pumpkin, but found that the floor of the pumpkin still had a bump in the center, from the stem, she supposed. She grabbed one of the remaining knives and began scraping at the flesh in the pumpkin. Then her hand, slick from the juices of the gourd, slipped on the handle of the knife. Her hand slid down the hilt and onto the blade. She felt the cool slice as the blade cut into her palm, and then the stinging pain as the juice hit the wound. She yelped and pulled her hand out, holding her fist closed. Red liquid squeezed between her fingers, and she felt her stomach turn.

"Are you all right?"

She forced a weak smile. "Sure, yes, I just," she swallowed hard and held her hand up.

"Wow, okay, your face is looking a little, um, here, let's sit you down," he said pulling out a chair and guiding her into it.

She gave up trying to look good and settled for trying to remain conscious and keep the contents in her stomach down. She leaned over her lap, her burning hand held away from her body, knowing full well that if she saw the blood again, she would faint dead away.

She felt him at her side, and he gently pulled her hair away from the nape of her neck and put a damp towel in its place. "I'm going to get you something to drink. You just sit here."

"This is so embarrassing," Ainsley muttered.

She heard him open the refrigerator and the rattling of a glass. A cold sweat had broken out all over her body, and she found herself taking deep breaths. "Here is your drink," he said, holding a glass with orange juice and a straw close to her. "You need some sugar. You're blood pressure has gone down to nothing."

She forced herself to take a tiny sip of the juice, feeling the cold slide down her throat. Then she took a second. She breathed slowly, thinking she didn't want anything to drink, just to feel better.

He bent over her and took the towel away, bringing it back a moment later. "Drink a little more," he said, and she felt his warm hand close over her clinched fist. "Let me see," he said gently.

She carefully opened her fist, feeling the burn again. "It's not the pain," she said breathlessly. "It's the idea of it."

"I know. It's fine." She felt something dab against her hand and winced. "Sorry," he said gently. "It's not so bad. I'll clean it up quick."

She tried to concentrate on sipping the juice. She was still feeling waves of lightheadedness, but it seemed to be slightly better. She tried to keep her mind off of her hand, instead concentrating of the warmth of his side presence to her, the smell of him, like laundry detergent and spicy cologne.

"How about some bandaids?" he asked.

"In the cabinet in the bathroom," she said, still bent double with her head level with her knees.

THE COCKATOO CALLED

He was back a moment later. He gently took her hand, and she felt the rattle of paper as he unwrapped a few Bandaids. She felt the reassuring pressure of the adhesive as he applied the bandages. A moment later, she felt him wiping up her hand. "Okay, you're all set. But we need to get you lying down for a minute until you start feeling better."

She nodded but didn't move. She didn't want to go upright.

"I'm going to lift you up," he said. "Just for a minute."

She felt him next to her. Then he put one arm under her legs and another around her back. She was surprised that he was able to lift her so easily. She was an average woman. Average height, average weight. But he was able to take her into the living room and lay her down on the couch with relative ease. He settled her down on the cushions. She felt him add a pillow under her head but kept her eyes closed for a moment.

"How do you feel now?" he asked.

She was embarrassed, but relieved she hadn't vomited on him. At least she hadn't done that. "I'll be okay," she breathed. "I'm so sorry."

"Nothing to be sorry about," he said. "I'm just going to clean up a bit."

She heard him rattling around in the kitchen. After a few minutes, she sat up slightly on the couch and pushed her hair away from her face. She took a second to glance at her hand, but was relieved to see that he had gotten rid of every speck of blood. There was a line of at least five Bandaids marching across her palm, overlapping. It completely covered the wound.

He came back in, holding her orange juice. "One more drink," he said, sitting next to her on the couch.

She took the drink from the straw obediently. "You're a good nurse," she said.

"I am," he agreed. "I have an excellent bedside manner. And I can juggle."

"That's all you need," she agreed.

He bent and gently pushed her hair from her forehead. "You look much better with some color in your cheeks," he said smiling. He leaned over and pressed his lips to her forehead. "Much better," he said, and she felt the color rush into her face.

"I thought that we were going to order pizza," she said, changing the subject.

"Anchovies and olives," he said cheerfully and laughed at her expression. "Alright, then, we'll compromise."

*****

The pizza was delicious. It was ordered from a locally owned restaurant that was situated almost within walking distance from Ainsley's home. Of course, considering how terrible she felt, embarrassed at having almost passed out because of a mere flesh wound, she would have been satisfied with cardboard. The only positive outcome, in her opinion, was the totally platonic kiss that Gabe had given her which had pushed her over the edge from crush to true love in one gentle shove. Not that she would have ever admitted to the feeling, but wow, it felt good. Crazy, but good.

Gabe had done a wonderful job on the kitchen. He had managed to clean up the pumpkin mess, and whatever mess that she had created with the knife. He had then taken the carved pumpkin out onto the porch leaving it, with the candle inside and unlit.

After dinner, Ainsley pulled out the bags of candy that she had bought earlier in the week, opened them, and dumped them into a big mixing bowl. When she returned to the kitchen, Gabe was rinsing the bowl of seeds from the pumpkin.

"You don't have to do that," she exclaimed seeing him working at her sink.

"Are you kidding? I've never had these before. I want to try them. If I don't get them tonight, I'll have to live unfulfilled for the rest of my days."

She laughed a little. "It is a risk," she said. "So you've never had these before?"

"No, I've heard of it, but this is new for me." He held out the bowl. "Does this look right?"

"Perfect," she said. "And I'm going to let you light the candle in the Jack-o-lantern. The kids should start coming soon, at least the little ones. The older trick-or-treaters will be here later."

"And you said that you didn't know how many you would get?" he asked, snatching a miniature Snickers bar out of the bowl and ripping it open.

"The neighbors said that this road would be pretty busy. I'll have enough candy, though. Unless you have an uncontrollable chocolate binge," she said grinning.

"Not uncontrollable," he said smiling back.

She emptied the candy bags from the bowl on a table next to the front door and returned to the kitchen to switch on the stove to pre-heat it. While it was warming, she put foil out on a cookie sheet and sprayed some butter flavored cooking oil on it. Gabe dumped out the seeds on the pan and together they spread them out evenly. Once salted, they popped

THE COCKATOO CALLED

the cookie sheet with the pumpkin seeds into the oven and went back to the living room. As soon as Ainsley had switched on the TV set, the doorbell rang. She swung it open, and to her delight, there were five toddlers dressed up as Disney characters standing on her porch. She gave each of them several pieces of candy after hearing their particular rendition of trick-or –treat in sweet childish tones.

After they had gone, Gabe slumped back on the couch in that way that tall people did. His legs seemed to go on and on, and Ainsley stifled a smile. She sat on the chair close by, facing the door so that she would see any new visitors.

"I talked to Uncle Topper's lawyer this afternoon," Gabe said. "I'm going to run over there and get the keys in the morning. I also talked to Jack. He's back in town on Friday, so I'm going to go out to the house and meet him there Saturday."

Ainsley looked at him thoughtfully. "So do you think that he can help you get into the desk? Maybe find the address book?"

"And get his opinion," Gabe agreed. "Do you want to ride along?"

"Sure!" She hoped she didn't sound too eager.

From behind her, she heard Dali exclaim, "Yes!"

"I don't think you're invited this time, Bird," Gabe replied. "He's hating that he can't get out right now," he said, looking past her at the bird in the cage.

"If I thought for sure he wouldn't try to head out the door when we opened it, I might let him out but," she said, and as if on cue, the doorbell rang again.

CHAPTER EIGHT

By nine o'clock, they were out of candy, and the only kids coming to the door were ones that Ainsley was pretty sure had been there before. Catching seconds had become a rite of passage with the middle school crowd, and for them, there were few things funnier than pulling one over on the adults. But she had handed out what candy she had left anyway, better them gorging on it than her, and then closed the door firmly. She switched off her porch light to signal that they had closed up shop, and went to retrieve the bird from his cage. After a few cuddles, she handed him over to Gabe.

"So you didn't see Dali while your Uncle was around?" she asked watching him cradle the bird close to his chest.

"No, my business was getting busy and time was limited, so I'd meet Uncle Topper at his favorite restaurant. We would have dinner out, just catch up some on the news, but I wasn't visiting his house so much anymore. I know that Jack was, though. So if there is anything significant missing, I'm sure that Jack would notice."

She looked at Gabe a little cautiously, afraid of his reaction, but she had to ask. "And you trust him completely?"

"Jack?" Gabe looked relaxed, the bird cuddled in his arms. "I wouldn't trust him farther than I could throw him about most things, but about this, yes, I do. He may have had something of a checkered past, but he cared about Uncle Topper, and saved him more than once. And I mean that literally. Uncle Topper told me some rather crazy stories." He gently fluffed the bird's feathers. "Jack will help, especially if he thinks that someone is out to get this guy." Gabe said confidently.

Gabe was exactly right in that respect.

*****

THE COCKATOO CALLED

"You think they broke in to get the bird? That's insane!" Jack had arrived at Uncle Topper's house, a large crate holding Hemingway stowed in his passenger seat. It didn't surprise Ainsley that he drove a massive truck, a huge dually that had definitely seen better days. The exhaust that it belched was an unpleasant slate gray, and the engine sounded like it was very unhappy. But the sheer size of the vehicle, combined with its dull black paint job, made it seem like some beached ship, sanded down and weathered by the elements. He had jumped down from the cab of the truck, moving like a man half his age, and taken the crate from the seat. Ainsley and Gabe had watched this from the porch, but as he approached, Gabe had jogged down the steps to meet him. They opted to go first into the library, Jack seemingly entranced in memories as he walked into the foyer.

"We got Barney here when we were visiting Africa," he said, putting a heavy hand on the head of the lion. "They were shutting down a local bar, and he needed a home. Paid handsomely for this guy."

Gabe grinned. "I had wondered. I know Uncle Topper wasn't much of a hunter."

"Ha! Hunter? Nah, too squeamish by half. He would have rather be eaten by old Barney here then raise a weapon to him!" He brought the bird into the library, sat him on the desk, and opened the crate.

Hemingway stepped out like royalty holding court. He came out onto the flat of the desk and fluffed his feathers, slightly aggravated. He watched the group of people with one light golden eye, head cocked.

"Will Hemingway bite me?" Ainsley asked, drawing a little closer to the bird.

"Well now, that would depend," Jack said, gently stroking the bird's head, fluffing the feathers until Hemingway seemed to have a collar of red.

"Depend on what?" Ainsley had stilled, looking at the bird's intelligent eye.

"That I don't know. He's gotten me a time or two, drawn a little blood, but then, he could have taken the whole finger, so I don't blame him for that!"

"Oh!" Ainsley still stood frozen.

"You got to remember about these guys," Jack continued conversationally, "they're smart and independent. They have an idea about what they like and don't like. And their hormones rule them too. Can't say I understand him, but, he and I, well, we have an agreement. I do what he wants me to do, and he puts up with me!" He chuckled to himself, and the bird turned and grabbed a finger in its massive beak.

The gesture was a gentle one, though, and Ainsley could tell that they did indeed have a singular relationship.

"Topper wanted to have one of his own, but I told him that he needed something that would be less work than old Hemingway here. That's why we picked a 'too. Not an easy bird, that's for sure, but a little more hands on."

"Hemingway has always been fine with me," Gabe observed, looking a little more cautiously at the bird.

"Some people he likes, some he doesn't. I can read him pretty well. He has limits to what he'll tolerate with anyone. The only person I've ever seen him be totally in love with is my little girl. Not that the feeling is mutual. But he'd let her pluck him bald and bake him in the oven, I think."

"Really." Ainsley tried to picture Jack's daughter. Was she a pierced and tattooed character like her father? It wouldn't take too much to picture the two of them sailing on a pirate ship, Hemingway perched on a shoulder, face to the wind.

"My Genevieve doesn't care for our Hemingway," he said grinning. "But he does love our girl. Must think she's part of his flock."

"So do you see anything missing in here?" Gabe asked, changing the topic abruptly. He was scanning the room carefully, but Ainsley could see nothing out of place, at least, not since their last visit.

"Well, now, I don't think so," Jack said, standing hands on hips. "Nothing that comes immediately to mind. Your Uncle had so many things, though. I could be wrong." He turned on his heel, striding from one corner of the room to another, head down, then looking back toward the many bookcases. "But it's not just anything that they're after, right? You think that somebody is trying to steal the bird from you?"

"We think that someone wanted what Uncle Topper had given me. Or they think that he gave me. It's just too much of a coincidence! I never had anyone try to break in before I got Dali, but since then, I know of at least three times that they've come in. Of course, the first time they took Dali and I was so surprised by the mess of it all, I didn't know if they had gotten anything else. It was such a disaster that it took me a while to finish checking out my stuff. After all that time, I honestly couldn't name anything that I found missing. That's why I feel sure that someone thinks that I have something of Topper's." Gabe looked unhappy. "And it's also why we wanted to come out here. Because if someone was after something of Uncle Topper's, we figured if I don't have it, it must still be here."

"But Topper only left you the bird so far? Right?" Jack asked.

THE COCKATOO CALLED

"Nothing else has come out of the estate?"

"As far as I know," Gabe said, "nothing has been distributed. Nothing has been moved from the house, any of his accounts, anything, really. And I've talked to most of the other cousins."

Jack crossed his arms over his massive chest, his long beard tucked down. "Okay, so we'll take a look around." He frowned. "But it makes me sick. Someone stealing from a dead man like that. And from Topper!" He shook his gray head, face grave. Hemingway made an aggravated squawk, and Jack seemed to agree with the sentiment. "We need to nail these bastards!"

Ainsley and Gabe had been there just days ago, but Jack wasn't to be hurried. Every room had memories attached to it, every collection an adventure. They decided to start with the desk, and Gabe sorted through the huge ring of keys that the lawyers had given him.

"Got it," Gabe said at last, poking a little key in the lock and hearing the click of the turning mechanism.

"Got what?" Jack had Hemingway on his shoulder, looking that much more the pirate, and was standing in front of the open cabinet door.

"The desk is open," Gabe said over his shoulder.

"Won't find anything there," Jack said dismissively. "He only came in here to smoke and think. Anything good he kept upstairs."

"Where did he keep his records?" Ainsley asked, looking toward the big man.

"Huh? Records?"

"Papers. Where would he have kept his files?"

"Ah. Well, he had all his bills, taxes and the like, up in his room."

Gabe had gotten the lid rolled up on the desk and was rummaging through the cubbies. He had a stack of papers before him, but was shaking his head as he paged through them. "These are old. I mean, really old."

"He kept everything," Jack agreed. "That desk came from his father. I imagine the papers are from him."

Gabe nodded. "These are ancient," he agreed. "They might be nice for some kind of historian, but they're not going to help us at all."

"Well, if you're looking for our papers, the stuff he collected while we were out sowing our oats, you'd see that upstairs, I'd wager." Jack closed the cabinet door. "Eh, Hemingway?" he said.

"So we should go upstairs to his room again?" Ainsley looked between the two men.

"I want to get a look at some of those pictures," Jack agreed. "Been awhile."

They walked up the stairs single file. Jack led with Hemingway still on his shoulder. The bird's long ruby tail was like a ribbon down Jack's jacket, a badge of honor. Hemingway would flap his extravagant wings on occasion, and Ainsley could almost feel the draft from his movement.

The doors were open. The great antique doors that had blocked the view of the interior of the bedroom when they had come before were now standing ajar. Gabe stopped short on the threshold. Ainsley tried to think back to their last visit. They had closed the door. She could remember Gabe pulling the doors to and hearing the clunk as the panels met in the middle. It had stood out in her mind, that sound. So why were they open now? Of course, she reasoned silently to herself, there were the caretakers that were coming to care for the property. They might have come up here for some reason. Check to make sure that all was undisturbed? Drop by to ensure that the house was still sound? But something didn't feel right.

Together they walked into the room and froze. If there had been any doubt before, it was gone. The room was in fine order, except for the walls. The photos had been the most outstanding characteristic of the room when they had come before, but now it had been destroyed. Pictures and frames lay in tangles over the hard wood floor, glass littering the surface like so many hard-edged diamonds. It looked as though someone had, at first, opened the frames to pull out the pictures and then discarded them both on the floor when they hadn't found what they wanted. But farther into the room, the frustration became evident because many of the pictures had just been swept off the walls, flung far from where they had originally hung. Some of the frames had cracked open on impact. Many of the glass fronts were broken. A few photographs had been ripped in pieces.

"Oh, Lord have mercy," Jack said in a growl.

Gabe uttered a curse under his breath.

Hemingway gave an echoing squawk as though putting in his opinion of the destruction.

"Well now," Jack said from the doorway, "it does seem that we have some bad goings on here."

The police arrived half an hour after their call to take a report and to photograph the mess. Gabe was confident as he explained their presence at the house and Ainsley felt relieved that they had contacted the lawyers before their visit. In spite of these assurances, the police were quick to call the law firm. The officer in charge explained that they needed to make sure that Gabe had proof of their claim that they had come to the house with permission. It wasn't breaking and entering if you had the approval of the executor of the estate.

Ainsley hadn't been involved in anything like it, and sat on the edge of her chair as the police took their statements. But she was concerned that there would be little that they could do. Jack could only attest that he did not see anything missing from the premises. Whatever the person had been after when they had come to the house, they couldn't predict that it had been found. That was unless Gabe and Ainsley had completely missed their target, which they agreed was possible. The house was huge, and the collections equally massive.

The group was told that they could help clean up the mess as soon as all the evidence was gathered. But the investigation wasn't like any CSI episode. The police did take pictures and write notes, but there were no exhaustive fingerprinting or mapping of the crime scene. It was simply a case of vandalism unless the family found something missing from Uncle Topper's belongings, and as such, Ainsley doubted that the case would be pursued.

After the police left, Gabe and Ainsley just looked at one another.

"Well, I want to look at some of those pictures," Jack said. His face was creased with emotion, and Ainsley felt a surge of sympathy for him. "I have to go through them. Can't believe someone would do this. Makes no sense."

Ainsley surveyed the mess with Gabe. Jack had stepped into the room and had picked up a few photographs, paging through them slowly. Hemingway was still perched on Jack's shoulder, but he had fortunately been a perfect gentleman when the police had talked with them. Ainsley now felt like she needed to help the older man. He looked so sad, and it struck her how much he was missing his friend.

"Let's get some garbage bags," she said quickly. "We can get rid of the broken frames and salvage whatever can be reused. But we'll pick up the pictures; we'll want to get them in order."

"Okay," Gabe agreed. "I'll go get the bags." He disappeared down the stairs and Jack straightened, gaining resolve.

"I'll get out the stand and set Hemingway up. He'll need some water. But he'll wait just fine." He walked through the mess, dropping the photographs he was holding onto the pool table. He went into the little room where Ainsley and Gabe had noticed the extra cage the last time they had been there, and came out a minute later with a bird stand. It had a giant metal pan beneath and a perch with a bowl stationed at either end. Jack carried it next to the pool table and transferred the bird to a perch. He tugged one of the bowls free and took it into the adjoining bathroom where he filled it with water.

"It looks like Uncle Topper had everything set up for Hemingway to visit," Ainsley noted.

"Oh, yeah, he's had this for a while. I'm guessing that Dali used it some, but this has been here for years." He gently ran his hand down the bird's back. "He liked Hemingway. And he liked us to come visit." He stopped speaking and blinked his eyes a little.

Ainsley didn't know what to say. It just seemed cruel that someone would come in and destroy so many memories. She started gathering photographs, stacking them neatly on the pool table to be sorted. It would take some time to figure out which photographs went with which. When Gabe returned, he started gathering the broken pieces of the frames and dropping them in the bag. He had found a broom and dustpan as well to collect the little pieces of glass and wood.

Jack had started at the other end of the room and was gathering photos as well, moving more slowly as he scanned the shots. He would occasionally give a little laugh or shake his head.

After all of the pictures had been laid out on the pool table, Ainsley helped Gabe finish picking up the frames. There were some that could be used again, but many that couldn't. Of course, she didn't know what would happen to all of them when the will was read. Would someone keep the pictures in this house? Or would the house be sold and all of the things inside divided among the family members?

"I don't see the picture that we had taken in Mexico," Jack said frowning at a set of pictures laid out on the felt.

"What did it look like?" Gabe asked, taking his place next to the table.

"It was Topper and me. We had Hemingway with us too. We were in the market. Shopping again," Jack flipped through a few more pictures. "It was hung with some of these," he said gesturing to the other photos.

Gabe and Jack looked over some of the pictures. They began rummaging through the stacks, resorting and stacking. "There are some other ones missing," Gabe said frowning. "The ones from the safari," he said. "I remember those from last time we were here. And some of the shots from inside this house," he noted.

"I know the ones you mean," Jack agreed. "And I don't see the ones we had from Spain." He grinned. "Despite all those crazy stories Topper liked to tell, we did meet some famous people. Salvador Dali was just one of them."

"You met Salvador Dali?" Ainsley was surprised.

THE COCKATOO CALLED

"Uh, yeah," Jack said. "We met a lot of unusual people over the years. Old Topper got around, and Salvador Dali was known to hang out with the rich and famous. Can't say they were best friends, but they definitely rubbed elbows."

"I thought that was just a tall tale," Gabe protested.

"Ah, no, boy." Jack admonished, shaking his head. "We met a lot of red carpet folks. Movie people, music people, authors, artists, anyone with a little fame and money like to hang around together."

"Did you talk to Dali?" Ainsley was looking at the eccentric looking man, his large hands deftly flipping through the photos. She had seen pictures and knew that this look wasn't new for him. Jack had always looked like a gypsy pirate in pictures. He was just younger in most of them. Perhaps it was this flash mixed with the big personality that had helped him enter the realm of the rich and famous. And Dali had been famous. She had studied Salvador Dali briefly in some of her high school classes, and his very reputation had helped her recall his art. And to say that he was an eccentric was a major understatement of the term. Dali had been a genius, but a wild and creative man who had brought scandal and sensationalism everywhere he went.

"Not me," Jack said. "I saw the man, but I was a little busy at the time. Talking with some of the other movie people," He grinned.

"Did Uncle Topper have a picture with Dali? Or from that trip?" Gabe had a stack of black and white photos in front of him.

"Not with the artist himself, but we had some from the trip. And now that you mention it, we had some with Dali in the pictures." He looked thoughtful. "There were a whole lot of people at that party. Who knows what we might have gotten in that shot. I just recall a few of the group pictures. Lots of pretty young girls." Jack shrugged. "But I don't see them here. Looks like someone went through and took a bunch of different pictures."

"You're sure that they're not in any of the piles?" Ainsley asked, puzzled.

"Not seeing them," Jack confirmed. He looked to where Gabe had spread out another set of photos. "What about you?"

"I'm sure I'm not seeing them." Gabe was frowning. "I've gone through here twice. I know which ones I saw last time, and I know that some of them aren't here. We didn't throw out any of the pictures." Gabe looked frustrated.

"So do you think that whoever made the mess, took the pictures too?" Ainsley asked the two men.

"Looks like," Jack said. "I can tell there are some missing, but I don't know how many. Might have been their plan all along. If they were taking things, we wouldn't know what was missing."

"Then we need to figure out which ones are missing. It might give us an idea of what they were after." Gabe picked up some pictures, shaking his head. "This is going to be a challenge."

"What about the papers, the address book. Do you think that they took that too?" Ainsley watched as Gabe digested her question.

"Better look for that now," Gabe replied. "Where did you say Uncle Topper left his papers?" he asked Jack.

"In there with the night cage," Jack said, gesturing behind him. "Doubt you'll need the keys," he commented when Gabe dug the key ring from his pocket. "He didn't lock up much."

Gabe headed into the little room and Ainsley followed. The cage was sitting on an old desk, a rough looking piece of furniture. Ainsley wondered if it had come with Uncle Topper into the house when he bought it since it certainly didn't go with the more grandiose style of the house. And Gabe had told her that the bulk of the original furnishings had come with the house when Uncle Topper had bought the estate. Topper had kept them all and just added his flair along with the traditional pieces.

"My guess is this is it," Gabe said, tugging one of the drawers open.

"I think you might be right." Ainsley looked into the drawer doubtfully. "But is it organized at all?"

Papers were bristling from the drawer like jagged teeth from an elongated mouth. Different colors, textures, and prints marked the files. "I see some years on the folders. Maybe it's in chronological order." Gabe tugged at some of the papers, dislodging a few. "These are from two years ago," he said dismissively. "Let's see, what year would we be looking for?"

Ainsley shrugged, but then her face cleared. "We can ask Jack if he knows the year that your Uncle claims he got the painting."

"Okay, I'll ask," Gabe said quickly, strolling out of the tiny room. He was back a moment later. "Jack is guessing late 1960s or early 1970s."

"Okay, well, let's see." Ainsley slowly paged through the drawer. "These are too new. This drawer only goes back to the 1980s"

"We can try the drawer underneath," Gabe said, and Ainsley nodded as she pushed the other drawer closed.

Gabe pulled open the next drawer and looked through the next set of files. "Looks like these are a little older." He pulled out a few folders. "1979, 1978, this one is thick, 1977." Ainsley looked at him as

THE COCKATOO CALLED

he bit his lip thoughtfully. "Let's pull 1976 and earlier."

It took them a few minutes and a lot of coordination to remove the files they wanted without scattering papers all over the floor.

"What are we going to do with these?" Ainsley asked. She had a tall stack of the papers in her arms.

"We'll take these out to my car. I'm not leaving anything here that I think we might need." He looked up from his stack of files. "These are not in English," he observed.

Ainsley edged closer. "It looks like Spanish." She huffed out her breath. "I can't read a bit of it," she smiled ruefully.

"We might have found some papers from one of Uncle Topper's trips," Gabe explained. "I don't know if you were with him," he gestured with the papers.

"Let me check them," Jack said. He grabbed a few papers from the top of the stack. "Spain, ah, I remember it well!"

"So you were with him?" Gabe's voice sounded relieved.

"On this one I was," Jack said thoughtfully. "In fact, we had some pictures from this one." He turned and went back to the pool table. "But I can't remember if I saw those."

"What did they look like?" Ainsley followed the men to the side of the pool table.

"There were at least two," Jack began, "and Hemingway was in one of them." He started shuffling through one of the many stacks of photos. "It was in black and white, but easy to tell where we were, kind of tropical looking background, pretty stucco house."

In silence, the three of them went through the pictures, pausing a few times to show Jack some of the photos.

"I don't see them," Jack said frowning. "I can't understand why anyone would want to take some old pictures like that."

"Makes as much sense as anything else," Gabe said.

"So, what else do we need to look for?" Ainsley asked, gathering the photos into their stacks.

"The address book?" Gabe turned back towards the little room.

"Oh right," Ainsley agreed. "I almost forgot what we had come for."

Gabe was rummaging around through the desk, and then stopped. "His book was always black leather, wasn't it?"

"That'd be the one," Jack agreed.

"Then I think I found it!" He held up a battered book, the leather cover soft and bent.

Jack looked over and nodded. "Yep," he agreed, "and I'm guessing that you plan to take that as well."

Gabe nodded. "We're going to have some homework," he said, but he was smiling.

"Let's put these downstairs before we go into any other rooms," Gabe said. "We can leave them in the library."

They left Jack in the bedroom with Hemingway and went down the stairs. At the bottom, Ainsley hesitated. "I'm so sorry about Jack. This is hard for him," she said in a soft voice.

"It is," Gabe agreed, "but Jack wouldn't want to be left out. And if something strange is going on, he could be a potential target. He needs to know that."

Ainsley nodded, realizing for the first time that she hadn't even thought about the older man that way. Could he be in danger as well? And what about Gabe? Would they eventually give up searching his things and decide to ask him directly?

When they went back upstairs, they found Jack in the doorway of another of the bedrooms. He had the bird again on his shoulder and was rubbing his eyes. "Will ya look at that," he pointed out, and Gabe and Ainsley looked into the room. It was a guestroom, they supposed, but it was immediately obvious whose room it was. The furniture was heavy oak pieces, the decorations some models of ships, one taking up nearly the whole top of the expansive dresser. But the biggest piece, aside from the enormous bed covered in a heavy navy blue spread, was a birdcage. It went from floor to well above Gabe's impressive height. Inside were twisted pieces of ropes, perches for its occupant, and a big silver bell.

"Look what he got you, Hemingway," Jack said, walking into the room.

Ainsley came in beside them, stopping next to the cage. It was huge; four times the size of Dali's borrowed cage, and easily big enough to fit a full-grown person standing straight up. "That is enormous," she said, swinging the door open.

"Nice of the old man," Jack muttered, still emotional.

"Yes, he was," Gabe agreed.

They were silent for a moment, each with their memories. Ainsley's thought was mostly tinged with regret; regret that she had never met this man. He seemed to be truly extraordinary.

They didn't want to leave until they had gotten to venture into the rest of the house. There were eight more bedrooms with sumptuous remodeled bathrooms on the upper floor. On the first floor, there were

THE COCKATOO CALLED

the rooms that they had already explored along with an elegant dining room and a pantry off the kitchen. They went down into the basement for only a cursory glance since the light wasn't good, and it was chilly down there in the unfinished space. And despite the fact that Ainsley hadn't seen some of the rooms before that day, she had to agree that it looked like the intruders had only gone as far as the bedroom.

"Either they found what they were looking for, or they gave up," Gabe speculated.

"I think they got what they wanted from upstairs," Ainsley agreed, "but they're still looking for something more. And whatever it is, it has to be related to what they think your uncle left you."

"I'm telling you," Jack interrupted, "they think that there was a painting. They think that you have it since you have the bird."

Ainsley had to agree. It made a strange sort of sense.

"What will you do now?" she asked Gabe.

"I guess I'll keep looking. I've rigged up a security system in my apartment, so hopefully if anyone tries anything, I'll get some kind of warning. And we have all of this information to go through." He shrugged.

"Then we're ready to leave now?" Ainsley noticed that Jack was looking suddenly older.

"Sure," she said. "I'm ready to go too."

Hemingway docilely went into his crate as though he could read his friend's emotion. Together, they went out the front door, with Gabe following switching off the lights and locking the door.

Gabe walked with Jack to his big truck and stood by as the bird was loaded into the passenger seat. Ainsley stood back and watched as the men shook hands, feeling like they might need a moment to speak without her presence.

She and Gabe stood by and watched as Jack pulled away from the house, his truck rattling and belching as he went down the driveway. Then he turned behind the clump of evergreens, and was gone.

"So are you just going to take the papers home?" Ainsley asked as she slipped into the car, looking at the files on the back seat.

"Yeah. I thought I'd just go through them at my apartment." Gabe glanced at her. "Why? Don't you think that I should?"

"If someone happens to want to get to them, I would worry that they would go after them at your apartment. They've been there before."

"You're right." He started the car, backing out of his space. "You're right about the papers. I should put them somewhere safe."

"Do you have somewhere else you can keep them, lock them up?"

"I have a bank box," he said after a moment. "I could put them in there. But I can't exactly get them out easily to read."

"Do you have a copier?"

So they spent the rest of the afternoon making hundreds of copies in one of the massive machines at the copy store and then stowing the originals in a bank box.

THE COCKATOO CALLED

CHAPTER NINE

November had stormed in with cool and rain, but warmed midweek. Ainsley took Dali out to visit with Patti at the Feeders Supply store. She had seen the interesting harness that Hemingway had worn, allowing him to be taken to various places without fear of losing him. But she didn't want to chance anything, so she decided to go talk to someone who dealt with birds all of the time.

Patti was pleased to see them. "So you're back! And what has happened with your young gentleman friend?" she teased.

"He's still around," Ainsley replied grinning. "But I wanted to ask you about something." She described meeting Hemingway and the contraption that he wore.

"That is a harness," Patti agreed. "We have a few here, but I don't know if we have one to fit a cockatoo." She hesitated. "Let me look. We did have a shipment of bird things come in earlier this week," she went down the now familiar aisle, parrot toys lining the short walls to either side. She stopped midway down and stood with her arms crossed, scanning the selection. Then she moved, quickly scooping up one lone package that had been resting on the bottom shelf as though forgotten. "Here!" She was grinning with triumph. "Our lucky day. This was sent by accident. We had some harnesses for rabbits ordered, and this one came in the mix. Ordinarily we don't order these unless we have a specific request."

Patti pulled open the package and pulled out the harness, which looked to Ainsley like a set of strings. She shook it out and held it up for Ainsley to see.

"Some birds love these, and some will have none of it, so we'll have to see what your fella thinks." She brought it to the front of the store with Ainsley trailing behind, Dali still in the crate.

"Are you ready?" she asked.

Ainsley opened the door of the crate and let Dali out, amused as he looked between the two of them. Patti bent and pulled out a stuffed parrot from under the counter. Ainsley laughed as Dali examined the newcomer.

"What's that for?" Ainsley asked curiously.

"This is our demo birdy," Patti replied.

She showed Ainsley how the harness would loop around the bird, crossing over his chest and tucking beneath his wings. She demonstrated twice on the stuffed bird and then handed the toy and the harness to Ainsley while she cuddled with Dali.

Ainsley tried herself, and with some mistakes, managed to get the harness on and tightened around the stuffed parrot. "Why do I think that this might be a little more challenging with the real thing?" she asked, looking at Dali.

"If he doesn't like it," Patti said, "just try a little at a time. 'Toos are easier than a lot of birds. You just need to go slow and make sure that he doesn't chew it up while your back is turned."

Pattie introduced the harness to Dali, gently looping it over him. "This is as far as I would go at first. And I would practice him wearing it in the house for short amounts of time, making sure he can't get out, before I would have him wear it anywhere else."

Dali tolerated the harness for a moment before growing impatient and struggling a little to spread his wings.

"That's all we do for today!" Patti exclaimed, dropping a fond kiss on the top of the bird's head.

Ainsley had never been to Gabe's apartment, but when he asked her if she wanted to come by to help him go through some of the papers that they had taken from his Uncle's house, she wanted to go. She liked Gabe. Actually, she liked him, and just like any other girl looking at a promising relationship, she wanted to know more about this man.

Of course, there was always the faint possibility that he might have some skeletons in his closet, and that would bear looking into too, so she had an ulterior motive as well. Or a second ulterior motive if nosiness counted as a valid first.

However, years of self-conscious meditation had her pausing. Going through files would mean all that paperwork, all that reading. And if history had taught her anything, it was that guarding her abilities and disabilities were crucial in the tender beginnings of a relationship.

She sighed and huffed out a breath. She knew she was smart, very intelligent in fact. As the saying went, her mother had had her tested, and the results had become frighteningly consistent after grade three. She wasn't lazy, she wasn't stupid, and she had a learning disability, dyslexia.

And years of trying to cope with it had, in fact, helped her develop into the person that she was. She was persistent, almost too much, and stubborn to a fault. She had worked hard to prove herself in the classroom, to be as capable as other students, and in the fight, had sharpened her edge. The struggle that came along with dyslexia was a many-limbed thing that stretched out over her whole life. It had impacted her personality, helped her polish a thin shell to keep her dignity whole. It had made her independent, a problem solver, an out of the box thinker. But it had also made her brittle, a little bitter, and a whole lot self-conscious. She guarded her problem carefully, sharing it with few people. Her teachers had known, her parents, her closest friends. Dr. Blandford knew, and had hired her with full disclosure, because Ainsley had thought it only fair to give her the chance to say no.

But her co-workers knew only of a slight difficulty, and she hadn't decided what she wanted to tell Gabe. She didn't want to see the change in his eyes, the way he looked at her. She didn't want to see the pity, the hesitation, or the curiosity.

Her final decision wasn't much of a conclusion. She would go. She would visit his apartment, see a little bit into his life. But she still wasn't sure what she wanted to share with him. That would all depend on him.

*****

She drove her car, following the directions from her dash mounted GPS even though she generally knew the apartment complex that Gabe lived in. Dyslexia had many facets to it, and she had succeeded in capturing almost every single one. She had a poor sense of direction. She struggled, not with the mechanics of driving, but with the overall plotting of the trip. She tended to learn one route to and from places, and use it consistently until it was automatic. If there was a detour, it was likely to send her into a mild anxiety attack. She had been known to call her father and read street signs until he could help her find her way to a familiar path. With the use of the GPS, she was relieved of much of the pressure, but she still had difficulties if she went the wrong way or ended up in a neighborhood with cookie cutter houses. She lived by landmarks, not by directions, so driving anywhere unfamiliar was a challenge.

Luckily, Gabe lived close and she was accustomed to traveling down the main road in her day-to-day life. She certainly didn't need any more stress just now. She turned into his apartment complex and scanned the numbers on the buildings; looking for the one he had given her. It was a fine place, a little too expensive because of the location, but still an okay neighborhood. The whole complex had been built sometime in the seventies when odd angled wood sided buildings were the rage. It had gone from being modern and edgy to slightly worn out and tired. The wood had been patched and repainted, the bushes trimmed recently, and it looked like a middle aged lady fighting hard to reverse time and losing a little in the fight.

After Ainsley parked, she sat in her car for a moment, breathing deeply. The little drive had grated on her nerves, and she needed to get her composure. She wiped her hands on her jeans in a nervous gesture and looked over toward Dali's crate.

"We're here," she told the bird, her voice a little breathy. "You're finally home."

Gabe's apartment was on the lower level, which provided a tiny patio space that he liked. When he opened the door, Ainsley was surprised to see that he had oven mitts and was carrying a big fork on a long handle.

"Dali, don't worry, I think you're the second course," she joked and held up the carrier so the bird could peer through the front. "I didn't know you'd be cooking," she said as she stepped into the apartment after him.

"I wanted to impress you with my culinary prowess," he bragged smiling. Then he looked in the cage and lifted a brow, "he doesn't have enough meat on his bones to make him worth it," he bantered back. "I hope you're hungry. I'm making ribs. They're my specialty."

So much for impressing him with her ladylike table manners. She loved ribs, but knew full well that they were possibly the messiest things that he could have chosen for them to eat.

"You didn't have to cook," she admonished him, following him into the kitchen.

"I like to cook," he said, putting the fork and oven mitts down. "And since I have you here to work, I figured feeding you was the least that I could do." He bent down and looked into the crate while Dali observed him critically. "What are you looking at, Bird?"

"You should see what we're learning to do!" Ainsley exclaimed, opening the cage door for the bird to step out. "We have tried a harness three times."

"A harness? Like the thing that Hemingway wears?"

"Yeah, I got one from Patti. She showed me how they are supposed to fit, and we've been practicing tolerating the feel of it. His favorite treats seem to be little sunflower seeds. So far it hasn't been too hard to get him to cooperate." She smiled ruefully. "I mean, he hasn't actually worn it yet, but he let me put it around him. He wants to chew on it mostly, but I think he'll get used to the idea."

"You're going to look like some kind of bird lady," Gabe said grinning.

Ainsley stopped a moment, entranced by that lovely smile. Then she shook her head. "I'm thinking about taking up dressing like a pirate."

"You'd have to dress like a wench," he replied, "like corsets and lacy stockings." He stopped, pretending to think, "You know, now that you mention it, that might not be a bad look!" Gabe lifted his eyebrows and smiled rakishly, and Ainsley had to laugh.

"I'll remember that," Ainsley answered, but she felt the red creeping into her cheeks.

The bird made a fussy sound and Gabe took him from Ainsley, holding him against his chest. "You want to show Ainsley your other home?" he asked the bird. He led her into a little living room where the most prominent feature, aside from a giant flat screen TV that would have been more at home in a private theater, was a large cage. It was made from metal, no doubt out of necessity, but the metal had been curved and formed to look like an elaborate pagoda.

"Holy cow," Ainsley said, staring at the cage. "That's what he was living in?"

"Apparently, yes. That is the palace that he was calling home. It probably wouldn't look quite so ostentatious in the house, but here I think it's a little overwhelming." He shrugged slightly. "But he came with it, and I heard it wasn't good to change their homes unless you need to."

Ainsley walked a little closer, looking more carefully at the cage. He was right. In Uncle Topper's house, it wouldn't have looked out of place. With the dark antique woodwork, the collection of everything from everywhere, a mammoth elaborate cage would have blended right in with the rest of the environment. But here in the little apartment with the 70s quirky angles and the traditional furniture, it looked as odd as a spaceship landing in someone's living room.

"This is something else," she said. The cage was as tall as she was, and the lower tray hung just a foot off the floor. It had multiple levels, with a skirt of metal that stuck out from the main portion of the cage to catch any stray seeds or pellets that the bird might throw. "I feel a little bad now," she continued. "The thing he's staying in at my place is half this size."

"I haven't heard him complain," Gabe said. He reached out and unlatched the cage door. Then he held his arm next to the door of the cage so Dali could climb onto the top of the door. "This is his favorite place to hang out if I'm not with him," he said.

Dali did look comfortable. He shifted from foot to foot, looking around the apartment and then up at them. Gabe took out one of the food cups to fill with water and gestured to a small cabinet next to the cage.

"His food is in there if you want to give him some," he said. "He might be hungry, but then again, he might just be waiting to see what we're having."

Ainsley opened the cabinet and looked inside. Although the cabinet probably came from Gabe himself, the contents did not. There was a heavy crockery jar of what looked to be similar pellets as the ones that she fed Dali. There were also a couple paper bags that revealed different nuts and seeds, some of which she didn't recognize. On another shelf was a toy made from coconut pieces and some fancy straw sculpture. Ainsley suspected that this might have been a souvenir bought for a spoiled pet while Uncle Topper had been traveling. She wondered if Jack had been on that trip. And she wondered too if Hemingway had a matching toy of his own. "I'll put some pellets in the bowl, but don't expect this kind of luxury when you go back home with me," she told the bird. And although birds don't smile, he seemed to be laughing at her.

After they had cared for the bird, Gabe went back outside to check on the ribs. He had put two foil wrapped baked potatoes on the grill, and a pan with canned green beans was boiling softly on the stove.

"This isn't fancy, but it'll be good," Gabe said confidently.

"It's a home cooked meal," Ainsley agreed. "I wouldn't dream of complaining."

"Well, it's almost ready," Gabe said.

They set the tiny table in companionable silence, and then Gabe exited onto the little balcony with plates. When he returned, he had a large slab of ribs and the wrapped potatoes steaming in the cooling air. He slid the door closed.

"I've got some oven mitts in the drawer if you want to grab some and bring out the beans. We'll just put the pan on the table." He frowned to himself. "I don't even think I have any serving bowls, so fancy is out of the question."

"The pan is fine," Ainsley said, rummaging through a drawer until she found what she was looking for. "At my house, I eat out of cardboard about half the time." She carried the simmering beans out to the table and placed them on a hot pad. With a flourish, Gabe set down his platter and gestured for her to take a seat.

"Dinner is served," he said grandly.

The food was good. Ainsley was pleasantly surprised at Gabe's accomplishments in the kitchen, and thought to herself that she would have to think of something good to serve when he came to her house to have dinner. She smiled to herself. She was just assuming that he would be coming to her house.

"So have you gone through any of the receipts yet?" she asked, taking a bite of the buttery potato.

"I've laid them out and tried to figure out what goes with what in the piles, but that's as far as I got." He paused and sighed. "It would help if we knew anything about this fabled painting. Like when he supposedly bought it, or where. As it is, he seemed to have taken multiple trips to different places almost every year, including last one. And although I know that the real Salvador Dali was from Spain, he was also a traveler, living here in the United States for some time. Their paths could have crossed at any number of times, and that's assuming again that Uncle Topper bought the painting from Dali himself."

"I was reading up about that too," Ainsley added, a little self-conscious because she was stretching the truth. "And I read that in 1974, Dali had a bad split with some of his associates, and Dali's business manager sold many of his works without his permission. I don't know if it would match our timeline, but that might have been a way for your Uncle to get one of the original works."

"I read about that too," Gabe agreed. "I just Googled it," he grinned. "But I did learn a whole lot more about the artist than I ever knew before. And I know that his work is worth quite a bit of money, which would be a motive for someone to come after that particular piece. What I don't understand is, if you needed cash, why wouldn't they have taken some of that other stuff that Uncle Topper had? I mean, I don't know what all of it is worth, but that house is brimming with collectibles."

"Maybe they knew of that specific thing and had a buyer already set up. Or maybe they are some kind of art collector and want to keep the painting. It could be a lot of things." Ainsley thought about the house and all of its various contents. "And Jack said that he had heard that your Uncle owned the painting. But he'd never seen it himself. That seems strange too. If Jack, who is arguably your Uncle's best friend, hadn't seen the painting in person, I wonder if anyone else has?"

"I don't know." Gabe hesitated. "I've called some of the cousins about the will and what to do with Uncle Topper's estate, but I haven't asked anyone about the painting. It just seemed a little awkward to talk about it. But I might have someone else to ask. My Aunt Violet was the closest to Uncle Topper when he passed away. She's the closest in age to Uncle Topper too, and they were two of a kind. If Jack doesn't know anything, our next best bet is Aunt Vi."

Once dinner was over, Ainsley stood next to Gabe in companionable silence, washing dishes as he dried them and put them away. He was neat, but not compulsively so. His dishes were a no nonsense white, not quite plastic but close to it, that she bet had been a gift from some practical sister or perhaps his mother. Instead of going back into the living room, they went next to what had once been a second bedroom but was now an office. The room was surprisingly big, however, and Gabe explained that it was part of the master suite.

"I decided that since I would be working from home, I wanted the office to be as big as possible."

The room was wall-to-wall desks and bookshelves. There were two computers that seemed to be working simultaneously, both with elaborate drawings set up on the screen. On the desk beside them were large drawings that had been unfurled from a roll and now lay in layers of sheets. Ainsley knew very little about architecture, aside from the occasional city tours she had taken, so the nuts and bolts of the actual design process was foreign to her. But she supposed that all of the drawings would eventually be put together to create something great.

"Nice office," she said appreciatively.

"I like it. Especially since I have to be in here all day long." He pointed to a little table by the corner. On top of it was an elaborate bird stand made mostly by PVC pipes covered with some type of tape. "This is Dali's official perch," he said. "I got it online. Not the most gorgeous thing, but Dali loves it." He frowned. "Speaking of which, I'd better run and get him."

He exited quickly, and Ainsley took a moment to look a little closer at the place. There were a few pictures on the desktop, and Ainsley noticed one that had a very clear picture of Uncle Topper. He had a bright smile, full of white teeth and charm, and by his side was a younger couple, arms around each other. There was a strong family resemblance.

"That's mom and dad," Gabe said. "They're snowbirds, so they're not in town right now."

"Snowbirds?"

"They live around here during the spring and summer, and come fall, they head out." He shrugged. "They have a nice little place on the beach that they've been renting for years."

"What about the holidays?" Ainsley asked, thinking about the

THE COCKATOO CALLED

upcoming busy season.

"We take turns. They'll come in and stay with my sister this year. Next year, they'll have us down there."

"Christmas in Florida? It's just not right."

"Where ever the family is, that's our motto anymore." He sighed. "As they've gotten older, they've spent more time in the warmer areas. I can't blame them for that, especially on some days in January. I do miss them when they're gone, though."

Ainsley felt a little twinge. It had been hard to move away from her parents, but it had been necessary. She didn't want to depend on them too much, and she knew that she could easily fall into that tempting trap. Her parents had been her advocates all through her education. They had been to every meeting, conferenced with teachers, gotten her tutoring to help her get through the classes, and spent many hours researching techniques that might help her. When she had graduated with her diploma, she had felt a little like they all were getting the hard earned award. But when she had needed to find work, she had felt their hovering a little too strongly. It was hard to separate after so many joint battles. The move was for all of them, really. It gave her the room that she needed to stand on her own, and the space that they needed to start living a little more for themselves.

"I agree," she said. "I love spending time with my family," she was smiling to herself. "But a little separation doesn't hurt."

Dali made a loud squawk, reminding Ainsley about what they were supposed to be doing.

Gabe seemed to come to the same conclusion. He quickly went over to the desk and started rolling up the set of drawings from the board.

"I'll get these cleaned up," he said. "Then we can spread out the rest of the paperwork and go through it." Ainsley felt the familiar tug of dread. She watched him as he started gathering his materials. After the papers were in a neat scroll, he deftly fastened them together with a pair of rubber bands. He tucked the rolls next to the desk and pulled out one of the more familiar stacks of folders that Ainsley and he had taken from Uncle Topper's house. He then began sorting the folders systematically, placing them according to year. "There were some papers that weren't in any folder." He laid out that stack separately.

Ainsley stood, her hands twisting unconsciously. The stack of files now looked monstrous. Too much for her to handle. Looking for files meant identifying labels, analyzing print. She drew in a deep breath and looked at the stack. Start with something simple. The files had been plainly labeled with years, and numbers laid out sequentially like that were manageable for Ainsley. But then she saw the loose papers, the print shifting on the page. Her face felt flushed, her hands cold as she stared at the impossibility of her role.

"Why don't you just take those papers and put them with the right folder," Gabe said, head down as he shuffled through information. "The folders all have the years on them, so organizing according to date is probably our best bet."

Ainsley squeezed her eyes tightly shut and then blinked, shaking herself angrily. This was ridiculous. She had never given up without a fight. She determinedly picked up a single sheet. There was a certain pattern to the formatting of the pages. The dates tended to be at the top, the top right, really. Using that idea, she started flipping through the papers a little more quickly. Yes, the dates weren't too hard to find. She had a certain limited set of things that they could say. The names of months were familiar. There was no decoding necessary for that. And the dates were arranged in a pattern of numbers. Those she could find. She continued to work on the loose papers while Gabe worked on the folders, adding labels where the tabs had been blurred, putting the year in large black letters on the front. Ainsley put the papers with dates in the corresponding folders, but still had a number of papers that weren't dated, and she started a separate pile. Somehow she would convince Gabe to go through these. She didn't want to get any of it wrong or make a mistake that would cost them time.

With the folders distributed and labeled, Gabe went to work on taking notes, beginning first on constructing a timeline. The much-needed organization was a great start.

He was halfway through the first page of the timeline when he looked up from his work. "According to this, Uncle Topper went to France, Germany, and England twice during 1970," Gabe observed. "In 1973, he was in nine different countries, and that doesn't include the traveling he did within the United States. 1975, 1976, both of these years he did a lot of traveling in the United States, virtually coast to coast. Considering the amounts of time he spent traveling, this might be a challenge."

"But we're looking for specific things, right?" Ainsley looked up from the stack of papers she was sorting. "Something about paintings, or art, or valuables, collectibles?" Her eyes were beginning to blur, and a familiar headache was coming on. She had been concentrating hard just to get her part done.

"Sure, we can maybe look for some of those words," he agreed.

"We'll have to compare his travels with the receipts. But it will be the receipt that proves something." She sighed. It was looking like a lot of work, and her help was going to be limited. If the information was in print, she could scan it into the computer. She had become a master of figuring out how to work around the actual reading of text. Using different computer applications, she could scan the pages, transfer the information to a printed document that could be searched, and enter the search words in that way. A computer would be able to scan much faster than she would anyway.

But there was a flaw in her plan. So many of the receipts were old, and therefore dated back to before printed documents were the standard. Most of these were handwritten notes on carbon copy paper that were bent and faded with time. Even the most sophisticated of computer programs might struggle to decipher the spidery, cursive scrawls that made up the text of these documents.

"We'll go through the folders first and look at the receipts." Gabe pulled one out and opened to the first pages. "We can clip them together, but if we see any of interest, we can put them on the top to refer to later."

"Okay," Ainsley said slowly. "Do you want me to look in one of the folders too? Just for the receipts, right?"

"Sure, yes. As good a place to start as any." He grabbed one of the other folders and slid it across the desk to her. He took his folder and brought it around to her side of the desk. He pulled out a cushy office chair and rolled it behind her. "The guest gets the good seat," he said smiling.

She took the chair and put the folder on her lap while he pulled up a second one and sat next to her.

After twenty minutes of sorting, Ainsley almost felt like she had accidently doomed their search. The receipts were everywhere, often misfiled, and so faded and wrinkled that some were virtually illegible. She was almost ready to give up when Gabe held out a written note. "Look at this," he said, sounding a little excited.

"What is it?" she asked.

"It's a letter. It's not very clear who it's from, but it does sound like Uncle Topper was buying something." Gabe leaned a little closer, so close that she could smell the spicy scent of his soap as he pointed to one of the lines on the paper. "Says he was going to pick up his painting on December 19th, 1975 in New York."

"But don't you think the painting could have been anything?" Ainsley said doubtfully, feeling guilty that she was so distracted by the warmth of Gabe sitting next to her.

"Well, sure," he said, excitement still in his voice, "but I'd like to think that this is what we're looking for. My uncle didn't collect a whole lot of art. You can tell by looking around the house that his preferences were different. So I can't imagine that there would be very many paintings, real ones, not prints, in his collection."

Ainsley looked at the handwritten script. The paper had aged into a mellow golden color, the blue ink faded to almost gray. The characters looped across the paper, some familiar shapes battling with each other.

"If you look at it logically," Gabe said, unaware of her inner debate, "all of these papers are more about his travels than everyday life. There aren't any receipts from the usual grocery trips or eating out. I'm thinking that the only ones that we will find are for the things he valued. Or the things he collected."

"So assuming that that note is about the painting," Ainsley said thoughtfully, "what does it tell us?"

Gabe scanned the paper. "The date is December 1975. That would be after Dali's split with his business manager." Gabe frowned. "I can't read the signature. But this looks like the address is in New York. So I imagine a first step might be to look at the background of the art and the artist."

"You know, there is a Dali museum here in the United States," Ainsley said slowly. "It's in Florida."

"Then we should go."

Ainsley stared at him. "We should go to Florida?" Her eyes strayed to the chilly landscape out the curtained window.

"Sure. Why not? It's a quick flight."

"Well," Her mind was a little stuck. Her first thought was her job and then the expense. She didn't have hundreds of dollars sitting around for the flight. She did have vacation time available, but she had planned on visiting her parents for a few days.

"I have a friend with a plane. He's good, and he needs the time in the air. We can fly up one day and come back the next if we need to. I'll chip in for the gas, so you won't be out any money."

Ainsley had never done anything quite so impulsive. Never. But now it seemed like a real possibility. Her mind froze, but she heard the words before she could think it over. "Then I'll go," she said.

CHAPTER TEN

Aunt Violet, at the respected age of 83, had prided herself as the current matriarch, albeit through the gradual dying out of others in her family. Although she missed her siblings, she firmly believed that this life was a temporary place anyway, a stepping-stone that would eventually lead to their reunion at the pearly gate.

Or, as she would say, "I'll see all those old bastards eventually anyway. For now, I need to cause some scandal that I can talk about when I get there."

Aunt Vi lived in a retirement home very close to Gabe's apartment. It had been built with the idea that the proximity to shopping and other recreational activities would have a positive effect on the residents, and in general, this assumption was proving to be true. The apartments were almost always full; the people living there pleased that they could gather for in house activities as well as take a handy bus to go to various other outings in an all-inclusive and reasonable price.

Gabe called before they decided to go over to visit. He told Ainsley confidently that it wasn't necessary, except for the fact that his aunt might choose to go on one of the many outings and miss their visit.

"She has more of a social life than I do," he said over the phone. "I have to check in with her just to make sure she'll be home before I come by." His grandmother had passed away at the young age of fifty-six, and he barely remembered her. It was his Uncle Topper and his Aunt Vi and a few of the other brothers and sisters that had been his surrogate grandparents on his father's side.

"Are you sure she'll be okay with my coming along?" Ainsley had asked, feeling a little like she was intruding on a family visit.

"Are you kidding? When I was in high school, she wanted me to bring over my friends all the time. She would take us on shopping trips and to the movies, as long as I chose something she would want to see."

"So she likes visitors," Ainsley said.

"That is putting it mildly. She loves visitors. And she loves going out. And she loves just about any excitement. She's pretty much ready at any time to do something."

"She sounds great."

"She is."

They agreed to meet the following day, and Ainsley had stood smiling, phone still in her hand, feeling young and silly and good all at once. She wasn't sure that she needed to be on this fact-finding trip. In fact, her role in this spontaneous investigation was a little strange to begin with, but she wasn't going to argue. She wanted to see Gabe, and if her silly heart was going to insist on it, she wasn't going to hold herself back.

Gabe was just on time, which was just one of the things that Ainsley liked about him. He was considerate, and that went a far way in her book, showing that he cared about her time. Of course, it didn't hurt that he was handsome, but that might make her sound shallow, and she definitely didn't want to seem like a pretty face would turn her head.

She let Gabe into her little house, grateful that she had taken the evening before to clean up and change the papers in Dali's cage. The bird was now holding court at the table, skating around on the new plastic tablecloth that she had bought to protect the old wood. It seemed inevitable that wherever the big bird would go, he would bring a certain amount of destruction with him. To help save her furniture, she had invested in coverings for the table, the back and arms of the chair, and the top of her dresser. If he wanted to chew on something, she didn't want it to be something that she wanted to keep nice, or worse yet, something that would hurt the bird. He was an indiscriminant chewer, even on his best day.

Now he had a set of plastic measuring cups that he was slinging around. He would hop with his prize to the edge of the table and then dump it over the side, turning and watching the cup as it fell. He was only satisfied when someone picked up the cup and returned it to him so he could repeat the process. It was a strange birdy hobby, but it kept him from eating her furniture, so Ainsley was willing to buy in.

"Hey, Birdy bird," Gabe said cheerfully, dropping down into a chair next to the table.

Dali rushed up to him, skipping in his hurry, scattering a few loose papers and scraps of treats that Ainsley had given him. Gabe picked the bird up and held him close.

"He is so funny about that," Ainsley said smiling. "He will follow

THE COCKATOO CALLED

me around the house just so I pick him up and hold him."

"Yeah, he didn't want me to leave either. He followed me every time I left the room." He looked up at Ainsley as she moved around the kitchen, putting away her cup from her morning coffee. "Thanks for helping me with this," he said. "I know this all seems crazy, like a weird mystery movie, but I, well, I'm glad that you are helping me."

"I wouldn't miss it," Ainsley said truthfully. "When I found Dali out in my back yard, I had no idea what it would lead to, but so far," she was smiling, "it's been worth it."

"Good, I'm glad you think so," Gabe said. "And just wait, if you think it's been interesting so far, you will love to meet Aunt Violet."

*****

They found Aunt Vi in her room. She was tucked in a wingback armchair that seemed to cradle her frail body, and wrapped in a hand crocheted afghan she had made herself. This time, to keep her hands busy, she had a game boy, several years out of date, and was playing some game that emitted high pitched beeps and a tinny song.

"Gabriel!" she exclaimed, seeing her great-nephew. "It's about time you showed up. You promised me a McDonald's shake last time you were here. I intend to take you up on that. I do have a craving for some chocolate." She looked at them over her red-rimmed glasses. "Actually, I'm thinking a Big Mac too."

"Sure, Aunt Vi," Gabe agreed. "When will you be ready to go?"

"Well, now," she said, throwing back the blanket. Her clothes underneath were not the typical old lady gear. She had on light blue polyester pants, a bright red tee shirt with a white sweater. Her white tennis shoes were terribly clean, her socks bright red like her shirt. She looked like she had dressed for the occasion. Seeing Gabe's look of surprise she said, "I'm hungry, let's go!"

Gabe held his arm out like some old fashioned gentleman, and his aunt took his arm. She slowly stood and smiled, her false teeth white and straight against her red lipstick.

"And aren't you going to introduce me to your girl there?"

Gabe smiled his adorable smile and Ainsley felt her insides turn to something warm and soft. "Aunt Violet, this is Ainsley. Ainsley, this is my Aunt Violet."

"So nice to meet some of Gabriel's friends," Aunt Vi responded, beaming again.

They went out through the double doors into the watery sunlight.

The rain had let up in early morning, but the wetness had persisted in the slushy leaves and soaked concrete. The temperature had dipped into the 60s. It was a perfect fall day; a damp but perfect day. Ainsley took a deep breath of the clean air and sighed. McDonald's might not have been her favorite pick for places to eat, but it was looking like this was going to be its little adventure. Gabe moved slowly with his Aunt on his arm. Ainsley followed behind, moving ahead of them only to open the door on their way out of the building and again when they reached the car.

Once in the car, Ainsley in the back while Aunt Vi sat in the passenger seat, Gabe fired up the engine. A blast of music came from the radio, and Ainsley saw with amazement that Aunt Vi had picked the station and was turning the volume up.

"Okay, now that's what I like!" she exclaimed, and Gabe pulled out of the lot.

A Big Mac and chocolate shake later, Aunt Vi was contentedly sitting back in the booth. Ainsley had a sundae in front of her and was relishing the artificial ice cream with true enjoyment.

"Aunt Vi," Gabe began. "I have been looking into some of Uncle Topper's things. We were over at his house, kind of checking up on the place. Jack told us about Uncle Topper's collection, about the Dali painting that Uncle Topper said he had."

"Jack!" Aunt Vi said happily. "I love that Jack! How is he?"

"Jack? He's good, great," Gabe responded. "We saw him just a week ago."

"Tell him that he needs to visit me again," she scolded. "Does he still have that giant bird of his?"

"Hemingway? Yes, he still has him. They go almost everywhere together." Gabe was smiling slightly.

"Crazy man, carrying a bird everywhere you go. But there you are, I imagine everyone has their little eccentricities. His just has more feathers than most." She puffed out a breath through very red lips. "You tell him to come, even if he has to bring that bird along."

"We will," Gabe agreed. "I promise I won't forget. But Aunt Vi, what about the story? Did Uncle Topper have a real Salvador Dali painting?"

She looked suddenly a little older, a little more serious. "Silly old man," she scoffed. "He would buy a bottle of tap water if someone told him that it was special." She looked at them through the thick lenses of her glasses. "I never saw the painting myself," she said slowly. "Oh, I heard about it plenty. He even wanted to pose for the paper. Stand next to that picture so everyone could see what he had found. He had gotten it framed and planned to put it up in his bedroom along with the rest of his pictures. You have seen those haven't you? His whole life plastered on the walls up there. But then he suddenly changed his mind. Wouldn't talk about the painting. People started asking questions then. Was the painting real? Why was he backing out now?" She shook her head slowly. "And then it was over, he wouldn't speak of it any longer. He was done with it. And he just moved on." She shrugged her frail shoulders. "And that was the end of it. He never talked about it again."

"Did you see it?" Gabe asked, leaning forward, hands folded on the table in front of him.

"No," she said. "Back then I was too busy minding my life. He told me about it. Said it was a portrait of a young woman that he had seen and decided that he wanted. Not that I know much about that particular painter. He did those drippy clocks didn't he?"

"They are some of his best known works, yes," Ainsley agreed.

Aunt Vi looked a little irritated. "Painters can't just paint what they see anymore. It has to be changed to suit them. I'd just as soon have a paint by number of kittens than some of the stuff they call art these days."

Ainsley dropped her head to hide her smile. She knew it wasn't an unusual stance on the opinion of modern art these days, but it was a little startling to hear it stated so directly.

"But why do you think Uncle Topper suddenly changed his mind about the painting? Why did he go from wanting it put in the paper to not displaying it at all?" Gabe had his chin in his hand and a lock of hair had fallen across his forehead. He pushed it back unconsciously, his eyes showing how far his thoughts had wandered.

"Why indeed," Aunt Vi replied. "Maybe he knew that he had been duped? Or maybe he got it in a less than legal way and was afraid he might get in trouble for it. He did tend to act first and think about the consequences later." She pulled the straw loose from her cup and it made a loud blurping sound. "All I know is that I visited that old house of his, and he never showed me that picture. I didn't ask about it either. Wasn't of that much interest to me."

Gabe glanced at Ainsley. "I wonder if it was just a story. I wonder now if the painting ever existed."

"Oh, it existed, all right," Aunt Vi said firmly. "Topper said it was the find of his life, even if I never did see it. I think it was just more trouble than it was worth."

*****

They walked Aunt Violet back into the building and to the door of her little room. She didn't ask them in, and for that, Ainsley was grateful. They kept the heat chugging along in the building, no doubt to satisfy their more thin blooded residents, but for the visitors, it was a little too stuffy. The air outside felt refreshingly cool in contrast. Ainsley spent a few moments feeling the damp breeze blow her hair back and breathed a sigh of relief.

Back in the car, Gabe turned to Ainsley. "I don't know that we learned much," he said making a wry face.

"I think we learned a lot, really," Ainsley argued. "I mean, it's not that we found out new information, but she seemed sure that the painting exists. And that means that we're on the right track."

"So now on to Florida? Or do you have any other ideas?"

Ainsley glanced out the window. "Besides the few people that we've talked to, do you know who else might have an idea about what your uncle was doing?"

"Aunt Vi knows family stuff, but I'm guessing that Jack would know the rest. And we didn't ask him any details when we saw him before. Maybe it would be worth another conversation."

"Okay, then a visit with Jack. And the Florida museum." She frowned. "And there are parts of the house that we never went to. The basement? The attic? Does the house have more storage? It seems like if he had the painting and then wanted to hide it, like your aunt was saying, he might choose somewhere like that rather than out in the open."

"That is true. We haven't looked everywhere in that house, that's for sure. It's a big place, and if he were having problems because of the painting, he wouldn't have it just lying out there in the open. Aunt Vi said she thought he had it framed. I guess I had just assumed it was in a frame hanging on some wall, but now, well, I might be wrong. If he had it framed, it would probably still be in storage, but if he never did get it done, it might be just laid out somewhere."

Ainsley pictured the massive house. To search that whole place would take some serious time. And she felt like time was limited. Because if they were thinking about going back there to search, then whoever they believed was after the painting, and whoever had broken into Gabe's apartment, would come to the same conclusion. They would be back.

"So we need to call Jack and see when he can meet us," Ainsley began, but noticed Gabe was shaking his head.

"Jack is out of town just now. I think he said he would be gone until Thursday. He had some kind of meeting that he said he couldn't miss. I

THE COCKATOO CALLED

don't know what that was about."

"Well when did you want to try for Florida?"

"I have a deadline for a project that I am doing locally on Wednesday. I have to have some drawings ready for the meeting. After that, I'll have some time before the next set is due. What does your work look like?"

Ainsley watched as he deftly maneuvered out of the parking space. "I suppose if it is on the weekend, it wouldn't matter when I went. I don't have many plans until later in the month." She thought about the holidays and the family gatherings that would be planned. "Once we get closer to Thanksgiving, I'll probably be heading home to see my parents."

Gabe nodded. "Okay, then that gives us a couple of weekends to deal with. I'll call my guy and see what we can arrange between now and then."

*****

The plane was set to leave at 10:30, but the advantage to flying in a private plane was a little bit of flexibility. That was also, as it turned out, a disadvantage as well. Gabe's friend who flew planes also fixed them for a living and was half an hour late. By the time he had gotten to the airport, Jack had caught up with them, duffel bag slung over one broad shoulder, animal carrier in his other hand.

Ainsley could see the other employees at the airport ogling them as they strolled down the pavement to the little plane. Jack pretty much stood out wherever he went, and today was no exception. He had added a hat to his wardrobe, a jaunty cap with a short brim in front to cover his balding dome of a head. He still wore jeans and heavy work boots, and today his shirt was a rusty red color. The bird was making protesting squawks from within the crate.

Gabe had laughingly told Ainsley about his earlier conversation with Jack. It seemed that the opportunity to get a free ride to Tampa, where the temperatures were a balmy 83, was too much for Jack to resist. Instead of agreeing to meet them somewhere locally, Jack had decided that he would be better spending his time giving them a guided tour of Tampa.

"I just agreed to his idea. I couldn't think of any reason that he shouldn't come along, and I figured that he could be some help," Gabe had admitted over the phone. "I've learned over the years that Jack can be a handy man to hang around. He seems to know just about everyone."

Jack didn't know anyone at the airport, however, and when they made noises about boarding the plane with an animal, he just chuckled at their concerns. "He's a bird, for God's sake! If any of us should be comfortable with flying, it would be my boy here."

When they finally met the pilot, they had to rush to the plane in order to make up time. But the man wasn't to be hurried. He made a careful observation of the plane, completing a thorough safety check before they boarded.

By the door, Gabe made more formal introductions. "Josh, this is my friend Ainsley, Ainsley, this is Josh. He was my roommate in college for one very memorable year."

"That was before I flunked out," Josh said sheepishly. He blushed a little, which clashed with his tightly curled red hair.

"You were too smart for the university," Gabe said grinning. "Josh here got great test scores, he just didn't care to learn about Shakespeare or essay construction."

"That is true," Josh agreed. "And don't worry about the flying. I'm way better with mechanics than I ever was with a pen and paper."

Jack had stood to the side during this exchange, looking over the plane with pure enjoyment. His voice floated from over a wing. "I always thought I'd like to fly one of these things," he said loudly. "Haven't ever taken lessons, but I imagine I could pick it up pretty good."

Josh looked toward the voice, watching as Jack stepped around from the side of the plane. "They do have lessons here," he said, eyebrows up, "if you're serious about learning."

"Would save a whole lot of cash on commercial flights," Jack said, warming to the idea.

"It's an expensive hobby though," Josh replied. "You have to pay for the lessons, the fuel, for leasing the time with the plane…"

"What about buying a plane?" Jack asked quickly.

"You could do that," Josh agreed. "Is that something you would want to do?"

"Don't know, could be," Jack said, a grin splitting his beard. "Guess I'm looking into it."

They climbed into the little plane, and Josh made a final check. Once inside, he made sure they were all buckled up appropriately, and then spent more time clicking switches, checking dials, and writing information on a pad of paper.

"All ready?" he asked cheerfully, and then the engine roared to life.

Gabe sat next to Ainsley, giving Jack the seat next to Josh so that he could watch the younger man as he maneuvered the plane into position.

"Does flying make you nervous?" Gabe was looking at her, eyes dark.

"A little, but nothing terrible like my problem with blood," she replied lightly. "I promise that I won't pass out on you this time. I can handle this."

She could feel a surge of nerves as the plane started moving, and another stronger jolt as the speed increased. By the time that the wheels had left the pavement, she had grabbed Gabe's hand and was holding on to him tightly. He wasn't complaining, however, and gave her a grin that showed just a little reckless excitement in the experience.

"It'll even out in a second!" he shouted over the noise, leaning close to her.

She nodded silently. It was a heady and scary feeling, but she was enjoying it just a little.

The flight did even out, and as they were flying low enough, they were treated to some beautiful scenery out the plane windows. It was too noisy to talk much, so Ainsley spent time snapping pictures through the glass.

When they finally started to descend, Ainsley was feeling more relaxed. The landing, however, was another rather nerve-racking experience, and she was grateful when she could step from the plane and feel the earth firm beneath her feet.

"Smell that?" Jack exclaimed as they stood on the warmed pavement. "That's the smell of Florida! Even this far from the ocean, you can smell the heat and the salt." He took another deep breath, his chest puffing with the inhalation. "Love it here."

"When was the last time you were here?" Gabe asked, helping Josh unload their small bags.

"About six months ago," Jack's face had grown a little more serious. "But just a year ago I was here with Topper. He was looking something up, and I wanted to catch a quick fishing trip. He went into town, and I went out on the water." He shook his head. "It was the last time Topper got to come out here."

They were all silent for a moment, thinking of the man absent from their party, but the one that had drawn them together unintentionally.

"We'll have a car waiting," Gabe said, pushing past his thoughts. "We can drop you wherever you want," he told Josh.

"I'm good," Josh said. "I have a friend coming by to pick me up in an hour or so. I want to make sure the plane is in good shape to leave."

"Okay then," Gabe said. "We'll see you in two days?"

"Meet you in the airport," Josh agreed. The men shook hands, Jack included, and they started across the heated pavement, leaving Josh tending to the plane.

THE COCKATOO CALLED

CHAPTER ELEVEN

The rental car was hot inside, uncomfortable, with fake leather seats and a tiny back seat. Ainsley took the back since her legs were short compared to the men, and Jack drove. She realized as they emerged from the airport parking area to the main road, that having Jack as the driver might not have been the best choice. Like everything else he did, Jack drove fast and with panache, rushing around curves and turning abruptly into traffic, leaving horns wailing in his wake.

He gestured as he spoke as well, and Ainsley looked over to the seat next to her to see how the bird was taking the rather wild ride. Hemingway was in his carrier, strapped into the seat of the car with a makeshift harness that threaded into the seat belt. Jack was a man of surprises, but his insistence on the safety of his pet was rather nice.

"Are you handling all of this okay, Birdy?" Ainsley asked, peering into the cage.

Hemingway appeared to be concentrating on maintaining his footing on the slick bottom of the plastic crate, one huge claw wrapped around the wire door of the crate as they took corners at high speeds. His one eye peered at her between the bars but he made no comment. Seeing him gave Ainsley a twinge of guilt for leaving Dali behind. But Theresa had a key to her house and promised to go by to feed him and keep him company. 'Birdy sitting', she had said, would give her a chance to practice her parenting skills that she was afraid she might lose if she continued to be single. Ainsley had laughed at that. Theresa was far from ready to be settling down, in her opinion, but stranger things had happened.

The drive was not long, but felt far longer after being jostled in the back of the car. Even Hemingway looked annoyed when Jack came around to the back seat and slid in next to Ainsley.

"I gotta get his harness on him so he can go into the museum like a civilized visitor," Jack explained.

"Do you think that they're going to let him in?" Ainsley looked at the big bird in the crate, thinking of the havoc that beak and those claws could cause to valuable paintings.

"Have to," Jack replied. "He's a service animal. They can't refuse him."

"Service animal?"

"I had him trained. He's a seizure animal. He can detect if someone is goin' to have a seizure and tell them."

"Oh!" Ainsley felt a little flustered. "I didn't realize that you had seizures."

"I don't," Jack said, "but no one has to know that."

"Then does he detect the seizures?" Ainsley asked, head cocked and looking at the older man, beginning to feel a little suspicious.

"Well, now, that would be a good question. I imagine about the time someone started falling, he'd be clued in that something wasn't right." He grinned and winked.

"So you made it all up!" Ainsley exclaimed.

"Not that either, girl," Jack said, still smiling. As he spoke, he opened the door to the cage and Hemingway stepped out onto his proffered hand. "My neighbor, a Miss Mandy McMahan, had this old dog Prince. Prince was about the ugliest example of mixed breeding that I ever did see. But he was smart. And when she found that she had seizures, well, the people at the training place gave her Prince. He was to tell her when she was going to have a seizure, and she'd sit down and call for help. Worked like a charm, get it, Prince Charming?" He chuckled at his own joke. "Prince likely saved her life."

"I've heard of dogs doing that," Ainsley said doubtfully. "But never birds."

"I might have borrowed the certificate and changed it a bit so that I could bring old Hemingway around with me," Jack admitted. "He's not as talented as Prince, but a damn sight prettier, aren't you fella?" He had gotten out the harness and Ainsley watched intrigued as he fit the loop over the bird. She and Dali were nowhere near that good at using the harness. She had managed to talk the bird into wearing it while steadily supplying the favorite treats, but they hadn't yet tested it out in the open.

As for the rest of the lie, Ainsley was a little torn about how to view Jack's story. Jack was lying to get his bird admitted to places, which was certainly not right, but she guessed that as long as he could control the bird, it wasn't such a bad thing. In the scope of the danger they were in, it did seem to be a little transgression compared to breaking and entering

THE COCKATOO CALLED

and stealing property.

"And there we go, ready to see the town," Jack said, propping the door open and stepping back into the sunlight.

Ainsley slipped out as well, and Gabe closed the driver's door behind him and triggered the lock. The museum rose before them, gleaming white in the sunlight.

As it turned out, the museum was full of information, but most of it just reinforced what they had already learned. The dry history that they had gleaned from the internet was fleshed out with photographs and brilliant works of art. Ainsley was shocked at how much talent she could see in the paintings despite her ignorance of technique and tone.

Dali's work was varied, crazy, emotional, frightening, and undeniably brilliant. When they had finished the tour, Ainsley had breathed a sigh of relief. Going into such a place with Gabe was a pleasure, but Jack and Hemingway were predictably unpredictable, and she was just happy that they hadn't caused any destruction on their quick tour.

With the museum in their rear view mirror, Ainsley relaxed a little and laid her head back on the seat. Gabe was driving. He had caught her panicked look when Jack had started unlocking the door and made up a story about how Jack needed to be their navigator so that they could get around town safely. If Jack was suspicious about their reasoning, he didn't say.

"So now for lunch," Jack said grandly. "I've got just the place."

It wasn't so surprising that the restaurant was very similar to the place that Jack had chosen while they were at home. It also wasn't a shock when the man behind the bar smiled at Jack, waved them to a table, and addressed both the man and the bird by name.

"Well, how are you, you old bastard?" the wiry man greeted Jack, taking his free hand in an enthusiastic shake. "Oh, pardon my language," he said quickly, seeing Ainsley as she ducked in behind Gabe.

She smiled, her eyes skimming the decidedly beachy themed restaurant around them. Most of the windows were open to the air, and the smell of sun and salt were intense against the odor of old damp wood. A slight tang of fish also wafted through the windows, and Ainsley could see the water at a distance.

"Casper, it's good to see your ugly face," Jack said grinning. "It's been a while."

"You were lucky you caught me here," Casper replied. "Heading out tomorrow to go up north to visit some friends in Georgia."

"Can't imagine why you'd want to leave paradise," Jack said shaking his head sadly.

"I have to work here in paradise," the other man replied. His face showed years of living and working in the sun, the skin brown and seamed, his broad nose a little crooked with a stripe of white where he doubtlessly perched sunglasses to cut down on the glare. His hair was the same color as his skin, shot through with some iron gray, a little long and definitely in need of a trim. "The last time you were here, you had Topper dragging behind. You guys were up to something, if I recall correctly. How is the old man?"

Jack's face showed a flash of pain, "Oh, he passed, Casper," he said gruffly.

Casper froze, then his face fell as well. "Sorry to hear that, man, sorry as I can be. Topper was a great old guy."

"He was," Jack responded, taking the moment for a silent salute. "And this is his nephew, Gabe." Jack pulled out a chair for Ainsley in front of the bar and they all took seats while Jack settled himself. "Gabe and this little lady came out here to visit some of the old haunts that Topper and I liked."

"Then I'm honored that you came here." Casper didn't ask Jack what he wanted to drink, just poured him a tall glass of some dark, frosty beer and put it on the bar in front of him. "And what can I get you?" he asked Ainsley.

She looked behind him at the boggling array of liquor bottles and taps. She was thirsty, and the ride had made her tense up like a rubber band stretched to its limit. But she didn't know what she wanted to order, and was faintly embarrassed to be so indecisive.

"You like a menu?" Casper asked, pulling out a paper from behind the bar and placing it on the wooden top in front of Ainsley. Gabe leaned close to her and read with her.

Ainsley felt a little surge of dismay. On a normal day, she could decipher a menu, but she generally chose restaurants where she knew the offerings and could choose without even considering the printed choices. If she planned to go to a new place, especially one that offered more complicated faire, she would look up the menu on-line so that she could have time to study it. Although this place offered a limited variety of items, she was tired, and was having trouble focusing on the small print.

"If you like wine, maybe you'd like a hard cider. They're cold and not too dry, a little sweet," Gabe suggested, his breath close to her ear, tickling. "I don't think they even sell real wine here."

"Sounds perfect," she agreed, relieved that he had taken her hesitation as indecision, "and I'm going to run to the lady's room." She

THE COCKATOO CALLED

slipped from her stool and headed across the wooden floors, noticing with a little amusement that there was sand in the seams of the wood. The ocean and the beach were kings here, and would invade every little element of the place if they could.

The bathroom was old, spare but clean enough. The floor was still gritty with sand, but it smelled of soap and the ever-present scent of the ocean. She used the facilities and then stood at the mirror, patting at her hair helplessly. The humidity of Kentucky was nothing compared to Florida. Now her pale hair curled like crazy, sticking to her neck where she had dabbed some water to help cool her down. Her eyes in the mirror looked dark, her freckles, a feature she had inherited from her red headed mother, stood out on her pale skin. She would have to watch herself in the sun. Even totally dressed, any time outdoors would cause her cheeks to redden and her neck to burn.

With one hand she tucked her purse under her arm and checked her phone. She didn't have any new messages. She had told her mother where she was going and promised to call when they had landed. Her mother was worried, of course. She quickly sent off a text saying that she was fine and having a great time. On second thought, she found a picture that she had taken of Gabe as he was strolling out of the museum and added that to send to her mother. She imagined that it would make her parents feel better, to know that their young, single daughter was going off to visit the beach with a handsome young man rather than a pirate with a parrot, or worse yet, with the purpose of looking for art thieves. She found herself grinning. Her parents were pretty great. It would never occur to them that she would be following some man around with nefarious plans in mind. And she had been leading them along a little, guiding them to a slightly slanted conclusion. When she had told them that she was going to his apartment for dinner, was visiting his great aunt, or was going to help him care for his uncle's estate, she had deliberately let them believe that this was all part of a courtship, not a pursuit of a mystery. She looked down at the phone screen as a response came back, an emoji smiley face. Her mother had learned how to use the symbols fairly recently, and now they were laced into almost every conversation.

WHEN WILL YOU BE BACK?

The text was punctuated by a tiny palm tree symbol.

I'M GOING TO STAY HERE UNTIL MONDAY MORNING. I'LL BE HOME AFTER THAT.

Spell check and auto correct were a beautiful thing, she thought with an ironic smile. She hesitated in her typing and pictured her mother's arched eyebrows, her observant hazel eyes scanning the screen for any indication of improper behavior.

WE'RE STAYING AT A HOLIDAY INN. SEPARATE ROOMS OF COURSE.

That was the truth, although they hadn't checked in yet. She knew she'd call her mom from there. She might go for days not speaking with her parents while she lived her daily mundane life, but just now with everything going on, she was keeping them updated.

YOU WILL LET US KNOW WHEN YOU SETTLE IN? Another smiley face, this one with a wink.

SURE. She added her little symbols, a beach with a wave, a little seashell, a fish, and a smile. She turned off the screen and tucked the phone back in her pocket.

When she returned to the table, the men appeared to be in deep conversation. Their drinks had arrived, and the bottle stood in a pool of dampness. The air was thick with it. Jack was on his second glass of the dark beer; Gabe was drinking a soft drink.

"Hey, we went ahead and ordered," Gabe said, apologizing with his eyes.

"Only one thing good here anyway," Jack blustered. "Fish. You gotta eat fish if you come here. Otherwise, might as well go up to McDonalds."

"So we're having fish," Gabe said smothering a smile.

"That sounds fine with me," Ainsley assured him. "I like seafood."

"Told Gabe that you would. Not sensible any other way. So what's your next stop?" Jack was leaning back in the chair, balanced on the two back legs. Next to him, perched on the back of a second chair, was Hemingway. He looked a little rumpled after all of his adventures earlier in the day.

"Well, you mentioned that you had some places that you always liked to go with Uncle Topper," Gabe began, "I figured we'd start there."

"The marina, that'd be one," Jack agreed. "And there was this antique shop that Topper always went to. A good friend of ours owns it. He liked to find some bargains when we went there, but he did sell or barter a few things too. Good people. Always willing to let him get his hands on something he wanted. Of course, they weren't getting the short end of the stick either. With all of his gallivanting, Topper had plenty to bargain with."

"Really? I thought most of the things that he bought ended up going home and into his collections." Gabe took a long drink from his soda.

"Most he kept, but there were a few things that he decided wasn't worth getting them home. And then there were the investments." Jack's eyebrows went up at the term and he grinned. "If he thought he could make a trade, well, that's what he would do. He got to the point where he knew what some of the other collectors were interested in and would buy things for them. Well, not for them, but things that he thought that they'd take as a trade. Then they might do the same."

"Did he have a lot of collector friends?" Gabe was tracing patterns in the moisture on his glass unconsciously.

"Topper had friends everywhere," Jack said, and heaved a sigh, making his beard twitch. "It was part of his charm."

When Casper brought the huge tray of food, an older woman accompanied him; her skin was as burnished as his but topped with artificially lightened hair in a curly halo around her face.

"And here we are," Casper exclaimed cheerfully. "Let me introduce to you my new bride, Debbie." Debbie helped unload the plates, nodding a greeting to the group as she worked.

"Casper, you devil! When did you get hitched? And such a beauty!" Jack was beaming at the older lady, and she colored a little under her tan.

"Keep your eyes and your hands to yourself," Casper warned Jack. "This one is mine. We've been married for almost six months, so she hadn't seen all of my bad habits yet. She still thinks I'm a catch!"

Debbie was smiling behind his back, and made a brief gesture indicating his lack of sanity.

"Well, if it doesn't work out with old Casper here," Jack began, and Casper set his plate before him with a little extra force.

"My Debbie doesn't like the northern states," Casper said quickly, but he was grinning as well.

"My loss," Jack said dolefully, and Ainsley had to chuckle at his expression.

The fish was delicious. The batter was crisp; the fish itself light and flakey, and the tartar sauce was homemade by Debbie, the information causing Jack to propose marriage on the spot. Ainsley enjoyed the lunch, sitting back full and satisfied when she was done, taking a few minutes to give scraps of fish to the bird perching next to her.

Hemingway was a perfect gentleman, especially when being fed. He took the pieces with a gentle beak and bobbed a thank you with each bite. He tried everything that was given to him, eyeing everyone's plate in case he had missed a sample. When they were done with the meal, Jack took the bird outside to have a break, which Ainsley assumed meant that Hemingway would relieve himself. He seemed to have great control, and had not made any messes since they had embarked on their trip.

Gabe was leaning over his phone, a map of the city zoomed in on the screen.

"Where to next?" Ainsley asked, trying to look with him.

He scooted the phone closer for her to see. "We're close to the hotel. I think we can go that way first, check in, and leave our things. We might take a break and go over some of the information and notes we have."

"The hotel is on the beach, right?" Ainsley hinted.

"There is that. Did you want to go out swimming?"

Ainsley hadn't been to Florida since she was a child, and certainly didn't want to leave without seeing the ocean and enjoying a little time on the beach. "Will we have time?"

"Sure, we can do that for a few hours. Seems a shame to be here and not go out at least for a while."

"And later?"

"We can grab dinner. I don't think we'll have time to go to any of the other places until tomorrow. But I'll call ahead to the antique shop to make sure we can talk to someone."

THE COCKATOO CALLED

CHAPTER TWELVE

The hotel was one of those chain buildings that would have looked at home in any city. The only nod to the actual location was the lush plantings and overhanging palm trees with tiny lizards scurrying up the trunks. The rooms were overly cooled with stale air and the towels were thin and well bleached. But the sliding door looked out onto a small concrete pool that then opened onto the beach just a few yards away.

Gabe's room was next to Ainsley's, but Jack had chosen to stay somewhere else. When asked, he just made an extravagant face, his bushy eyebrows reaching almost to his hairline, and smiled mysteriously.

Ainsley had dropped her bag on the bed next to the sliding doors and stood framed by the curtains, looking out into the blue green brown of the water. The ocean's sigh could clearly be heard through the glass, and when she pulled open the door, the stale air within the room was replaced with the moist breath of the sea.

She heard a door stutter open, close by and saw Gabe's dark head as he peered out through the opening.

"Not bad, huh?" he asked, grinning at her.

"This view is wonderful!" she replied.

"Yeah, since we're not yet in the high season, they still had some space left. I was lucky that they were side by side though." He stepped out onto the little sidewalk, the ocean wind blowing his hair.

She stepped out as well, taking a deep breath and turning her face toward the sun. "Really nice," she sighed.

"You'll have to watch for a sunburn," he said, seeing her face lit up. "Do you have any lotion?"

"I do," she agreed. "Are you ready to go out?" The ocean was drawing her and she felt like a kid all over again, eager to put her toes in the sand and feel the rush of the waves.

"Sure. It'll take me just a second to change." He pushed back his hair from his face and looked over at her. "Meet you out here in about 10 minutes?"

"Okay!"

She slipped back inside and closed the door and then the curtain. She didn't want any wandering person to be able to see her rummaging around in her room, although she had no intention of changing anywhere but the bathroom. The bedroom was way too open for her taste. She dug into her bag and pulled out her bathing suit. It was an old one piece. She hadn't had time to go buy anything new, and this suit was made more for swimming laps more than sunbathing. Besides, its practicality was also good since it was well made and had held up for a couple of years wear. She took it into the bathroom and quickly used the facilities and changed, pulling her hair into a ponytail and adding a pair of short shorts over the suit. She had a beat up pair of flip-flops that she pulled from the bag as well. She was sliding them on her feet when she heard a light knocking on her door. She slid the curtains open and smiled. It was Gabe, looking fit and tanned in a pair of swimming trunks with a towel slung over his shoulders. She stopped for a moment, admiring the view, before she slid open the door and motioned him inside.

"Ready to go?" he asked, his eyes skimming the room which was a twin to his own.

"I just need some sunscreen," she replied, and pulled out a full tube. She had bought it at the beginning of summer and used it religiously when she needed to work outside. Too many sunburns in her childhood had made her realize how quickly a day could be ruined if this step wasn't taken.

She squirted a blob of the lotion on her hands and quickly began covering her face, chest, arms and legs, making sure to cover each piece of exposed skin. She scraped the wisps of hair away from her face and applied the cream, rubbing it into her skin. Gabe was standing still, observing her, making her feel suddenly awkward and clumsy.

"Do you need any?" she asked, holding out the tube.

"I'm good," he said, smiling slightly. "Mid-day, I'd be more concerned, but I should be good this late in the day."

She nodded and squirted out a final glob, working on the back of her legs and her feet. "Have you ever gotten a sunburn on your feet? It really hurts!" she said, trying to cover her self-conscious feelings.

"Do you want me to get your back?"

She nodded. "Yes, thanks," she said quickly. There was no way that she could have managed to cover her back completely, she told herself sternly. It wasn't like she was just trying to flirt with him. He took the

THE COCKATOO CALLED

tube from her and went behind her.

"It might be cold."

She felt him slather on the lotion, his hands firm and efficient. She tried not to be embarrassed about the little shivers she felt. Must be getting pretty desperate to enjoy the moment quite so much, she thought grimly.

"Thanks," she said again, holding up her hair while he worked on the back of her neck.

"Sure," he gave one final pass of his hand over her back. "I think I got you." He stepped back and she turned, picking up the thin towel from the bathroom.

"Let's go!" she exclaimed, again feeling like she was a kid on summer vacation.

Together they went out the door, locking it behind them and taking the key in a little bag in which Ainsley had stowed a paperback book and extra lotion. Her sunglasses were perched on her head and she set them on her nose, watching the sun flash off the ocean like shards of mirrored glass.

The sand by the hotel was loose and hot, shifting onto her flip-flops and between her toes and she was relieved to reach the water's edge and shed the shoes. She walked slowly into the surf, feeling the chilled water of the gulf wash over her feet to her ankles. The wind blew off the water, pushing her hair from her face, making her taste salt on her lips. She grinned up at the sun. This was just what she needed.

"Nice," Gabe said smiling at her. She didn't know if he was referring to the beach or her, and she didn't care. She followed him into the sea, the cold momentarily taking her breath away, and then relaxed into the waves.

Gabe could swim. And he looked good doing it. Gabe with wet hair and a bare chest was worth watching. She spent the next couple hours wading in the water, splashing out to sit on her sandy towel, and wading back in. She was almost disappointed when her hunger overcame her fun, and she turned toward Gabe where he stretched out on a towel next to her. Most of him was in the sand, his long legs stretching out into furrows he had made while settling in.

"So where do you want to go eat?" he asked, turning his head and looking at her, his eyelashes spiky with seawater.

"I don't care," she replied, propping herself up on her elbows. "Do you have any suggestions?"

"Nope, but I'm sure Jack would if we asked him."

"Are we meeting Jack?" she asked, wondering if she was feeling regretful about that or relieved.

"No, I think he had other plans. You'll have to tolerate just me."

She slanted him a glance, "I think I'll be okay."

"Good," he said. He glanced at his watch, a waterproof chunky timepiece that would have looked ridiculous on a smaller man. "Are you ready?"

At her nod, they climbed to their feet; shook out the sandy towels to take back to the hotel, and Ainsley found her flip-flops and slid them on, sand and all. She took one final regretful glance toward the beach, feeling like she was saying farewell to a friend.

They went back to the hotel to take quick showers, and met just outside the door to go out for dinner. The rental car seemed much larger without Jack. The evening had cooled a little and Ainsley rolled the window down. She knew her hair would be a wild mess, but it was barely dry from her shower, and with the rampant humidity, it was bound to frizz anyway. With the extra sun, some of the red would be visible among the golden strands, strawberry blond, as her mom called it. The change was almost instantaneous in the summer, that and the freckles.

"Okay, so what kind of food do you feel like?" Gabe glanced at her as he drove.

"I don't have any preference," she replied, watching the flashing lights as they drove by shops and restaurants embellished with gaudy signs and slick advertisements.

"Italian sound good?"

"Perfect," she agreed, as she felt her stomach rumble in agreement.

*****

She drank a glass of wine and took a deep breath, the smell of garlic and butter infusing the air. The bread was homemade, with a crispy crust and soft middle. The waitress delivered the salads with a flourish, and Ainsley thanked her. They had chosen well. The place was homey without being overdone, and almost every table was taken.

"This is good," Gabe said, sampling the salad.

"I'm glad the guy at the desk suggested it," she agreed.

"And he seemed to have a good idea about where else we could do some research. I think that local library might have information that would be harder to find somewhere else."

Ainsley agreed. The library a few blocks away from the museum was well stocked with books about Dali that might have been more obscure than what they could have found elsewhere. But since he was their local

THE COCKATOO CALLED

celebrity, with people coming from across the country to visit the museum, they were providing some additional resources for anyone interested in his art.

"And did you get to find out about the antique shop?" Ainsley asked.

"Jack gave me the name of the place and I called. The owner was already gone for the day, but he's due to be back tomorrow. I told them that I would call in the morning to figure out when it was best to stop by. Jack also said that we could run out to the marina and take a look at their boat. He said he was going by sometime tonight to check it out. Sounded like he'd like to take it out on the water."

"He's living up to his pirate look," Ainsley said grinning.

"He's trying," Gabe looked at her, a small frown creasing his brow. "Would you want to go out on the boat? I didn't know if we would have time, but I hated disappointing Jack since we came all the way down here."

"If you trust Jack not to get us stranded on some desert island, I think I'll be fine," Ainsley said. "Well, and if the weather holds up."

"We'll check the forecast before we go anywhere," Gabe agreed. "And now let's talk about something else. It seems like whenever we're together, we're talking about my uncle or the painting, or Jack."

"Or Dali," Ainsley said quickly. "But Theresa said that he was doing fine."

"Tell me about you," Gabe said, his eyes picking up the warm light from the candle glittering on the table.

"Oh, big subject," she said lightly. "You know a lot about me."

"But I don't. I know you grew up close by, but why did you move? You don't seem to be that devoted to your job."

"I like my job," she said defensively. "I just wanted to get away a little. I needed to try to be a little more independent, and my parents would have a hard time with that if I were living at their back door. So I decided that I could move away, but just not too far. This way, we all get the space we need, but I can visit as much as I'd like."

"That makes sense. And you're an only child?"

"One and only," Ainsley said with a small smile. "My parents wanted more children, but it just didn't work out that way. But I had lots of cousins growing up. And some of my family live in Louisville, so I see them regularly."

"No big scandals in your family tree?"

"I think one of my grandfather's relatives was a bootlegger, but that's about as good as we get," she replied. She felt a little awkward with the conversation. She did have something that she had been holding out, that she hadn't wanted to tell him about. But she wasn't about to start in on the sob story of how difficult her life had been when she was younger. Better for him to see her for what she was now. "What about you?" she asked.

His response was delayed as the waitress came by to whisk away their salad plates and bring in the larger dinner plates heaped with steaming pasta. For a moment, they were totally distracted by their dishes, trading tastes and samples.

"So what about your family?" Ainsley asked at last. "It sounds like you all are pretty close."

Gabe nodded thoughtfully. "We get along pretty well. I see them as often as Mom can get us together when everyone is in town. Come summer, we see each other almost every weekend." He busied himself winding a strand of spaghetti around his fork. "Really, my mom's side of the family is the tamer group. There aren't very many of them, and her brother became an accountant. It's my dad's family that has all of the interesting people."

"Like your Aunt Vi and Uncle Topper."

"Like them," he said smiling. "I hope my assorted family members haven't scared you off. We are just a normal American family."

"Scared me off? Do I look like I'm scared off?"

He reached over and covered her hand with his own. "I'm glad that you came on this trip," he said.

She felt the heat trip up her neck and to her cheeks. His eyes were catching the light and she could swear that she could see stars in them. His hand was warm and firm, his touch saying so much.

"I'm glad I came too," she responded, and meant every word.

*****

After dinner they drove back to the hotel, racing with the sun so that they could see it set over the water. Leaving her purse and shoes in the car, they ran across the sand until the ocean breeze was stirring their hair with gentle fingers.

The sun looked like a perfect globe of light as it danced on the lip of the ocean before dipping behind the gulf. The waves were tame, a shimmer in the distance, and Ainsley caught her breath. She hadn't realized she was still holding Gabe's hand until she felt him shift next to her.

"Your face is perfect, and your hair is on fire," he said, his voice just a little breathless.

THE COCKATOO CALLED

"I'd say you were drunk, but you didn't have any wine," she responded, trying to keep her voice light.

"If this were an old movie, I would say I am drunk, on your beauty. But I don't think that I can pull off the line." His lips quirked in a smile. "You are beautiful, you know."

She ducked her head, glad that the flames from the sun gave her an excuse for the glow. A cry from children dancing in the surf had her looking up and out into the distance. She felt his fingers, gentle on her cheek, turning her face back toward him. The kiss was little more than a brush of lips, but it started a bloom of heat deep inside Ainsley. So sweet, so perfect. She leaned closer, stepping into his embrace, feeling one of his hands drop from her face and slide down her shoulder to settle on her back, pulling her even closer. The next kiss was deeper, pulling her under, washing her over with waves of warmth.

They stood for the golden minutes of the sunset until the sky's flames were doused with gray. Then they traced their way back to the hotel, hand in hand. They stopped at the car to grab Ainsley's purse and she slid her shoes on. She dug into her bag and pulled out the key to her room, an old-fashioned door key, out of place in this time of automatic door locks and key cards.

"We might have an early morning tomorrow," Gabe said, halting at the door to her room.

"Just let me know," she replied, trying to string her thoughts together.

"I'll call you as soon as I know something. We'll grab breakfast first."

She tried to wipe the foolish smile off of her face, but couldn't seem to contain her emotions. "I'll see you then," she said, her hand on the knob.

He grabbed her other hand and pulled her a little closer for a quick hard kiss. "Goodnight," he said.

She used the key, fumbling a little, and unlocked the door with him behind her, a step back, ever the gentleman. She slipped inside and stopped with the door still open. "Well, goodnight," she said a little breathlessly. Then she closed the door, stopping with her head down for a moment, trying again to catch her emotions.

"You need to lock the door," she heard his voice through the panel, still just outside. Obediently, she twisted the lock, then added the chain for security. She thought she heard his footsteps retreating, but then heard the distinct sound of the door next to hers being opened. She liked the idea that he was just next door. And the walls were thin enough for her to hear him moving around inside. With strangers, it might have been intrusive or uncomfortable to know every move of her neighbor, but now it was reassuring in the strange city. And to be perfectly honest, she just liked that he was there. She sighed. What a perfect evening it had been. She dropped her purse on the bed and smiled all the way to the bathroom.

She switched on the light and looked at herself in the artificial glow. She looked pretty. Her eyes were bright, her hair a wild halo of curls, her skin slightly rosy. She looked at her little makeup bag, pulling it open and finding her toothpaste. Her toothbrush was already unwrapped and propped up in a glass. She dug in the bag again, searching for lotion. She would take another shower to get rid of the salt and sand. Her eyes went to the shower behind her and she thought of the little sample size shampoo and conditioner she had left in there. She was tugging down a fresh washcloth, bleached white and thin to the touch, when the sway of the shower curtain behind her caught her eye. She frowned. She knew she had left the curtain open with her swimming suit hanging from the curtain rod after her ocean swim and shower. She had wanted to dry the suit before she would need to pack it for home. Someone from housekeeping must have come in and neatened up. Unconsciously, she shook her head. But no, the towels that she had used on the beach were still lying in a sandy heap on the floor. She had tucked them out of the way so that she wouldn't track too much sand into the room, but they were easily seen, and housekeeping would have certainly taken them. Other signs of her inhabiting the room were still visible, the unwrapped soap next to the sink, the washcloth from earlier folded and laid out, still damp, on the counter.

Without thinking, she turned and jerked the shower curtain open, thinking only of her swimming suit and where it could have fallen. But her eyes didn't land on any suit. There was something in the shower, something white and feathered and broken. Her cry sounded a little like a squeal, and then just a heaving of breaths. She stumbled backwards, one hand over her mouth, the other hitting the counter, swiping over the surface until the ice bucket and glasses that had been left on the convenient tray were sent flying, landing with a crash and clatter on the floor. Her shoes crunched over the glass as she continued backing out of the room, small whimpers escaping her.

The banging on the door had her spinning, eyes wide with terror.

"Ainsley? Ainsley are you all right?"

"Gabe," she said, too softly for him to hear, but it was reassuring for her to hear her voice. She rushed to the door, her now clumsy hands fumbling at the locks. As soon as the door was open, she threw herself at him, feeling his arms go around her tightly.

"What happened? Are you hurt? Ainsley, are you hurt?"

She pulled back slightly and looked into his pale face. "No, not hurt. I'm okay, it's just," she looked over her shoulder, feeling a wave of nausea wash over her. Her mind was unwillingly going over the scene, the white feathers, the limp body, not Dali, surely it wasn't big enough to be her sweet bird.

"What?" He gently held her shoulders, looking down into her face. "What is it?"

"In the shower," she said through clenched teeth.

He went around her frozen figure, and she heard him curse when he stepped around the broken glass and looked into the tub. "What the...!"

She slowly approached the bathroom door, standing back a little. "Someone was in here. Someone broke in. Gabe, is it...?"

"It's a seagull," he said grimly. "Someone must have caught one and killed it. Looks like the neck was broken."

She wrapped her arms around her middle, taking deep breaths. It was a gull, just a wild bird. Not Dali, not her bird. But still, someone had killed a living thing just to get to her. Someone had put it here to scare her, and she was falling for it in a big way. Her anger starting swelling, a hot wave that blew the chill from her bones.

"They left it here for me. Someone wanted to scare me. Why?"

Gabe stepped carefully around the glass and the upturned ice bucket and closed the bathroom door after himself. "It seems pretty obvious to me," he said, moving quickly. "Someone doesn't want us here. They are trying to threaten us. They don't like what we're doing. And using the bird," he shook his head and grimaced, "that's just disgusting." He stepped out into the room. "We can't stay here now. I don't think that they'd go after us, killing the bird was a coward's act, but they might think about going a little farther to get their message across."

"We need to call the police," Ainsley said decisively. "Maybe they left some kind of clue."

"The police are going to look at this, and then look at us." Gabe paced from the window to the bed, pausing to look blindly at the television. "If we call them, we're going to be up most of the night filling out complaints. We'll have to call the office here at the hotel too. They might have their questions." He strolled to the window and pulled the curtains closed with a little too much force, causing the heavy fabric to swing stiffly. He muttered a curse and reached into his pocket, pulling out his cell phone.

"Who are you going to call?" Ainsley asked.

Gabe looked up at her for a moment, his eyes steady. "I'm calling Jack. He needs to know what is going on. And he may know more than he's let on, I can't tell. But now they are going after you, and this is getting a little too personal."

"You think the bird was a reference to Dali?"

"Don't you?" He paced again, hitting the call button on his phone.

Ainsley rubbed her hands over her face, stifling her anger and trying to think logically. She couldn't stay here. They wouldn't be staying in the room. There was no way that would work. She went over to her suitcase and began gathering her things, putting off going close to the bathroom until she had cleared out the rest of her things.

Gabe was talking to Jack, but his side of the conversation amounted to explaining what they had found in the shower, and then a lot of silent nodding.

"Don't go in the bathroom again," Gabe said as an aside as he watched her pack. "I'll help you in a second."

Ainsley nodded and sank down on the side of the bed. She felt a mild sense of shock, and pulled out her cell phone. She texted a few lines, no doubt with odd auto corrections, to her parents just to let them know that she was fine. She just needed to touch base with home, with normality. She next texted Theresa asking about Dali. The missive was short, but rewarded with a funny picture of the bird eating something that looked suspiciously like pizza. Theresa had responded quickly, and it made Ainsley feel better.

"Jack's coming over here and taking you to his place," Gabe said first. "He was staying with a friend, and said that we can bunk there tonight. But he wanted to see this first," he gestured vaguely to the bathroom and its deceased occupant.

"What about the police?"

"I don't think it would do us much good at this point," Gabe said. "I think we'd do just as well to clean up a little and check out. I'll take pictures to have for proof."

Ainsley nodded, watching as he came over to the bed and dropped next to her. He put an arm around her and she leaned into his warmth.

"This was just a stupid warning," he said gruffly. "Someone is not happy about what we were doing, and they must have known how this would upset you. So they left it for you to find."

"A warning for what?" Ainsley said breathlessly.

"It's a warning about what we're doing in Florida. I think whoever was getting into my place in Louisville has decided to follow us here."

THE COCKATOO CALLED

"What are we going to do?" her voice was strong, and a little angry.

"We're going to figure out what the hell is going on," Gabe responded, pulling her a little closer. "And we're going to get back at these bastards."

CHAPTER THIRTEEN

Jack traveled with his friend to the hotel ensconced in what appeared to be an antique Cadillac, which was the first surprise. The second was seeing who his friend actually was. Ainsley had pictured another pirate, or a sailor at least, wind-swept and rough, maybe with an eye patch. With fatigue and slight shock setting in, she was prepared for any outlandish character to burst out of the sedate and highly polished luxury car. But her assumptions were unfounded when she saw that the man that accompanied Jack was a thin refined gentleman with warm brown eyes, a neat slightly outdated suit, and an unlit pipe clamped in his teeth. His hairline had crept ever higher until his bald pate showed through the thin strands, but he had a splendid mustache that was shaped and curled in a distinctly rakish manner. Ainsley only hoped that he never lit the pipe for fear that this decoration would go up in smoke.

Jack swung out of the car and immediately swept into Ainsley's room, his face dark with anger. His cursing was much louder and more creative than Ainsley had heard, and when he came out, he was shaking his head, his hands clenched in tight fists at his sides.

"They are cowards, that's what they are. Taking it out on some poor innocent animal. They're worse than animals themselves. When I find out who did this…" He swung in Ainsley's direction. "Are you all right, my girl?"

Ainsley nodded. "I'm fine. It was just a shock. But I'm okay now. I'm just ready to go."

Jack took her arm gently. "Then you'll go," he said decisively. "This is my good friend Abraham Macintosh. He will take you back to his house while we finish with this."

"Oh, that's not necessary," she protested.

"No, you go on. You can get settled at his house."

Ainsley was pretty sure that she could have talked Gabe into letting her stay, but Jack was another story all together. She suspected that he came from the same mold as her father, the take-charge kind of person.

"All right," she said, "but I need to get the rest of my things together." She wanted to make sure of something else. She wanted to be sure that she hadn't missed something important because of her immediate and intense reaction to the scene in her bathroom. She needed to make sure that all of her things were still there and undisturbed, that no one had used the animal cruelty to cover up for a more subtle invasion. She slipped back in the room and Jack followed. Mr. Macintosh was lingering outside the door, very calm in the wake of Jack's explosion. Gabe stood in the doorway to the bathroom.

"Your bag is here," he said as she came up behind him. In his big hand he held the makeup bag that she had stuffed with all of her most intimate things, her makeup, her lotions, and soaps. The shampoo would still be in the shower, but she wasn't about to ask for it. And her toothbrush was mixed in with glass shards and sand on the floor. She took the little bag from him, not opening it, but tucking it under her arm.

"Can I just look around for a minute?"

He nodded and stepped back, allowing her in. "Watch the glass," he said.

She eased into the room, trying to avoid the bigger bits of glass, her eyes scanning the sink, the counter, and finally the tub where the curtain was pulled back. She could see nothing out of place beyond what she had noticed before. The linens were just as she had left them, the towels, the washcloths, and the mat draped over the side of the tub. Her little bottle of shampoo and conditioner were still perched on the lip of the tub, and she could see her bathing suit in a heap by the drain. Someone had just let it fall when they had moved the curtain.

She stood very still and forced herself to look at the bird. It was hanging by a cord, and when she looked closer, she could see that it was the telephone cord that usually plugged into the wall. It had been knotted loosely around the bird's neck, and it seemed obvious from this angle that the bird had been dead already when it had been hung there. It looked still but not yet stiff, its feather's rumpled and bent, its dark eye already glazing. A thin trickle of blood seemed to trace from somewhere around its breast and slide down its body, ending with a scarlet droplet suspended from one claw. She didn't know why it was bleeding. The broken neck certainly wouldn't have caused it. But the blood was still red enough to appear fresh, and it made her shudder slightly.

"We'll get this cleaned up," Gabe said, and laid a gentle hand on her shoulder. "You head out with Mr. Macintosh, and I'll meet you there."

Ainsley nodded. She wouldn't be doing much more here. All that was left was to sweep up the glass and dispose of the bird. She had packed most of the rest of her belongings, and she wouldn't be taking the rest. She didn't want to ever see that bathing suit again, or this hotel, for that matter. This sad scene would forever taint all of her memories.

*****

Gabe handed her bag into the Cadillac as she settled into the front seat. He dropped a kiss on her forehead and looked at her closely.

"I'll be coming along in just a few minutes. Okay?"

"I'm fine, Gabe." She kept her voice firm and her eyes even on his. She was done being frightened.

He smiled and stood, pushing the door closed. Mr. Macintosh had already started the engine, and it purred with well-maintained precision.

"Are you ready?" he asked.

"Yes, thanks," Ainsley agreed. She was watching out the window as they pulled away from the parking lot, thinking with regret of the beautiful memory ruined.

"Jack tells me that you are very good with Hemingway," Mr. Macintosh's voice broke into her thoughts. She realized that he might have been talking to her before while she had been lost in thought.

"He's great," Ainsley said forcing a smile. "A little scary, but great."

"Jack dotes on the bird, but I have to admit, I've become fond of the old fellow myself."

"Do you have a bird too?"

"A parrot? Like Hemingway?" he smiled a little, "Oh my, no." He glanced at her as he drove. "Hemingway is fine for an occasional guest, but I couldn't deal with him as a permanent roommate. He's terribly loud, and he can make a significant mess when he gets upset." He seemed to pause, to think for another moment. "Actually, he is a mess most of the time."

Ainsley was smiling now, warming a little. "Yes, I have been looking out for Gabe's uncle's bird, Dali. He can be very messy and loud when he's in a mood."

"Dali? That would be the cockatoo that Jack insisted Topper needed."

"So you were friends with Uncle Topper too?"

"Jack and Topper came to visit Florida frequently. I've known Jack for years! Too many years, I sometimes think." He pursed his lips thoughtfully. "Topper visited with me, came along with Jack, on

THE COCKATOO CALLED

occasion. He was quite the traveler! He had some of the most outlandish stories, but I quite enjoyed those as well."

Ainsley nodded and smiled to herself. "I never got to meet Gabe's uncle," she said ruefully.

"Young Gabe is the spitting image of him."

Ainsley was silent for a while, seeing the blur of scenery as it melted into the darkness. When they pulled off onto a drive, Ainsley had to rouse herself out of her mesmerized state. The long day behind her, coupled with the stress of the evening, was making her brain sluggish and her eyes grainy.

"And here we are!" Mr. Macintosh climbed out of the car almost as soon as the sound of the engine died away and was opening Ainsley's door before she had unbuckled her seatbelt. Not that she thought he minded. He seemed to be of that generation where opening doors for ladies was just something you did, something that every gentleman of any age should do. "I'll get your bag," he said, ushering her toward the door.

She nodded sleepily. His home was surrounded by local plantings including towering palms meticulously groomed, but his front lawn was not a lawn at all, but covered in pea size gravel that rattled like ice in a glass when they stepped between flat stones on the way to the wooden deck. The deck itself was built in two levels ending in a wall of glass windows. In the darkness, golden orbs of light seemed to bloom from the greenery, illuminating their way up the deck steps. Mr. Macintosh opened the door with a soft click and then hit a switch within, bathing the room with light.

Ainsley paused at the door, her purse hanging from her shoulder, her cell phone in her hand. She was suddenly aware that she had willingly left the hotel with this virtual stranger, but for the life of her, she couldn't be concerned about Mr. Macintosh. There was just something so gentle about him, an old fashioned air that made her feel as she had in the presence of her grandfather. The funny thing was, the two men didn't physically resemble one another at all. And one glance at the interior of Mr. Macintosh's house showed her that Mr. Macintosh was very different in other ways as well.

The front room was a glassed in atrium of sorts, full of lush plants and wicker furniture that created a tropical oasis. Through a second set of glass doors, Ainsley could see the actual living room, a large space with an overstuffed sectional couch situated in front of an enormous flat screen TV. The décor there was fiercely modern, almost stark. Mr. Macintosh ushered her through the front room and swung open the glass doors so that she could step into the air-conditioned cool of his house. Black and white tiles stretched from the living room into the open kitchen. From the middle of the space, a wooden stairway with metal rails, supported mostly by a metal frame, split the room. At the top of the stairway, a balcony with a half wall stretched in either direction ending in a door on each side. Ainsley supposed that these were the bedrooms since the bottom floor appeared to be mostly open.

"You're welcome to stay in my room for the night," Mr. Macintosh said gallantly, and Ainsley had a brief flash of herself taking the man's bed. She suspected that he would have flannel sheets, and it probably smelled of Vicks.

"Oh, no, thanks," she said faintly. "This looks fine right here. I'll just stretch out on the couch."

"Jack has been using the guest room and I'm sure that he'd be willing to…"

"No, really. I'll be fine right here." She went over to the huge couch and sat down, just to illustrate her point. She was fairly surprised at how comfortable it was. She let out an inadvertent sigh. "This is nice," she said a little dreamily.

"It's a fine piece," he agreed. "Would you like something to drink? Some hot tea perhaps?"

It suddenly sounded like a very good idea. Tea. That sounded comforting in an old world kind of way. "That would be nice," she said and smiled.

"Good." He took her bag and placed it carefully by the couch. "Then I'll start some water."

She thought she must have nodded off while he was rattling around in the kitchen because when she pried her eyes open, Gabe and Jack were coming in the door. There was a tray on the table in front of her with a white mug, a small pot with golden honey, and a little pitcher of cream. Gabe dropped his bag on the floor next to hers and sat next to her on the couch.

"Wow," he said grinning as he sank into the cushions. "This is some house."

"I like it," Mr. Macintosh said smiling lightly. "Can I get you anything to drink?"

"Beer, man, I could use a beer," Jack dropped onto the other section of the couch.

"Gabe?"

"That would be great, Mr. Macintosh."

"Call me Mac," the older man said, "and I'll get the beer."

THE COCKATOO CALLED

He went back to the kitchen and Ainsley bent over her cup, finding an Earl Gray tea bag on the tray next to the mug. She dropped it into the cup and lazily bobbed it in the water. The brown stained the water and smelled of comfort.

When Mac came out, he had two dark bottles of beer and another hot mug of tea. He sat in one of the chairs placed close to the rest and looked at Jack.

"Is everything cleaned up?" he asked.

"Yes, we buried the bird. Didn't feel right about it unless it was taken care of." Gabe sighed a little. "We took pictures for our records," he stretched out his long legs and ran a hand over his face.

"One thing at a time, boy," Jack said, and took a draw on his beer. "We'll take care of one thing at a time."

"So we'll still do our investigation," Gabe agreed, "and then we'll head home."

"I hope we find something tomorrow," Ainsley said.

"We will," Gabe reassured her.

They sat for a time in silence, each lost in their thoughts as Ainsley felt her eyes grow heavy again.

Jack finished his beer and stood. "I'm going on up," he said. "Okay for you young ones to stay up 'till all hours, but old men need their rest."

"Agreed." Mac stood slowly. "Come with me, young lady, and I'll show you around." He led Ainsley back to a full bathroom, another modern wonder, with a glassed shower and fluffy white towels. "Feel free to use all of the facilities," he said. "There are extra toiletries in the cabinet."

"Thank you so much," Ainsley said earnestly.

"It is no bother," he said. "Please make yourself at home." He paused and looked at her. "This attack on you was totally uncalled for, totally wrong. But you're safe here."

She nodded, feeling tears threaten. She knew it was because she was tired, but still, she felt a little silly for the reaction. Mac patted her briskly on the back and headed back out.

Ainsley used the bathroom, and after seeing the display of possible choices for shampoos and soaps, decided that she would take a shower as she had planned earlier in the evening. When she returned to the living room, Gabe was standing holding a stack of blankets and pillows.

"I'll take this couch if you want the other," he said casually, putting the blankets on the glass table and taking the top one.

"That sounds fine," she said, conscious just that she was so very tired. She took her bag with her to the bathroom and rummaged around for her supplies. This time she used one of the toothbrushes that Mac had in the closet, and chose new shampoo and conditioners as well as soaps. The water was nice and hot, the steam rising in billows. She made sure that the door was locked before shedding her clothes and stepping under the spray. She hadn't thought that she would like the clear shower doors, but they did give her an unobstructed view of the closed bathroom door, which was reassuring after the events of the evening before.

She took a longer shower than normal, and when she stepped out she felt tired, but much more relaxed. She put on her shorts and tee shirt that she had brought as sleeping attire. It wasn't sexy, not even a little attractive, but it was soft and comfortable. She took a moment to towel dry her hair as best she could and then gave up, hanging the towel back on the rack. Taking her bundled clothes with her, she went to the living room. The lights had been dimmed, but it was still easy to see Gabe sprawled out on the couch, a blanket pulled up to his chin. His eyes were closed, long dark lashes more evident as he dozed.

She put her clothes and bag on the floor and sat on the other couch. Someone, Gabe presumably, had spread out a blanket on the couch and put a pillow at one end, the one closest to where his head rested. She found her phone in her purse and put it on the glass table next to her, careful not to make any additional noise. With a sigh of relief, she then swung her legs onto the couch and sank back into the generous cushions.

*****

She didn't know what she had been dreaming about. Something dark and threatening, chasing her down corridor after corridor. Her heart was beating too fast, her breath coming too hard. She pulled herself up and put one hand to her head, pushing the hair from her face. Her dream was still fresh enough that she could examine it, how the red door had loomed open, the white fluttering of a bird, but behind her the heavy steps of someone who would not stop, would not rest.

"Hey, you okay?"

She hadn't realized that she had wakened him when she sat up, blanket clutched to her chest, her breath a little too fast and too loud. But Gabe's voice distracted her, and she turned her head to look at him in the hushed darkness.

"Yeah," she said in a whisper. "Yeah, I'm," she hesitated. "It was just a dream."

She watched him unfold from the couch, his blanket dropping back. He was wearing sweatpants, hanging low, and a thin tee shirt that was

THE COCKATOO CALLED

frayed at the neck. His hair was spiked with sleep. He sat heavily next to her, his eyes still blurry.

"Nightmare?"

"Yeah," she said nodding. She let her head drop to her hand.

She felt him gently put his arm around her and pull her into his warm body. "Sorry about that."

"It's not your fault," she replied leaning against him.

"It's not? Are you sure?" He pulled her close and she felt him lay his cheek against her forehead.

"It's not, and yes, I'm sure," she said softly.

"Okay, but let's just sit here for a minute. Warm you up."

She nodded silently. She felt him gently tug her back until she was curled up against him. She sighed in the warmth. He pulled the blanket up around them both and settled back. She laid her head against his chest, hearing the steady beat, reassuring and alive. The dream seemed to fade gently, and with it, came sleep.

Ainsley shifted a little and felt the body next to her move, an arm tightening around her. Her eyes popped open and she found herself staring into a strange room. Her mind tumbled as the night came back to her.

She felt Gabe shift next to her. She had to admit, it felt nice cuddled up like this. She had slept heavily when she had finally fallen back to sleep, and Gabe had been a steady presence, reassuring and solid at her back. Now she could tell that morning had come fully. A harsh stripe of sun turned the well-polished floor into a mirror, painfully bright. She was also aware of the rise and fall of a voice, a grumbling sound punctuated by the unmistakable squawk of a bird. Reluctantly, she eased away from Gabe's warmth and sat up, pushing her curls out of her face. She wasn't embarrassed about the night before. What had been left in her room had been unnecessarily cruel, a petty, nasty gesture from a despicable person. She wouldn't be swayed by such a disgusting spectacle, but it was natural that she had been upset about it.

She was on her feet, warily pushing her hair back again, when she heard the heavy tread of boots on the stairs and saw Jack descending. Hemingway was on his shoulder, looking a little disgruntled and damp.

"Ah, good morning," Jack greeted her, keeping his voice one notch lower than a roar.

"Hi," she said smiling.

Hemingway flapped his wings against the side of Jack's head and made a growling sound.

"Gave our boy a bath this morning and he wasn't in the mood. I'm afraid his has his feathers ruffled." His smile was crooked. "Literally."

Gabe stirred on the couch, heaving himself into a sitting position and running his hand through his hair. To Ainsley, he looked adorable. She quickly had to look away so that her expression wouldn't betray her.

"Figured we'd have a quick bite to eat and then head down to the docks. Weather is reporting showers for later, so it'd be better if we were out of there before the rain sets in." Jack looked at Gabe, eyebrows rising like hairy parentheses. "You going to make it, boy?"

"Sure, fine," Gabe agreed and stood, his sweatpants falling a little on his hips. He rubbed his hand absently across his chest as he wandered toward the bathroom, and Ainsley stood and gathered her clothes.

"You can use the facilities upstairs if you want," Jack said. "I'm starting breakfast." She didn't want to ask where he would put the bird while he cooked. A few feathers in the food might be decorative, but not tasty.

She nodded her thanks and took her bundle of clothes and her suitcase upstairs with her. Jack's bed was already made, tucked tight like a soldier might fix it. There was another strange contraption made of PVC pipes in one corner like the one in Gabe's office, but this one was sitting on a platform of newspapers, sprinkled with seeds, nutshells, and bird droppings. This was apparently where the big bird had spent the night. And he must have behaved himself, because she could see no signs that he had torn up or otherwise destroyed any furniture in the starkly modern and pristine room.

She hurried through her morning routine, stopping for a moment to look at herself in the mirror critically. She was pale, but she would chalk that up to being tired and stressed. Her hair had been tamed into a ponytail at the nape of her neck, and the cool blue of the shirt she wore brought out the color in her eyes.

She took one final glance at the mirror and grabbed her belongings. They had a lot to do today before they would head back home.

At the base of the stairs, she paused. Gabe was coming out of the bathroom, his hair damp and showing a little curl at his neck. His glasses were a little steamed from the heat. He smelled of soap and laundry detergent, but his face was unshaven, but the look worked for him. He grinned when he caught sight of her, the smile lighting up his thin face, making her heart pick up an extra beat.

"Morning sunshine," he greeted her, and before she could respond, had dipped his head and pressed a firm kiss on her lips. "I'm starving," he continued, dropping an arm around her shoulder and gently steering her into the room. She pressed her lips tightly as though to keep the kiss

THE COCKATOO CALLED

for a moment longer and smiled inwardly.

Breakfast was more of a feast than she was accustomed to. She tended to settle with cereal and coffee on most days, so the platters of eggs, bacon, ham, pancakes, toast, fried potatoes with onions, and accompanying butter, jelly, syrup and all the other condiments was unusual for her. But she found that she was hungry, and ate her way through seconds before she sat back with her coffee to listen to the men plot the day.

"So we'll check out the boat first," Gabe said, pouring himself a second cup of coffee before dropping into the seat next to Ainsley. "I've already called the shop, and it looks like they can see us any time after noon. So from the Marina we can either go to the shop to visit Uncle Topper's friend or drop by the library." He took a sip of the coffee and glanced at Ainsley. "I guess it will all depend on how long it takes us to look over the boat."

"And I would like to see you all for dinner tonight before you leave," Mac said from his seat at the head of the table.

"You don't have to do that!" Ainsley exclaimed. "You've done so much for us already, letting us stay here, providing this huge breakfast."

"Jack bought most of the breakfast supplies and cooked it all. I don't get that many visitors, so I would enjoy having you one last time," Mac explained.

"We'll be here," Jack said before anyone could protest any further. "Mac is an excellent cook. We won't want to miss that. But for now we'll clean up and get going before the weather changes."

By the time they left the house, the kitchen was back to being almost spotless and the blue sky was now blanketed with some low slung clouds. The wind had picked up, bringing with it the breath of the ocean.

In the daylight, Ainsley could appreciate the house even more. It was close enough to the water to enjoy a fabulous view, but not in the congested and commercial part of the main strip. She was watching the water as they pulled out of the drive.

The marina was just a 20-minute drive from the house, easily identified by the dozens of tall masts spearing the threatening clouds. The boats were mostly privately owned, a few that could be rented out for a deep-sea fishing trip or a quick tour of the neighboring islands. It was a relatively small marina over all, but pretty well maintained.

Jack moved purposefully to a slip that housed a 30-foot vessel, a Pearson P 30 William Shaw Design, he enthusiastically informed them.

"This baby has everything a man could want," he said proudly. "It holds four people easily. Fiberglass monohull cruiser," he intoned.

"What year is this thing," Gabe asked, his eyes lighting up.

"1972," Jack said, "but don't let her age mislead you. She's a beaut and has been maintained perfectly. AM/FM radio, VHS player, three burner propane stove, and the icebox works great. She's ready for anything."

Ainsley knew very little about boats, and even less about crafts that were made to go out on the ocean, but to her, this one seemed especially nice. Even with the sails furled and tucked against the masts, she could imagine how majestic it would look skimming over the water, a pale shadow against the darker water.

"I wish we could take her out for a spin," Jack said dolefully. "But with this weather and our next stop waiting, there just won't be time."

Ainsley wasn't sure if she was relieved that she wasn't seeing the pirate in action, or sad that she missed the spectacle. Either way, it had been an experience that she wouldn't soon forget.

Jack strolled across the narrow deck and started down a set of stairs that led below. Inside, the cabin had been buttoned up neatly, each door and cabinet sealed. It took only a moment for Jack to pull out a sizable lockbox, sealed to protect the contents from the damp and salt.

Inside were stacks of papers, some new and some faded with age, and photographs rubber banded together in thick packets. Gabe took one of the bundles and pulled off the rubber band, blinking when the cracked material gave way and the photos tumbled to the floor. Ainsley dropped beside him and helped him pick up the pictures, trying not to become caught up in the black and white shot of lines of women in sequins or the colored picture of Hemingway perched on the mast of the boat, blue green shades of colors almost blending with the background of the sea.

"We might as well take the whole box," Jack said frowning. "Too much stuff here to go through."

Gabe nodded and dropped the pictures he was holding back into the box. "I'll just take these home. I can always put them back at his house after we look through them."

"And we'll look see around here, might be something else we want," Jack agreed.

Ainsley helped scoop the papers back in the box and then followed Gabe to the next room in the little cabin. The bed would have barely fit Uncle Topper's tall frame, but it was neatly made and ready for the next occupant. They took a few minutes rummaging through some of the cabinets and drawers, but didn't find anything that looked related to their search. Jack was moving slowly behind them, lost in thought or memories. He had left Hemingway back at the house, and looked

THE COCKATOO CALLED

somehow incomplete without his feathered companion.

Ainsley stood by one of the portholes and looked out at the water, the surface now chopped by waves like it was being stirred with thousands of butter knives slicing and spreading the water in dashes and dabs. She could feel the boat moving, the dip and sway of the water pushing at them, the motion increasing.

"I think the wind has picked up," she commented, looking at Gabe standing by the head of the bed.

"Yeah, I feel it," he agreed. "But I think we're done here for now." He took her elbow and ushered her back into the main room. "We'll take a look above board, but I doubt we'll find anything else."

Jack had the box under one arm and headed up the stairs first, handing the keys back to Gabe as he edged up the steps. "You hold on to these," he said.

Gabe looked at the older man and shook his head. "You're the best man to be watching out for the boat. It might need to be taken out to sea a few times, just so it remembers what it's used for. You keep the keys. When everything is settled, we'll talk about it more."

Jack nodded his head in understanding, his lips quirking in a little smile. "Might need to take the old girl out. Raise a toast to Old Topper with some of the gang."

"He would have liked that," Gabe agreed, and then followed Jack out onto the deck.

In the open air, Ainsley could see why the boat had increased its rocking. The wind was stirring the waves, beating quickening rhythm against the dock and the hulls of the boats. She had to hold onto the walls and rails to steady herself, and the wind whipped her pale curls around her face. While she waited on deck, the men completed a hurried search of the rest of the boat, finding nothing more than the necessary tackle for fishing, the day to day equipment for the maintenance of the boat, and the detritus left by guests lounging on sun-bleached chairs. They climbed down from the boat onto the dock, Gabe holding Ainsley's hand in a firm grasp to keep her balanced. She was relieved when they were finally on the hard ground, but still felt a slight sway beneath her feet as though she were still navigating the shifting deck.

"Rain's going to break at any time," Jack said, the wind picking up the flat of his beard like a scruffy mat. "We'd better get on."

The rain started in fat warm drops just as they swung the car doors open, and Ainsley hurriedly slipped in and slammed the door.

"To the library next? Or the antique store?"

"The library, I think," Gabe said, and held onto the dashboard as the car rocketed across the parking lot. "It won't take much time since it's a pretty small branch. Then we can grab lunch before going to see the antique store."

THE COCKATOO CALLED

CHAPTER FOURTEEN

Ainsley heaved a sigh and dropped the stack of papers on the table in front of her. Since leaving the boat and coming into the slightly stuffy confines of the branch library, the time had seemed to slow and now she was pouring over documents that didn't seem to want to stay in focus. She pushed back from the table, her hand going to her hair. She shoved the curls back away from her face with the back of her hand. Her fingers were already darkened with ink. At first the reading hadn't been too bad. She had been responsible for scanning headlines looking for any references to the painting. But once the articles had been selected, her job became much more difficult. Now she needed to read through the material, and her disability was rearing its head.

"You okay?" Gabe's question startled her from her ruminations.

"Sure, just tired," she responded. But he was studying her, watching her, concern plainly showing in his expression. She felt a flush creep into her cheeks and knew her emotions were showing. She was getting tired of pretending. She didn't like any kind of deception, even if it was from omission. Say something, she thought grimly. She hurried on, trying not to think too deeply. "Gabe, I, well, there's something that you should know about me." Suddenly her stomach was pitching, and she knew then how much she was falling for this guy. She didn't want him to look at her differently. She didn't want to see him change his opinion of her. She couldn't stand knowing that he thought less of her.

He had turned to look at her more closely, and she had to drop her gaze. "Tell me about what?"

"Me," she said rushing on. "I mean, it isn't that big a deal, but you should know." She felt a little surge of anger, the spark of stubbornness that had driven her to succeed in school, to surpass classmates that had nothing to prove, nothing more to fight for than the diploma that said that they had succeeded.

He was just watching her, and she couldn't stand the concern in his eye. She had done exactly what she hadn't wanted to do. She had made an issue of it.

"I have a learning disability." She looked at him as she spoke, measuring his reactions. "I'm dyslexic. Reading like this just isn't my thing." She couldn't decipher his expression. And it hurt somewhere that she didn't want to acknowledge. "I mean, I get by, but it isn't something that I like to advertise."

She was trying to make light of it, trying to cover, but suddenly she was feeling her throat close with emotion. She cleared her throat and blinked her eyes. He hadn't spoken so she rushed on to cover the gap of silence. "I've seen the way people look at me when they learn that I can't, no, that it's hard for me to read. They can't understand it, that I can't do something that comes pretty naturally to everyone else." She felt her brittle smile and she cleared her throat again, making a quick dismissive motion with her hand. "So it's just something that I don't discuss." Her chin had gone up a notch, pride altering her posture.

"So that's what it is!" His expression surprised her, a loosening of muscles in his face that made him seem years younger. The answer stunned her into momentary silence.

"What…what is?" she asked, feeling the words twist in her mouth.

"What the problem is!" He leaned over the table so that he was closer to her. He caught one of her hands as she twisted the corner of some papers between her fingers in a nervous gesture.

"Problem?" She licked her lips nervously, but turned her hand so that she could grasp his fingers.

"I knew that you were upset. Good God, you've been casting me the strangest looks for the past hour. I could tell that you were holding something back. I was waiting for the tirade to start, to be perfectly honest. I had thought at first that you were angry with me, somehow resentful that I had brought all of this down on you. Like it was all my fault," he nodded toward the papers around them, "which it is!"

"You're fault?" she was so relieved at his response that she was starting to feel rather stupid again, trying to follow his thought process.

"If I hadn't asked you to keep Dali, you wouldn't be here right now. The man might have kept trying to find what he wanted, but that would have been between him and me, and you would have never run into all of this." He spread his hand out again, gesturing to the stacks of articles and papers on the table. "But instead, you have Dali to look after, and you're helping me with trying to figure out what is going on. And you're in Florida instead of getting ready for the Holiday! And now with the threats, you've become as much a part of this as I am. And it's a dangerous place to be." His other hand tightened around hers. "By keeping you with me, looking for answers, I've also put you in danger. I know that now. And I thought that you had come to that conclusion too. That it was the reason you were holding back with me. You seemed so," his long fingers curled around hers as he struggled to find the right word, "restrained sometimes, like you didn't want to let me know what you were thinking."

"I was," Ainsley said slowly, thoughtfully. "But I was thinking about my problems. I don't blame you for any of this! It isn't your fault that this crazy person is trying to take something that you don't even have."

"And it isn't your fault that you have problems reading," he scolded gently. "Look, I know you're smart. You have a very quick mind. You think of things that I don't, and you remember facts and details that I would never be able to keep track of." His other hand came up to cup her fingers, holding her hands between his. "I respect you more than you know, but it's more about your character, really. You're brave, and strong, and you want to do what's right. You haven't hesitated to help me with this."

"But the dyslexia slows me down," she protested.

"I don't see that," he said seriously. "My best friend had a learning disability. We worked together all through high school. He could out think me, out logic me, with one lobe of his brain tied behind his back." He was grinning now. "And I would write for him when he would get stuck. I got A's, he got A's, it was a win-win."

The relief she felt made her almost giddy. The black cloud that seemed to hover in the secret part of her brain that was still the self-conscious little girl seemed to disperse.

Gabe tugged gently on her hands. "I'm ready for a break," he said still smiling a little. "So let's just take our copies and get out of here. There's no reason that we need to stay in here to work. We can grab something for lunch now, and then head over to the shop. We'll wade through the rest of the information later."

*****

Ainsley was playing around with the last few leaves of spinach in her bowl, feeling tired and happy and worried all at once. Gabe had polished off his burger and was lingering over french fries drowned in ketchup as he eyed her across the table.

"When I talked to Jack earlier, he said he wanted to meet us at the antique shop," Gabe told her. "I asked if he was bringing Hemingway, but he wouldn't give me a straight answer. We'll just have to wait and see about that." He took a long pull of his beer. "I don't know if I should text him and tell him that we're on our way. I'm not sure if he uses texting."

Ainsley smiled. "Jack seems to be heading into the twentieth century. He probably uses text messages," she replied. "And I think it will be helpful for him to be there. He already knows this guy, so it won't come off as being totally out of left field if Jack's with us."

"True." Gabe pulled out his phone and quickly typed a message, sending it to Jack and placing the phone on the table. He seemed to think of something, but was reluctant to ask. Finally he said, "do you have problems reading texts too?"

Ainsley shrugged. "Short things are fine. When they get longer, it gets a little more challenging. My parents and friends type mainly in caps. It helps me read more easily."

"I guess technology has been a big help for you in some ways."

"Sure, in a lot of ways," Ainsley agreed. "I use the cell phone all the time. I can use the voice programs to start searches, use a GPS, send texts and emails, all of that. And then it has text to speech that reads emails for me, reads the texts if I want it to, or gives information for searches. I have programs on my computer too. I used some things while I was in school, but technology has come such a far way even in a few years and keeps changing too."

"So it's gotten easier as you've gotten older, I guess."

"Sure," Ainsley pushed her salad bowl away from her and pulled her drink forward, taking a sip through the straw. "When I was a kid, it was so hard. No one could understand what was going on with me, and when I was young, I could just memorize what common words looked like. I mean, I could fake it to some extent. And for some time, it seemed like that was the best thing for me to do. I just guessed my way through until the Third grade." She shrugged and put her chin in her hand, leaning over the table. "You know how kids are. I thought that if I let on that I wasn't understanding something I would get in trouble."

"My friend was like that too," Gabe said. "He tried not to let the teachers know that he didn't understand the books when he was little. He memorized some of them so that it looked like he was reading. But when he got older, he couldn't just guess about the content. But he was lucky. His mom was a teacher and figured him out. She took on the whole school system to get the help that he needed."

"He was lucky then," Ainsley said frowning. "I was busy trying to cover up my problems, which I'm sure made it much harder for my mom to help me. When I was eight, my teacher told my mother that I had a bad attitude. Can you imagine? A bad attitude at that age. Most kids are still worrying about coloring between the lines. But not me. I knew that something was wrong. Maybe that was the worst part. I figured out that there was something different about me early."

"That had to have been hard."

"It was." Ainsley put her fork down. "For most of that year, I was in and out of the quiet space" she made air quotes around the words quiet space and her face reflected her disdain. "It was like being sent in the corner except for little kid style. I think she had good intentions when she put me there. She wanted to be able to concentrate, and she always encouraged me to work harder, but she didn't realize that I was. I was working hard. I just wasn't getting it."

Gabe put his hand on hers, stilling the agitated movement. "I am sorry."

She smiled weakly. "It's not your problem. And it's something that I've learned to cope with." She smiled ruefully. "And usually, I don't hesitate to tell people about it. If they don't understand the problem, than that's their problem. But with you," she bit her lip, her eyes dropping.

"Well, all I know is that you are pretty amazing," he smiled at her, a broad beautiful smile. "I won't be underestimating you, that's for sure, but you have to let me know when there is something that you are having difficulty with." He pushed his plate away and looked regretfully at the empty space. "And when we do our research, I'll just have to give you the hard part, going through the photos."

"It's a deal then," she agreed.

"In the meantime, we'll see what this guy at the antique store has to say." Gabe pulled out a paper with some words and numbers scrawled across it. "His name is Grady Sneider."

*****

The shop itself was utterly charming. The decking that led from the gravel lot to the front door looked like planking from an ancient ship, weathered and marked with time. The front door was propped open, letting in the breeze. Gabe went in first. Jack had assured them that he would meet them there, and Ainsley could already hear his voice from where she stood in the doorway. Gabe glanced back at Ainsley and smiled. She smiled back, enjoying the spontaneous expression on his face.

"Gabe, my boy, and here you are!" Jack was leaning against the counter, a collection of what looked to be old pocket watches spread out before him. "Ainsley, lovely to see you."

Ainsley felt her smile growing. There was just something so wonderfully warm about Jack. And after her lunch with Gabe, she felt as though a weight had been lifted off of her. It was ridiculous really. She hadn't known either of these men long enough to develop feelings for them. But here she was, enjoying their company, soaking up the enthusiasm. And to know that Gabe did not think any different of her despite learning of her problem, and her defensiveness about it, she felt like she could breathe a little more freely again.

"Hey Jack! Did Hemingway stay back at the house?" Gabe clasped the other man's hand in greeting.

"He was still acting up so I told him he'd have to stay back until he learned some manners." Jack held out a hand where a reddened welt could be seen on one of his thick fingers. "Gave me a love nip."

"That doesn't look very loving," Ainsley said, grimacing at the wound.

"He could have done much worse," Jack responded. "But enough about him. This is my friend Grady, Grady, this is Topper's nephew Gabe and his lovely young lady Ainsley."

"Nice to meet you," Ainsley said to the other man.

Grady smiled, showing the gold caps on his front two teeth. He had a rather round face with full cheeks and dark eyes that missed very little. A newsboy cap covered thinning hair, and he wore a vest, complete with pocket watch and chain that spanned a little round potbelly.

"Good to meet you as well," he greeted them. "I was sorry to hear of your uncle's passing," he told Gabe.

"Thanks," Gabe said, a fleeting expression of sadness darkening his face. "I miss him."

There was an unconscious moment of silence while the men were all lost in their memories, and then Grady brightened. "Jack tells me that you are looking up some of the collections that Topper had," he began.

"My uncle had a lot of interests, as I'm sure you know, and we've recently been going through his house. We found some information about a painting that he might have had. Even my Aunt Violet recalls something about it. I was just wondering what of it was true."

"You're talking about the Dali, I'm guessing?"

Gabe paused, slightly taken aback by the quick and definitive response. "Yes, that's exactly it."

"I'm not surprised! It was one of Topper's most prized possessions, at least for a little while. He bragged about it to most of us in the field. We heard the whole tall tale about his clandestine meeting with a representative of the artist's manager, how he got the painting under the cover of the stars. He was trying to decide how he wanted to display it, and had opinions flying about how best to care for it. And then, well, we didn't hear anything else about it at all."

"So did any of you get to see it?" Gabe was scanning the room as though the painting might have been hung there among the faded mirrors and framed lithographs.

"Not the real thing, although I'd love to have gotten a good look at it. But he did bring me a snapshot of it. He wanted my opinion. But art isn't my area. If it isn't an antique, I'm not your man, but I was still interested." Grady grinned, the smile making his cheeks a little rounder and his gold teeth catch the light in a wink.

"What was the picture of?" Ainsley blurted out the question before she thought about what she was going to say. She realized that this above all was one of her main questions. That the picture existed seemed almost sure now. That it had caused some real trouble in her life, had disrupted the peaceful flow of her existence and had brought her into this strange adventure that was a sure thing as well. But she had wondered, deep into the night while trying to talk herself into sleep, what was the picture of? What was it about this picture that would make someone go to such lengths to get their hands on it?

"It was a portrait, as well as I can recall," Grady replied, looking toward her. "A nude. It was a woman, standing at the window, the light just right, pretty thing."

Jack's face split into a grin, "a nude! That old codger!"

"No, no, it was very tasteful." His tone had taken on the ring of a collector, a little knowledgeable, a little in awe. "It was a beautiful thing. No one would mistake it for anything but what it was. It was a study of the human form, nothing scandalous about it." Grady gave a little sigh. "I tried to get Topper to bring it by here. I even told him that I would help him sell it, if that's what he chose to do. Now I have no idea what happened to it. A real shame."

"Was he thinking of selling it?" Gabe was looking closely at Grady, confused.

"He spoke about it at one time. But I doubt he'd have wanted to part with it. He said something about some trouble. Something about past sins." Grady took off his cap and swept his thin hair back with one chubby palm. "But like I told the other fellow that came here talking about that painting, I never saw it for myself, and I don't know what he ended up doing with it."

Ainsley caught the reference at the same time Gabe asked, "The other fellow? Was there someone else asking about the painting?"

"Not too recently," Grady said. "It would have been over a year ago. A man came in here asking about Topper and the painting. He said he had heard that the painting was of a nude. He had a general date when he thought it had been painted. He seemed to know a few details, but didn't act like he had ever seen the painting himself. He thought that Topper had owned it at one time, but had sold it. Was wondering if he had sold it through me. But I told him the same thing as I'm telling you. I never saw the painting in the flesh, so to speak, and I don't know any of the details about when or where it was painted."

"Who was this guy?"

"That I don't know. He left his card with me, but I knew that I would never see it again, so I'm afraid I just tossed it after he left. Seems to me that he was a professor at some college up north. He taught…" His words drifted off as he looked thoughtfully toward the ceiling, trying to wade through a year's worth of memories.

"Did he teach art?" Ainsley asked. It seemed like a reasonable assumption. If he were searching for the painting, then perhaps he was an art historian and wanted to track it down for an educational purpose.

"No," Grady said, still unfocused. "It wasn't art. I remember because that was my first guess."

He looked back at Ainsley and smiled. "I remember! It was theology! He was teaching at one of the seminaries! Not a Catholic one, maybe Baptist?"

"Well, that kind of blows our connection," Gabe said slowly. "I doubt any religion teacher would be chasing after a nude portrait by Dali."

"From what I've read about him, Dali had struggled with religion since he was a child. I think that his mother was very Catholic but his father was an atheist. I know that some of his earlier works were very anti-religion, but later, he did do some paintings that were influenced by Catholicism." Ainsley's head felt full of facts about the painter, but none of them seemed to want to fall together in any sort of pattern that made sense.

"Even so, the works that he did that had to do with Catholicism probably wouldn't have appealed to a seminary teacher unless it was a Catholic one."

"That I don't recall," Grady said. "But I agree that the subject matter didn't seem to meld with the way that the man presented himself."

THE COCKATOO CALLED

"And what was he like?" Gabe asked. "The professor?"

Grady shrugged. "I can't say. He was just an ordinary guy." He looked at Gabe. "I'm sorry, son, but I can't recall anything about him. Just a middle-aged guy with a forgettable face. Wish I could be of more help."

"Oh, you've helped a whole lot," Gabe said firmly. "We have been wondering about that painting, and at least now we know what it pictured. Do you have any idea where he bought it?"

"Spain," Grady responded positively. "He bought it in Spain in 1975. I know that for sure. He had just come back from the trip when he contacted me, and that was the year that I moved the store to this location. I was busy trying to get everything moved when he came by. But I knew I had to stop and listen to him. He was so thrilled about getting the painting. That's when he showed me the photo of it."

"Spain," Gabe said thoughtfully. "Well, it matches the receipt that we found. So we have that as well."

Ainsley was trying to picture all of the papers and photographs that she had seen. The line of history was gradually clearing. She could see more clearly now how Uncle Topper's story had evolved. He had bought the painting in Europe, a little victory for him since the painting was a rare prize. He might have bought it in a little questionable manner; it seemed that the exchange may have been a bit under the table, but it had been a success nonetheless. And Uncle Topper had been secure enough in the purchase that he had bragged about it to family and friends. The fact that he had told Grady about it and shown him the picture cemented the idea that the painting was genuine, at least as far as Topper knew, and he was proud of his purchase.

So he had the receipt for the painting, had rode with it for the delivery to his home, and had taken it into the house where he had displayed it at least long enough to photograph it. Presumably, it had remained in his house when he went to see his friend in Florida, and he had talked about the purchase with his sister Violet. He had even gone as far as to get the story in the newspaper, although, none of the articles that they had seen had shown a photograph of the painting or had told the title of the work.

And then something unexplained had happened.

Because Uncle Topper had abruptly stopped talking about the piece completely, it was as though it had never existed. It wasn't among his belongings in the house, and he hadn't sold it to anyone else to their knowledge. So what had happened to the painting? And where was it now? And what had caused such a change in Topper?

The questions seemed to loom more important now, even more than when Topper was alive. Because it seemed that someone was after the painting, and they weren't above hurting anyone that stood in their way.

CHAPTER FIFTEEN

Dinner started out as a quiet affair. Gabe seemed to be lost in thought, and Jack was frustrated that they hadn't found any more information about the painting or the person who was after it. In listening to his grumbling, Ainsley deduced that Jack seemed to have set his mind on the idea that they would have found all of the answers they needed on this little trip. Now the fact that they were going back virtually empty handed, except for a few random clues, was irritating him.

Ainsley felt a little different than her companions. She knew that they had finally figured out some facts about the painting. They knew the subject, at least generally, and they knew where the painting had been bought and when. They knew that they weren't the only ones that were looking for the painting, although, it seemed that the professor, whoever that had been, had not pursued the painting any further with Grady. But the main problem remained. Without having the painting in their possession, there was no way to act on the threat of the person who seemed determined to stop them. If they found the painting, at least then they would have the upper hand, the control.

"Eat up," Mac interrupted her thoughts. "The fish was fresh caught this morning, and it is my specialty!"

Ainsley summoned up a bright smile. "The food is delicious. Where did you learn to cook?"

"At my mother's side," Mac said winking. His usually pale face was flushed with pleasure and good wine. "This has been a hobby of mine for more years than I care to admit. So I want to know what you truly think!"

"It's wonderful!" Ainsley assured him again.

"It is good," Gabe said. "I don't always like seafood, but this is exceptional."

"You've done a great job, Macintosh. Now stop angling for compliments and give me some more of those potatoes!" Jack grumbled.

As Ainsley passed the bowl still heaped with sliced potatoes glazed with some delicious sauce, Mac asked, "And what are your plans now?"

Gabe looked up from his plate. "I guess we head home tomorrow. I have to get back to work, get caught up on my job. But we've got papers from the library to go through, and papers from the boat along with all of those pictures." He put his fork down. "I guess we'll go back out to the house too. If we don't find what we're looking for in the information we already have, there are plenty of nooks and crannies that Uncle Topper might have hidden more information."

"I'll keep my ears to the ground to see if I hear of any grumblings in the collecting world," Mac assured them. "Just because Topper didn't sell it through Grady or bring it here doesn't mean that he didn't sell it at all. It might have gone through some other channels."

"And if he did?" Ainsley felt a prickle of apprehension. "If he did sell the painting, then what? Do you think that the people who are after it will believe that? Do you think that they will give up?"

Gabe shook his head. "Without proof, I doubt that they will leave us alone." He put his hand through his hair. "But if we find proof, they might accept that. And since it seems like they've been on our tail since we started this, they'll probably know what we find as soon as we find it."

The thought made Ainsley uncomfortable. Was he right? Were they following them, listening in, watching them?

Gabe and Ainsley volunteered to do the kitchen cleanup. The sudden intimacy of being alone for the first time that day had Ainsley slightly off balance, but in a warm and tingly way. She could hear Jack's booming voice from upstairs where he argued with Hemingway. The cries that the bird made were easily audible downstairs, and Ainsley wondered how loud Dali would sound from outside her house. It was amazing the volume that came out of those relatively small bodies.

Gabe switched on the hot water and added a generous dollop of soap, watching the suds rise with the steam.

"You get to dry," he said, tossing her a towel.

"Okay," Ainsley agreed, catching the cloth and taking her place beside him.

"So are you glad that you came? To Florida, I mean."

"Sure," Ainsley looked at him with a sidelong glance. "It's been very interesting."

"It has," he agreed. "And I know that we haven't known each other long, but spending this time together has made me feel like I know you better now."

THE COCKATOO CALLED

"Me too," she replied, her eyes sliding away from the intimacy.

"This might not have been my ideal way to start dating someone, but it certainly has helped us get to know each other."

"Tight quarters and stress do bring out the best and worst in people," Ainsley agreed. Gabe passed her a clean plate and plunged his hands in the soapy water for another dish.

"So when we get home, I guess we'll be looking a little more at the house," he said. "Will you come along for that?"

"If you want me to," Ainsley agreed.

"I do." He flashed her a smile. "Although, I don't know if Dali is going to want you to go anywhere without him."

"He can come along," Ainsley said grimacing. "He might make a mess, but he'll probably enjoy seeing the house again. That is, if he remembers it. Do you think he will? Do you think birds remember where they've lived before?"

"I think so," Gabe said. "He knew me after we had been separated for weeks. I'd be surprised if he didn't show at least some sign that he remembered the place." He rinsed another plate and handed it to Ainsley. "How's he doing, by the way?"

"He seems to be fine. I feel like I've been gone for a week, but just two days is probably not upsetting him that much. And my friends are absolutely spoiling him."

Gabe cast her a sidelong look as he washed one of the crystal wineglasses that they had used at dinner. "You miss him, don't you?"

"Sure," Ainsley took the glass to dry. "I had no idea what having a bird around the house would be like. He's so much more of a pet than I expected. He has so much personality."

"Yeah, I knew what Hemingway was like, but Dali is completely different." He finished rinsing the last dish. Since Ainsley didn't know where all of the dishes went, there was a stack of cleaned and dried pieces stacked neatly on the counter. He considered them for a moment. "I guess we can let Mac put these away later," he said, and watched as Ainsley folded the towel and put it next to the sink. As she turned, Gabe caught her gently by the shoulders, turning her toward him. He pressed a quick kiss on her lips and released her. "Okay, job's done!" He caught her hand and pulled her with him away from the sink.

They could hear Jack in the living room now, laughing at something that Mac had said. The other man's voice was just an undertone, much more subdued than his boisterous friend. But Jack had a variety of friends. He and Topper had seemed to collect friends wherever they went, which was quite a life to have.

"I remember this one!" Mac had a photo in front of him, and Ainsley realized that the pictures and papers spread out on the low table in front of the couch were the ones they had collected from the boat that morning. Jack must have pulled them out to look at them. "Topper had been looking at buying his first sculpture for the back garden. We had gone to the studio, but the man had been so insufferable! Incredibly condescending. Topper had refused to work with him, but he did want a picture of this!" The photograph showed a young Topper next to a spectacularly ugly sculpture. The background was a fuzzy green shot with beams of sunlight. He flipped through a few other photographs and Ainsley sat on the chair opposite.

"Have you found anything interesting?" she asked.

"It's all interesting, my dear," Jack said smiling. He started spreading out the photos, laying them in an array of colors on the coffee table. Most were similar to the shots that they had seen adorning the walls of Uncle Topper's house, portraits of smiling people in a variety of backgrounds. Most of these photos, however, were more recently taken. In most, Topper looked much like he had in his last few pictures, an older gentleman, tall and a little gaunt, but still handsome. Ainsley was studying his face, still eerily similar to Gabe's, when she was jolted out of her thoughts by Gabe's voice.

"Bingo!" he called out. "Look at this!"

The photo he held was of a painting. It was unfortunate that the photographer hadn't spent the time to get the proper light exposure or focus, because while the subject of the painting was easily recognized, the brilliance of the artwork was not conveyed by this flat copy. Although, the details were not precise, it was obvious that this was the painting that Grady had spoken of earlier in the day. It was a painting of a woman, standing nude in the soft light from the window, her body turned demurely, but her face looking over one bare shoulder, her features easily read. She wasn't a particularly beautiful woman, but her strong bones would have held time at bay, and she would always be considered arresting or intriguing.

"That's got to be it," Ainsley breathed, looking over his shoulder at the picture. "The lost Dali."

*****

The next morning, Jack sat at the breakfast table pouring over the photograph while he sipped coffee.

"God awful headache," he grumbled. "Shouldn't have helped Mac

THE COCKATOO CALLED

with that bourbon last night."

"It was your Kentucky manners," Gabe said grinning.

"Hmmm," Jack responded. "And this picture is driving me crazy. I know that I've seen her before. Not the painting, I think I would have remembered that! But I think I've seen this girl. Dressed, I mean."

"You mean that you think that you know the model?" Gabe's eyebrows went up, surprised.

"I don't know that I know her," Jack said, still irritable. "But I recognize her. And not from this painting." He pushed the photograph away. "Can't think," he said, taking a long sip of the hot coffee.

"Could you have met her when you and Topper were traveling? Or maybe she was someone close to Dali himself. Didn't you say that Topper had been at some functions where Dali had visited? If she were someone close to the artist, you might have seen her there with him."

Jack put his head in his hands. "It sounds reasonable, but I think it was something else. Maybe I saw a picture of her." He huffed a big sigh. "I've got to go pack up Hemingway and all of his things. He's mad at me again this morning. I only yelled at him a little when he started calling at six AM, but it was just too damn early, and besides, he should know when I'm out late that I'm not going to get up and feed him as soon as the sun rises." He was still grumbling as he stood and pushed out his chair. "I'll see you all back down here in thirty. We'll head for the airport then."

The pictures and papers from the boat went into a satchel that also contained their research from the library. Ainsley was tempted to keep out the photo of the portrait, but in the end, slipped it with the rest. She needed to clear her head. She was due at work in the afternoon and hadn't slept well. She had been tempted to ask for Gabe to come to her again, to hold her while she slept so that her dreams wouldn't be shadowed by nightmarish birds and lost young girls. But she had resisted, her stubbornness, often a strength, but sometimes an irritating character fault, kept her in place, thrashing against the covers.

Now she felt like Jack was acting, like she had a sledgehammer beating a rhythm that only she could hear within her skull. She climbed into the car, but sat in the center of the backseat. She didn't need to get sick on the ride; she felt bad enough already. Luckily Gabe drove, while Jack sat next to him in the passenger seat and soon began snoring. Hemingway was cuddled down in his carrier, fluffy and irritated.

At the little airport, the pilot, Josh, was doing a few final checks around the plane when they approached. His grin was relaxed.

"Great day for a flight!" he exclaimed, white teeth flashing.

Jack grunted and started unloading their bags from the trunk.

"You have a good weekend?" Gabe asked, looking calm and unruffled in the balmy breeze.

"Sure did! And you?"

"We did well." Gabe turned as Jack pulled Hemingway's crate from the car and the bird gave a loud squawk. "I don't think the two of them are getting along this morning," he said as an aside.

Josh chuckled, "well the plane's ready to go when you are," he proclaimed.

Ainsley grabbed her remaining small bag and the satchel and nodded to Josh as she climbed aboard the plane.

"You alright?" Josh asked, seeing her expression.

"Just a little headache," she explained. "But thank you so much for the ride."

"No problem," he replied, and swung into the seat.

Before they took off, Josh checked to make sure that they were all strapped in properly. Ainsley popped a couple Tylenol, wincing as they went down, and then sat back in her seat. As the plane lifted, she glanced out the window and sighed.

*****

"Spill it!" Theresa exclaimed, as soon as Ainsley took her seat in the office chair. She still felt a little bad, both because her headache had yet to abate, and the mournful looks she had gotten from Dali when she had headed out the door. If she had harbored any doubts that the bird would forget her over her short absence, they were quickly dispelled as soon as she entered the apartment. His pacing, furious dancing, and loud vocalization told her that he knew exactly who she was. She had let him out of the cage and spent a few precious minutes cuddling with her feathered friend, inhaling the particular scent of his powdery feathers, and listening as he settled into her arms, mumbling in contentment.

He had been fairly despondent when she had tucked him back in the cage, although she had bribed him in with his favorite nut, an almond still in the shell. She had apologized to him for her absence, but felt him watching as she left. From right outside the door, she could hear him calling.

Now she looked to her friend and smiled ruefully, "give me some caffeine and I'll spill all," she told her.

"Deal," Theresa said quickly and disappeared into the back. The waiting room was populated with a little family, a mom with three teenaged kids, all hovering over cell phones that emitted beeps and rumbles, depending on the game. One boy occasionally snickered about something he was seeing on the screen.

Nan was in the back with a patient, starting their cleaning and prepping them for the Dentist. She was great with kids, and this girl, while she was over thirteen, was still nervous.

Theresa dropped into the seat next to Ainsley and handed her a sweating can of diet coke. She took it gratefully and took a long swig of the carbonated beverage, snorting a little as the bubbles hit the back of her throat.

"You're going to be disappointed," she said starting out. "We were there to do some research about his family. We ended up visiting the library and a museum. Not exactly fun in the sun."

"So you're telling me that you went to Florida and didn't go to the beach," Theresa said frowning.

"Well, no," Ainsley began.

Nan came hurrying up, "Oh no, you don't! You are not allowed to give any juicy details until I can hear," she protested.

"How about we go out after work for dinner?" Theresa looked hopeful. "It'll be a quick one because I know that you need to get home to your man," she looked at Nan, and then her lips twitched up in a smirk. "And you'll want to see Dali," she told Ainsley.

"You make that sound like it's weird," Ainsley teased back.

"No, he's cute," Theresa said grinning. "But I was hoping that we'd hear about a new man in your life. Not one with feathers, either."

Ainsley laughed in spite of her headache. "Okay, dinner, "she agreed.

*****

They settled for a cozy little restaurant in the heart of Middletown. The building had once been a home, and still maintained its original structure. It was finished with mismatched tables and chairs on the first floor, the second floor the show for antique trinkets, pretty baubles, candles, and handmade textiles. The floors were roughly finished hardwood and the walls painted pastel shades that reflected Easter egg tones. Ainsley met her friends in the front room where they were peering into the glass case by the cash register where a number of decadent desserts were on display.

"First we eat real food," Ainsley scolded. "Dessert is for after."

Nan turned regretfully from the case. "They put this here in front so that you can plan the important part first. You pick the dessert and then add the dinner that goes with it."

"Genius," Theresa joked.

The waitress, a teen with tight blue jeans and a snug tee that looked like she had never even sampled the goodies, smiled without comment and walked them back into the dining room. Ainsley sank gratefully in a wooden chair.

"So I hope that Dali wasn't too much trouble while I was gone," she began after the waitress left with their drink orders.

"He was really easy," her friend replied, "and you're dodging the topic. Tell all."

Ainsley wasn't sure what part of the story she was obligated to tell. Her friends had no idea of the intrigue that she had been involved in. And she was pretty sure she didn't want to go into the whole story. It sounded so outlandish when you weren't living the mystery and she wasn't one that enjoyed too much attention. So she skipped the Nancy Drew parts and told them about the flight down, meeting the pilot and Jack, who she explained was a friend of Gabe's. The rest of the trip she glassed over as a visit to some shops, an art museum, and of course, the beach.

"So tell the truth. Do you like him?" Theresa leaned over her plate of chicken salad on a bed of lettuce, unaware that she had been stabbing at it without consuming much for the last 10 minutes or so.

"Sure I like him," Ainsley said quickly.

Nan frowned.

"I like him," Ainsley admitted. "He's, wow, he's such a great guy. And he's smart, and funny, and um, handsome. And in a bathing suit," with that she just grinned and her friends both laughed with her.

"So are you officially 'dating'?" Theresa put air quotes around the word as she smirked.

"We are going out on dates," Ainsley hedged. "But don't get the wrong idea. I'm into relationships, so I'm taking this one slowly and with caution."

"Oh, we know you well enough," Nan replied. She was tearing up her sandwich into small bite sized pieces. "You're not the type to jump from man to man."

"Cute, isn't she?" Theresa winked at Nan.

"Funny," Ainsley interrupted. "But enough about my love life."

After dinner they returned to Ainsley's little house and popped open a bottle of wine. Dali was perched on the open door of his cage. He had gotten lots of skritches from the girls, and was grumbling happily.

THE COCKATOO CALLED

"So when is Gabe going to take him home?" Nan asked, gesturing with her wine glass toward the bird, sending the golden liquid splashing. She yelped and licked at her damp fingers.

"He's worried about leaving him in the apartment when he goes out," Ainsley said slowly.

"Why?"

Ainsley chewed her lip thoughtfully. "Well, you know how someone broke in and took Dali the first time?"

"Which is why you ended up with him to start with."

"Right," Ainsley agreed. "And we were lucky that it ended up like it did. We're still not sure why the bird ended up in my yard. We were assuming the he was let out, but he might have somehow escaped." She paused and looked at her feathered companion fondly. "But Gabe said he thought that someone might have come back and tried to force their way into his apartment again. He saw that his lock had been messed with. So now he's worried that if someone gets in, they might hurt Dali."

"Does he think it's the same person?" Theresa sounded aghast.

"I can't imagine that the same person would be robbed by two different thieves within a few months of each other."

"What are they after?" Nan was frowning.

"Good question," Ainsley said shaking her head. "That's our problem. He hasn't been able to figure out what they want, and why they would come back. So in the meantime, I'm keeping Dali here."

CHAPTER SIXTEEN

Ainsley pushed her hair back and popped the trunk of her car open to get to the boxes inside. Her mother had insisted, and she had reluctantly taken some of the holiday decorations that her parents had set aside for her use. So after dinner, her dad had lugged the boxes out, securing them in the trunk and then pausing to check out the tires, ask about her latest oil change, and peer under the hood as though he could eye any upcoming catastrophes that loomed with the aging vehicle.

She hefted the first box to her hip and balanced it as she tugged her keys from her pocket. The welcome light cast a golden glow in a halo on her stoop. At the back door she hesitated. The cool wind had whipped leaves in mounds around the door jam, but she noticed that there was a section of the door that was clear. She looked a little more closely but didn't see anything strange.

She had gotten paranoid, but she felt that it was with a good cause. Gabe had shown her the damage to his apartment door, and it had haunted her just a little. But her house was fine, right? No one would come here?

She unlocked her door and pushed it open, hearing Dali's welcoming call from within. She felt a wave of relief at the sound of his excited chatter. He was fine, she was fine, they were all going to make it through this just fine. She flicked the switch, flooding the room with light and letting it bleed out the door and into the yard beyond. It took three more trips to get the rest of the boxes in. She had only a week before Thanksgiving, and she was looking forward to the holiday. Her parents were planning on a big group, Aunts and Uncles and out of state cousins. She knew there would be questions, how did she like it, living on her own? Had she met some nice people? How was her job? They would have heard some of the information from her Uncle, but she was sure there would be more questions. And what about Gabe? She was sure to

THE COCKATOO CALLED

get a lot of teasing about that, but she kind of looked forward to it. Hearing her family's gentle teasing about Gabe made him seem more of her real life.

Shaking her head at her silly thoughts, she pushed the boxes further into the kitchen with her foot and pulled the door closed. She would need to go out on her own and buy some other decorations for the holiday, but this would be a good start. It was just another phase of making the place home, settling in, putting down her own roots.

She was tired now. She had worked for the full day and even though they hadn't been extremely busy, there was an abundance of paperwork that had to be dealt with. Not her favorite thing to do, but in this situation, it was a necessary evil. Her drive out to her parent's house had been automatic, but it had given her time to think. And her thoughts turned toward the mystery, the bird, and Gabe's family pretty much instantly. Was the painting real? A genuine Dali? And if Gabe's uncle had bought it, perhaps under the table, why had he decided to cover it up? He'd been so proud of it. Why the change? Had he been threatened himself?

She glanced around the well-lit kitchen and went back to the door, peering out the window one final time and locking it. It made her feel sad. Ordinarily, Middletown was one of those nice communities that you feel comfortable in. Good enough to leave the door unlocked, at least during the day. But now she wasn't feeling secure anywhere. She left the backlights on.

She left the door and turned back toward the boxes. She bent down and opened one of the boxes to look inside. Shiny garland sent out shards of light, glass balls packed in cardboard casing were tucked next to a larger box, grandma's Santa Claus tree topper that they had saved for Ainsley to use in her first home. She sighed and closed the box again. These would be fine stored in her spare bedroom until after Thanksgiving. And then maybe she'd have a little party, invite her friends to come over and help her decorate, Nan and Theresa, and perhaps Gabe?

She smiled at her thoughts and began taking the boxes into the other room. As she was lowering the last one to the floor, her phone began to vibrate in her pocket.

"Hi!" She knew the number, and just that made her heart speed up in a very sweet way.

"Ainsley, hey, it's Gabe."

"I saw your number," she said smile broadening unconsciously. "Don't tell me that you're calling to check on Dali today too!"

The phone call yesterday had been a short conversation. Gabe had claimed he wanted to see how Dali was, but Ainsley strongly suspected that it was something else. She felt it too. She just wanted to talk to him, prompted by her foolish heart. She loved that he was feeling the same.

"Um, yeah, well, I have a proposition for you."

"Really? Sounds intriguing."

"One last visit to Uncle Topper's fun house," Gabe admitted. "All expenses paid, and the company of an expert tour guide. That would be yours truly."

"And when would that be?"

"Would Saturday work for you? I don't want to take up all of your free time, but..."

"Saturday would be great," Ainsley agreed quickly. "I know that you wanted to get back in there soon. Do you have plans about where you want to search this time?"

"I talked to Jack. He was thinking that the attic was where Uncle Topper kept most of his old things that he wasn't displaying downstairs. The basement is too damp to store much of anything. Well, except for the liquor. I think he keeps some wine and other drinks down there."

"Count me in," Ainsley said. "The house is pretty fascinating."

They talked for longer, not saying much, but enjoying the connection. Ainsley walked with the phone into the living room so that Dali could make noises into the phone. He continued with his fascination for the lit screen, stretching out as far as possible in hopes of getting his beak on the piece of technology. Gabe spoke loudly on the other end, and when Dali seemed to finally recognize the voice, he grew very still, his dark eye focused on the phone, his crest rising and falling slowly.

"Then I'll see you later?" Gabe said to Ainsley when she had reclaimed the phone.

"You will," she replied, liking the smoothness of his voice as it hit her ear.

"Okay then, you sleep well."

"You too," she said, "night," and hung up before her poor heart could have a chance to make her say anything more incriminating.

She spent a few more moments choosing what to wear for the next day. She didn't want to overdress, but she wanted to look nice. Sexy? Well no, but cute, sure. She laid out her clothes and then pulled out her computer. The Kindle app had the handy read along feature, and she had gotten pretty involved with a novel she was reading. She settled on her couch and started to read, relaxation finally letting her mind travel. She had a lot to do the next day, so she would enjoy her evening.

*****

THE COCKATOO CALLED

"And it's raining," Ainsley murmured from her nest of covers. The sky was dull pewter, the clouds thick and barely moving. The rain fell in heavy sheets, unrelenting. Ainsley slipped out of bed and ran into the bathroom. A few minutes later, she was back in her room, sliding on her jeans and a deep purple top that she had laid out the night before because she knew it flattered her skin and light hair.

She could hear Dali in the other room and stopped by his cage to let him out. Holding out her arm, she let him climb onto her sleeve, frowning when she saw the fine white powder dusting her dark shirt. She shrugged ruefully and pulled him close for a snuggle. She would just have to dust off before Gabe got there, although he was sure to understand.

She went back in the kitchen and started the coffee pot while she finished getting ready. She perched Dali on the counter top as she applied light makeup. He liked the little plastic containers, so she had to make sure that while he sorted them, he didn't break into them and eat any of the content. She shooed him away from her brush as she fixed her hair, and then pulled out his comb to chew on while she gathered her curls into a loose ponytail at the nape of her neck.

When she turned away to find her shoes, she felt the flutter of feathers and saw that he had glided to the floor and was pursuing her. She picked up her shoes and carried them out to the living room with her where she deposited them next to the door. She was funny like that. She didn't like wearing shoes while she was in the house, and went around barefoot for most of the summer, both inside and out. But the weather was chilly this morning.

She poured herself a cup of coffee, amused to see that Dali had come into the kitchen and had climbed to the chair back, clearly waiting for his serving of oatmeal. She heated both bowls, adding cream and sugar to her own, and an ice cube to his to cool it down. As she fed him with a spoon, he dropped his wings and fluttered them like a baby bird being fed by its mother.

"Spoiled," she scolded, but smiled at him.

After he had eaten his fill, he stayed perched on the back of the chair while she ate her own, sipping coffee and checking her watch. Gabe would be there in another thirty minutes. And while she looked forward to seeing Gabe, she felt uneasy about the house. How safe was it? What was the likelihood that they would find anything? And, if they did, what would they do with it? She supposed they could publicly put it in a bank vault with the rest of Uncle Topper's papers until the will was read. If the painting was somehow impossible to get to, whoever wanted it would have to give up, wouldn't they?

Her head jerked up when she heard the knock at the door. Gabe stood on the porch; his hair pearled with beads of moisture. He was smiling and had a bakery bag in one hand.

"Come in," she said, closing the door behind him against the wet draft.

"Brought you something," he said, holding up the white bag.

"Are you trying to make me fat?" she asked.

"Fat and happy," he replied, "Although, you don't look like the type to gain weight easily."

She let the comment pass. She didn't gain weight incredibly easy, but she could put on a few pounds over the holiday and would have to watch her diet for a month or two to fit back into her pants. She wasn't some stick thin model type anyway. But she was generally comfortable with her body, or at least liked to think so. Now with the appreciative glance he was giving her, she felt her cheeks heat.

"Okay, so if you brought me something, what about your feathered friend here?" she asked tartly.

"Ah, Dali, you know I wouldn't forget you buddy," he said, standing close enough that the bird could climb from the chair back to his arm and cuddle his feathered head under Gabe's scruffy chin. "I brought him part of a bagel. He likes them toasted with jelly, you know. We had that lots of mornings, didn't we?" He was addressing the bird again as he handed Ainsley the bag. She had to chuckle when she pulled out two decadent Danish with white icing and some sort of sticky red center, and placed next to them a plain bagel.

"Okay, so we'll have a second breakfast, Bird," she said to the ridiculous creature cuddled up to Gabe's chest. "Do you want a cup of coffee?" she asked Gabe.

"Sure," he said, and dropped to a kitchen chair, still cradling the bird. "Are you ready for another treasure hunt?"

"I guess," she said, pouring a mug of coffee and putting it on the table in front of him. As she busied herself putting out plates with their pastries and toasting Dali's bagel, Gabe moved the bird back to his perch on the back of the kitchen chair, still stroking the bird's fluffy white head. "So have you heard from anyone else about the painting?" she asked.

"No, I mean, I have called in some cousins and phoned my uncle too. It was hard to put all of this delicately. Since he's executor, I didn't want it to sound like I was pressuring him to get the estate tied up. It's not my place, for one, and I know he's a busy man. But I keep thinking that the

THE COCKATOO CALLED

sooner the house is closed out and has changed hands, the sooner that this person will give up on the painting. Assuming that all of our guesses are right, and that is a big assumption, I know."

"Did he act like he knew when the estate would be closed?"

"We're still a few months away," Gabe said, shaking his head. "He's got the lawyers working on it, but it takes a lot of input from the bank and the government for that matter. Taxes for an estate like this are substantial. And with all of the possible people to inherit in the family, it's not like the whole thing will go down the line to one person."

Ainsley put the plate with the Danish in front of Gabe and another with the bagel, carefully spread with a thin coating of jelly, by Dali's chair. The bird tried desperately to lean down from his higher perch to reach the treat, but then lost his balance with a flurry of wing flapping and ended up on the table, skittering around on the slick surface. She moved her plate a little further away from the bird and slid into her seat. "I wish I could think of something that we could do to help the situation, but beyond finding the painting, I can't think of anything else. If we had any real proof of this person, we could go to the police. I'm sure they would have better resources to know what to do about it. But right now we don't have anything clear that shows that this person is doing what we say they're doing."

Gabe took a sip of coffee and shrugged. "I think we've done pretty well so far," he said encouragingly. "And besides the little threats, he hasn't ramped up his actions and no one has gotten hurt."

"If you don't count the poor sea bird in Florida," Ainsley said darkly.

"There is that," Gabe agreed. "But we've got more people helping us now. And we've got a better bead on what we're looking for. I feel like it's just a matter of time."

After they had finished their meal, Gabe stood to put Dali back in his cage while Ainsley cleaned up. By the time he was done babying the bird, adding a few treats to a dish to entice Dali in and petting his fluffy cheek through the cage bars, Ainsley had slipped on her shoes and found a light raincoat.

"Do you need an umbrella?" she asked, gesturing to a floral hook handled umbrella leaning up in the corner.

"Real men don't use umbrellas," Gabe replied, face comical. "At least not that kind."

Ainsley was chuckling as they walked out the door.

The drive to the house was a little harrowing. The rain waxed and waned, sometimes pelting them with heavy drops, sometimes just spatters, but enough that they had to keep their speed down. In the gloom, the house seemed more foreboding today, a little haunted.

"No lights on," Gabe observed. "I hope that they have remembered to pay the electricity bill. This place would be almost dangerous without power. I can't imagine exploring it with a flashlight..."

"Or a candle." Ainsley looked out into the rain. "It might have been the storm that took out the power."

"Let's just hope that they were frugal and turned off all of the lights to save money. I don't relish trying to find anything in the dark."

He pulled the car close to the front door and rummaged through the glove compartment until he pulled out a ring of keys. "Okay, you ready to dodge the raindrops?"

Ainsley nodded and stepped out of the car, pulling her hood up to cover her hair. The rain had slowed to a sullen drizzle again, but the steps were slick so she had to step carefully. By the time she had mounted the steps, Gabe had the door open and was reaching inside. She felt a wave of relief as light flooded the entry.

"Oh, great," she said smiling, and stepped inside, shedding her coat. Gabe followed her in and took the coat, hanging it on an antique coatrack just within the front doors. The hooks looked suspiciously like horns or antlers, but she didn't want to ponder their origin. Uncle Topper hadn't been a hunter, but he certainly wasn't above adopting things that had once been trophies for someone who had enjoyed that sport.

"Lights seem to be working, but man is it still dim in here. Must be the rain. I'm used to the sunlight helping." Gabe was looking around speculatively. "But everything seems alright. I don't see any signs that someone has tried to get in here." He paused to look more closely at the door, the handle and lock, obviously looking for signs that they had been tampered with.

"So what do you want to do first?" Ainsley asked, looking up the stairway.

"Let's take a quick tour around the first floor. I want to make sure that we don't see anything out of place. Then we can go up and check on Uncle Topper's room. If all that seems okay, we'll head to the attic. I think that will have to be our last stop, but if I remember correctly, the place is huge so we're not likely to get it all covered in one trip."

Mixed feelings, mixed feelings, Ainsley thought. She wasn't sure she liked the house as much as before. It seemed a little menacing in the dim lighting with the storm thundering outside. But then again, repeated trips meant more time spent with Gabe and more little peeks into his life. And like any woman who was smitten with a guy, she was anxious to know all that there was to know about Gabe.

THE COCKATOO CALLED

"Come on. We'll start in back and work our way to the front before going upstairs." They moved quickly to the rear of the house, through the dining room, the kitchen, the library, and a few other rooms that Ainsley could barely remember touring on their first adventure. When nothing appeared to be amiss, they went up the staircase, Gabe going first so that he could flip the switch and provide additional illumination at the top of the stairs in the hallway.

Uncle Topper's door was closed, which Ainsley took as a good sign. She was pretty sure it had been closed when they had left the last time, although there was no predicting whether or not the housekeepers had been there after their visit.

Gabe pushed it open and stepped through the doorway, his hand automatically reaching for the switch. The light fluttered on and then made an abrupt popping sound, throwing a blanket of darkness across the space.

Gabe muttered an expletive, and Ainsley felt her heart bounding within the confines of her chest. She was jumpy, but she felt that she had good cause.

"Light bulb," Gabe muttered. "Startled me a minute there." He seemed embarrassed by his utterances, and Ainsley smiled weakly.

"Scared me pretty good too," she agreed.

He cast her a grateful look, a little relieved smile, and took her hand loosely in his. "We can see a little from just the window," he said. The gray of the outer light was seeping in through the mostly closed curtains, but there was enough to see the outline of the furniture, the tidy little bed, the massive pool table, and the few pictures that still hung on the walls. Gabe strolled into the room, pulling Ainsley gently along with him, and dropping her hand for a moment, pulled the curtains apart, letting in more of the sickly daylight.

With that additional illumination, Ainsley could see that the room appeared very much as they had left it. The garbage bags of frames and glass had been removed, and of course, they had taken the stacks of photos with them, but nothing else seemed to be missing or moved.

"Okay, so I guess we can skip the rest of the bedrooms since we weren't in them earlier. Wouldn't know if anything was missing anyway. The access to the attic is over here."

Gabe headed toward the door, still holding Ainsley's hand, stopping at the open doorway to pull the doors to his Uncle's room closed behind them. Ainsley almost sighed. There had been something just a little sadder in the room, without the light, without all the photos reflecting a life well lived.

They went down the hallway briskly, Ainsley tagging behind a little, her eyes scanning the other closed doors until they reached the end of the hallway. The door here was narrower; she could tell that it wasn't meant to be another bedroom. When Gabe opened it, the air smelled different, dry and hot, with an almost visible tide of dust emanating from the dark recess. He leaned in and his fingers caught a switch, lighting up what appeared to be a narrow staircase that lead up to a tiny landing, and then twisted back on itself to continue up and away. Gabe didn't hesitate, but climbed the stairs quickly. His confidence reassured Ainsley who had to admit to being a little spooked by the unfinished and dusty treads that disappeared at the blind curve, not hinting at what lay beyond.

When they reached the head of the stairs, they were met by an open doorway, this door having been propped open by a stack of old and incredibly dusty books whose covers were too grimy to read.

"I don't think Uncle Topper came up here much," Gabe observed wryly.

"If ever," Ainsley agreed. "Have you ever been up here?"

"My cousin and I came up on dares a few times. It wasn't considered off limits, but wasn't encouraged either. It was usually when we had a family get together and the adults had gotten too involved with some kind of conversation that we weren't interested in." He hesitated and looked thoughtful. "I do remember there being a massive desk that was stuffed with papers in it. Can't remember exactly where it was though." He walked a little into the room but Ainsley hung back, letting her eyes adjust to the gloom. A second later, she heard a click and a bulb brightened above Gabe's head, a string hanging down just in front of him. He was grinning. "Found the light!"

"Good," she said, and joined him, her eyes widening as she looked around the room. The attic seemed to stretch out miles in front of them, no walls or doors obstructing the space except for a few jutting boards that no doubt supported some hidden structure of the house or encased a vent or other mechanical necessity. The light was only strong enough to illuminate a circle around it, the rest of the attic still in shadow. "Oh, wow," she breathed.

"Bigger than I remembered," Gabe said thoughtfully. "Or maybe we never went beyond this first section." He rubbed his chin as he looked ahead into the darkness. "Let me see if the other lights work."

Some did, but some, unfortunately, didn't. And a dead bulb meant a hole in the illumination that seemed to swallow up all the details of the space around it. Gabe had walked, it seemed, half a mile before she heard him wrestling with something, and when he stepped away, she could see

THE COCKATOO CALLED

the gray rectangle of a window. With the dotted lights, the long narrow space had the illusion of a funhouse where something creepy might spring from the shadows at any moment. While the collection downstairs could be chuckled over, dismissed as a whim of a wealthy and eccentric man, the objects stored upstairs seemed to take a more menacing air. And Ainsley knew very well that she was successfully freaking herself out. There was nothing up here that would harm her. But still, her mind argued, it was overwhelming.

Gabe traced his way back to her side. "So you did volunteer for this," he said, hands on hips, looking a little sheepish and a little apologetic.

"I did," she replied slowly. "But I didn't promise a lifetime of this."

He laughed. "It surely won't take that long," he said. "We'll look for a little while, see where we are, and then see what we need to do. It might be easy. Maybe he left it laid out somewhere."

"Like laying on a table with a big sign saying, 'valuable painting.'"

"Maybe not that obvious, but we can hope."

"Okay, so where do we start?" Ainsley wiped her slightly damp hands on the seat of her jeans and walked slowly toward the window on the opposite side of the attic.

"We start there," Gabe agreed, and together they hesitated before the sheet enshrouded furniture pushed farthest against the wall next to the window. When Gabe pulled the sheet loose, dust from years of stillness ballooned out in a pale cloud. Ainsley turned away and covered her face to avoid the worst of the dust. Even so, she found herself coughing a little while Gabe let out a mighty sneeze and then apologized. "Not my finest moment," he quipped.

"I'm definitely not hiring you to help me move any time soon."

"Sorry," he said, but he was smiling. He bent forward and dropped a kiss on her forehead. "I'll try to be more careful."

She couldn't help but forgive him. He was too cute for words. "Okay, but next time I take off the sheet."

She grew to regret that comment as they moved from piece to piece in the massive attic. It wasn't that there wasn't anything to look at or to sort through. There was plenty of that. Old pieces of furniture that spanned a century of styles, some in great condition and probably worth quite a bit, some broken and barley upright, suitable only for the garbage. And then there were some of the more recent additions. A giant stuffed bird, minus most of his feathers, was propped up against a wall. He appeared to be wearing a tie. Ainsley wondered if this had been one of the humorous pieces that Uncle Topper had gotten, only to be embarrassed when he brought Dali home and then relegated it to the attic. Other Uncle Topper oddities were the collection of coconut heads carved with grimacing faces, the giant model of what appeared to be the Great Pyramids and the Sphinx, and the mounted fish, a mammoth thing that had to have weighted over 100 pounds when it was caught. But beyond that, there were dozens of mirrors, old statuary, vases, clocks, lamps broken and whole, bed frames, wooden chests stuffed with linens and smelling of cedar and mothballs, and hundreds of books. But no paintings, no framed pictures, no canvases, nothing that could be the lost Dali.

"We've only made it through a third of this place," Gabe observed as he switched off one of the lights overhead. They had decided that rather than try to hunt through the house in search of new bulbs, they would exchange some of the working ones for the blown ones and then switch back as they moved along the space. It had worked fairly well, but as the illumination had been grouped in the farthest areas of the attic, the space next to the staircase seemed to recede into threatening shadows, and Ainsley had to work at keeping her imagination in check.

"What time is it?" Ainsley asked. In the dimness, with the rain a steady reminder of the gloom outside, it was hard to keep track of the time.

Gabe brought his lighted watch up. "It's after three. And I'm starving."

Ainsley nodded to herself. "Let's finish this bookcase and then head out," she said briskly. "We can always come back tomorrow."

"Tomorrow? Are you sure you want to spend your time coming out here again?"

"Tomorrow is fine," Ainsley said firmly. "Next week is Thanksgiving, and I doubt we'll have time to do anything then. I don't want this to wait any more than it needs to."

"About that," Gabe said slowly. "On the Saturday after Thanksgiving, my family has a tradition. We get together to make Christmas cookies in an all-day marathon. We roll them out, use cookie cutters, bake them, and then ice them and add decorations. They're the kind of cookies that are supposed to taste better after they age a little, so they're usually put away until the week before Christmas. But it's one of those things that our family always does. My sisters will be there. And my parents too. So I was wondering if you would want to come?"

Ainsley felt a little hesitation. She would be meeting with Gabe's family, who he obviously was very close to. She would be under the scrutiny of the two sisters who meant so much to him. She'd be on the cusp of a new stage in their relationship. At this point, it was either agree or?

THE COCKATOO CALLED

"Sure," she said smiling. "I'd love to come." Her heart had picked up the pace and she had to force herself to breathe more slowly. Meeting the family. Surely that couldn't be as scary as dealing with the threat she was facing now.

"Great," he said, but there was so much more behind the simple word. He bent, his lips skimming hers, ever so lightly. She smiled under the kiss. She felt his fingers brush her cheek and the kiss deepened. The attic was forgotten. The dust, cobwebs, creaky floor, and darkened nooks and crannies all slid to the back of her mind as she kissed him back, feeling the warmth flush her face and her heart increase.

The sound was so unexpected, so sharp and so loud, that she felt herself physically jump with the shock of it.

"What was that?" she blurted as Gabe spun around, facing the attic doorway, legs braced as though preparing for an attack.

"I don't know. Sounded like something big was dropped or fell over." Gabe started toward the stairs that led down to the second floor. "You stay up here. Just keep to the dark. Just in case."

He didn't say in case what, but disappeared down the stairs before she could protest. Ainsley obediently retreated behind one of the larger pieces of furniture, but instead of choosing one deeper in the room, she purposely chose one that was close enough to the stairs for her to hear what might be happening below. Gabe was crazy if he thought she was going to cower up here while he went off to a possible dangerous situation.

She pulled out her phone and held it clinched in her hand. She would call 911 if nothing else. Any kind of help, even if it turned out it wasn't needed, would be better than seeing something happen to Gabe.

She heard footsteps. The sound was a slow and cautious tread, someone uncertain of where they were going, or what they were doing. She was tempted to call out to see if it was Gabe returning, but the possibility that it wasn't Gabe, but someone else coming her way, kept her silent.

Then the sounds of movement drew nearer. They sounded heavy, labored. Uneven footfalls could be heard climbing the steps. A creak from where the old wood was protesting under the weight. The sliding shift of a misstep, another thump, and she could tell that they were almost to the head of the stairs. And it wasn't Gabe. Gabe would have called out. Gabe would have known that she was here and wouldn't have left her in the dark, frozen in fear, shrinking against the massive armoire that loomed over her.

At the top of the stairs, the steps stopped abruptly. She knew what they were seeing. The front part of the attic, the part where she hid in the uncertain camouflage of the shadows, was still mostly dark. They had moved most of the working bulbs to the other side, closest to the window, which was now only reflecting the dark gray dullness of the sky outside. It was obvious to anyone looking that someone had been here. But was it obvious that someone still was?

She felt the scrape of the shoes as a vibration under her knees. Her legs had gone numb, and her fingers gripped her phone so tightly that they were going numb as well. But a rattle from farther off had her catching her breath. This was a new sound, insistent and loud, it was clearly meant to be heard. In response, the footsteps nearer her began a quick retreat, over the attic floor and down the stairs, a rush of heavy footfalls on the wooden treads. Still she waited silent minutes before she slowly rose to her feet. Her heart was pounding so loudly that she doubted that she would have been able to hear anything over the drumming. But where was Gabe? Had he made the noise to draw the other person away?

All appeared as it had been before. The door was still propped open with the books, and the illumination from the lights in the stairway bled an etched rectangle on the floor of the attic. She went to stand at the head of the stairs, listening, listening, for the meeting of fists and flesh, the cry of attack, or pain, anything that let her know where Gabe was, or where the intruder had ended up.

When she heard nothing, she started her stealthy way down the steps, stopping at the bottom of the stairs and lingering in the doorway, listening intently. But nothing greeted her, so she carefully crept down the hallway, stopping at the red doors closing off Uncle Topper's room. From her vantage point, she could see the front door hanging open and the rain drenched exterior. She was still standing there at the top of the stairs when she saw a figure burst through the door, rain slickening dark hair.

"Gabe," she felt herself call out, unaware that she had been holding her breath until that very moment.

He turned and slammed the door behind him and then looked up to her, taking the steps two at a time. "He was here. Someone was here! I know it. But whenever I thought that I had figured out which room he was in, he wasn't. I couldn't ever get a definite location, but I could hear him. Did he come up there? Did he see you?"

He had stopped in front of her, and when he asked the question, his hands wrapped around the tops of her arms, bending down so that he could see her face more clearly.

THE COCKATOO CALLED

"I'm fine, just fine," she said quickly. "He did come up here, but I was hiding down behind some furniture, and he didn't stay. There was a noise from downstairs," she started.

"That was me," Gabe assured her. "I was trying to get his attention. I wanted him to come to me, but I didn't expect the noise to make him run."

"Are you sure it wasn't just a member of your family? Or the housekeepers?"

"They would have called out," Gabe said dismissively. "And besides, they all know my car by now. They would have known it was me." He was frowning as he dropped his hands by his sides. "No, whoever this was came here for a reason. And they didn't care that we were here. I don't like that."

She shivered realizing the implication. If they knew that someone was there, then they were obviously willing to confront them.

"Let's get out of here. Now."

Gabe took her elbow as they went back down the stairs. "What about the lights?" Ainsley asked as they headed out the front door. Gabe had his keys out and was locking the door behind them, but the porch lights illuminated his bent head.

"I'll leave them. I can get them when I come back tomorrow."

"When we come back," Ainsley amended.

He jerked at the door as though to assure himself that it was securely locked and looked down at Ainsley. His eyes were hard to read behind the lenses of his glasses. "I'm not sure if that's such a good idea. Both of us coming out here."

"That's the only way it is a good idea," Ainsley argued. "I'm not letting you come here by yourself, if that's what you're thinking. You'll just have to put up with me!" Without waiting for a reply, she headed out into the rain toward the car, hearing Gabe's quick steps behind her. She pulled open the door before he got to the car and had slid in and yanked the door closed before he made it to the driver's side. He folded his long frame into the driver's seat and turned to her, fresh droplets of water beading his glasses, one dripping off his nose.

"Are you going to let me talk you out of this?" he asked.

"What do you think?" she returned, buckling her seatbelt.

"Okay, so we'll talk about it later," he said quickly, and turned the key.

CHAPTER SEVENTEEN

She invited him in. Her house had become their typical meeting place, with Dali as the usual center of attention. But today, after a few greetings and petting him on his soft cheeks between the cage bars, they left him there and retired to the living room couch. Ainsley had gotten them each a towel and they took a few minutes trying to dry their damp clothes and hair.

Ainsley dropped her towel in a heap on the coffee table and looked at Gabe. "Do you want some coffee?" she asked, thinking of how chilled she had become despite the heat in the car.

"I do," Gabe said turning to her, "in a minute." His big hands framed her face and he pulled her close, his mouth settling on hers in a totally perfect way. Ainsley gave up trying to be composed and leaned into him, feeling his warmth, smelling the rain on his skin. She was just warming up, no, heating up nicely when he pulled away and tucked her in closer to his body.

"You know it would probably be better if you didn't go tomorrow," he said, nuzzling her neck, his arms tightening.

She drew back and looked into his eyes. With gentle fingers, she pulled off his glasses and sat them next to the crumpled towel on the coffee table. "You know that you're not going to win that argument," she scolded, and leaned in close. "We are in this together whether you want that or not." She looked at the little frown that marred his features and smiled a little. "The argument is done for now," she said with a mocking sternness. She bent close again and brushed her lips against his cheek. "Now return to what you were doing," she murmured against his skin.

"Ummm, yes ma'am," he growled low, and the subject was dropped.

*****

THE COCKATOO CALLED

The trill of the phone startled Ainsley out of a sound sleep. She wondered if she still had a smile on her face. The evening had been, well, she had enjoyed her time with Gabe, and it had been with great reluctance that she had let him leave.

She reached over to the cell phone plugged in by the bed and yanked the cord out while hitting the green accept button.

"Hello?"

"Ainsley?" Gabe's voice was sharp, totally awake.

"Yeah, yeah, it's me."

"Okay. That's good," he was breathing a little hard and she could hear the sound of, what was it, the hum of a motor in the background.

"Where are you?" she asked, pulling herself into a sitting position.

"On my way to Uncle Topper's," he said quickly.

"Why?" She felt slow and stupid coming out of such a deep sleep. She brushed a curl from her face, rubbing her eyes.

"I got a call. There's been a fire at the house."

"Oh, my God!" Her breath caught in her throat. "How bad? Was anyone there?"

"The housekeepers said that the fire alarm was hard wired into the house system. When the fire triggered the alarm, the fire department was automatically called. They notified the housekeepers because theirs was the number on record. They got ahold of me."

"But no one was there? At the house?"

"No. At least, there shouldn't have been anyone there. I'll find out more once I get there."

"Then I'll meet you there." She was already sliding out of bed, grabbing the jeans that she had left crumpled on the floor next to her bed.

"No!" Gabe's voice was loud. "No, I'll call you when I get there."

"Don't worry about that," she argued. "I know my way there. I'll just meet you. I can help."

"Ainsley, I don't know how safe this is. What if someone set the fire? What if this is all related? The house had been sitting empty for months and now suddenly, after we've been looking around in there, it's set on fire."

"You don't think it's something we did, do you?" Her mind was reviewing the day before, leaving the lights on in the attic, but had they left something else? Had they unintentionally started the blaze?

"No. The only lights we left on should have been fine. I think it was set. In fact, I'm almost sure it was. That's why I want you to stay at home. Keep your door locked. And I'll be out later."

Ainsley was shaking her head at him even though he couldn't see her. She had slipped on the jeans and was rummaging for a tee shirt in the dark. "You drive carefully," she said, avoiding his directions. "I'll talk to you in a little while." And she hung up.

He didn't call back as she finished dressing and putting her hair up in a hasty bun. She pulled on her shoes and grabbed a heavy sweatshirt. Her purse was hung on the hook next to the door and she grabbed it on the way out, stopping to lock the door behind her.

The rain had stopped. The pavement was still shiny and dark in places, reflecting the streetlamps in little bursts. She dropped into the driver's seat and fastened the seat belt. She pulled the door closed and started the engine, putting the car in reverse while glancing in the rear view mirror. No one was out in the middle of the night. For that, she was grateful. She felt like she could drive the way to Uncle Topper's pretty much without thinking. Her phone lay silent on the seat next to her, and she figured that Gabe had gotten to the house and was surveying the damage. Or else, the fire was still active, and he was hanging back, watching the memories burn. How awful that would be! The house, for all of its oddness, still had a lot of valuables inside, both intrinsically and sentimentally. Jack would be heartbroken. No doubt some of the other family members would be upset as well. And Gabe? She hoped that he wouldn't feel responsible for all of this. Because if he was right, if someone had deliberately set the fire because of their visit to the home, because of their search for the painting, then it was partly, perhaps, their fault.

Her thoughts were tumbling as she considered that angle. If the person after the Dali had set the fire, then that would mean that they had the painting, wouldn't it? They wouldn't set the home on fire if they thought that the painting was still there? It would destroy the painting along with everything else. So somehow, they knew that the painting wasn't in the house. But that brought up another equally disturbing question. If they knew that the painting was not there, that there was no way that Ainsley and Gabe would find it, why set the fire at all? To scare them? To warn them off? To give them a taste of what might be, what lengths that they would go to to prevent the painting from being found?

That was truly scary. Ainsley's house didn't have any fancy alarm to contact the fire department in a blink of an eye. She had the old battery powered devices that would warn her just in time to get out of the house before it went down in flames. And Dali? Her sweet bird with the sensitive lungs? Would just the fumes of a fire kill him?

She shuddered at the thought, but was relieved to see the drive ahead of her. All of this conjecture was doing her no good. Better to talk with

THE COCKATOO CALLED

Gabe, to see what had happened in the house, than to assume the worst.

The flash of lights from the trucks was garishly bright. There were two large trucks on site, and a greater number of other vehicles clogging the normally open driveway. Ainsley pulled her compact car in behind one of the more official looking sedans and switched off the engine. No one seemed to notice her. The firemen looked mostly finished with the fire, milling about gathering gear, shedding jackets. Other men were gathered in groups talking, some laughing, looking a little too much like a backyard picnic in Ainsley's opinion.

Beyond them bathed in its shadows was the house. There didn't appear to be any flames any longer. A dull red edging, embers caught in the wind, showed at one window, but the fire was definitely dying. And the fire had been the only light from within the walls of the house. Because now it stood, silent and dead, smoke snaking from windows and invisible seams. Ainsley was entranced by the look of it. Then she glanced back down at the movement around her. She stood frozen for a moment, her eyes scanning the groups looking for a familiar figure. But he spotted her before she saw him. He was walking toward her, his face in shadow so she couldn't read his expression, but she suspected that he was not happy.

"I thought that we agreed that you were going to stay at home," he said, his voice low. He caught her by the arms, punctuating the words with a hard embrace.

"I'm sorry," she murmured against his shoulder. Not sorry that she had come, but sorry that he had to watch the home burn. She had seen the way that he had looked at the place, had seen the odd pride, the fondness, the warmth that it had brought to his expression. Even if he didn't want to admit it, the house was a strong connection to an Uncle that he badly missed.

He pulled away. His hand went to her cheek and then tucked a lock of hair behind her ear. "You weren't going to listen to me anyway, were you?"

"If your request made sense, yes, I would listen. But this wasn't dangerous. I knew that there would be a lot of people here, including you. It's perfectly safe. And I didn't want you to be alone."

He nodded, and then turned as a man dressed in jeans and a tee shirt approached. "Gabe! Okay, we've got it under control. The men have been through, and it looks like everything's mostly out. Whatever is still burning is winding its way down now. There's been some damage, though. I'm not going to lie to you. And the water and extinguisher, well, it causes its own mess."

Gabe was nodding. "And now?" He looked tired.

"You called the law office? Left a message?"

"Yes, and I called my Uncle, the executer of the estate."

"Then that's all that needs to be done for now. You can't do anything more here. We'll be around for a while longer, cleaning up and making sure it's all taken care of. We'll let you know if there's anything else that we need. But for now, better for you to head back home. Call me tomorrow and we'll talk."

Gabe rubbed his face wearily. "Thanks for all of your help. You guys did a great job. I couldn't have asked for more." The men shook hands.

"I'll talk to you later then, and you have my number."

Gabe nodded and Ainsley watched as the man walked off to join the rest of his team. This was their job, she realized. And it seemed suddenly like a hard one. There was danger in putting out fires, that was for sure, but how many weeping families did they have to face, how many times did they have to say they were sorry for the family's loss, to see lives destroyed this way? She suddenly felt very grateful for her life, and put her arm around Gabe's waist for a quick embrace.

*****

Gabe rode with Ainsley back to her house. They had stayed another hour before leaving, but hadn't gone into the house, just watched the activity, the smoke lessen from a stream to a dribble. Gabe said he wanted to wait for daylight and hope that he would hear back from his Uncle or the law firm by then.

Ainsley opened the door to her little house and stepped back. "Come on in," she said, and closed the door behind him.

"I'll just crash on the couch," Gabe said, his face looking older with the strain. He looked a little gray, and Ainsley wondered how close to the fire he had gotten. Had he gone into the house? She wasn't going to ask him that now.

"That's fine," Ainsley responded. Her little house had the extra bedroom that she used for an office, but no guestroom. She didn't think he'd care. He looked just that tired. "I'll get some sheets and blankets out for you."

"Do you think I could take a quick shower? I smell like smoke."

"Of course," Ainsley said quickly. "Let me get things ready."

She went into her little bathroom and got out a fresh towel and washcloth. She unwrapped a new bar of soap and put it with the towel. Then, recalling a package of new toothbrushes that she had picked up at

THE COCKATOO CALLED

the grocery, she added that as well.

"It's ready," she told him.

"Thanks," he murmured and slipped past her.

While he showered, she found herself pacing her little house. Dali was moving restlessly in his cage, but she didn't want to get him off of his usual schedule, so she kept the lights dim. She took sheets and blankets out to the couch and started shifting the cushions and pillows until it resembled a bed. She heard the door open and Gabe stepped out, hair wet, wearing boxers and holding his bundle of clothes in front of him.

"I didn't have any PJs," he said shrugging.

"Sorry. I don't think mine will fit," she said smiling a little. He looked good in his boxers, so she wasn't complaining.

"My clothes smell like smoke," he said.

"You get comfortable, and I'll throw your things in to wash. I can dry them in the morning."

"Thanks," he said again.

She followed him into the living room and watched as he stretched out on the couch. He handed her the bundle of clothes, and she restrained herself from trying to tuck him in. She took the clothes into her tiny laundry room, dodging a couple pairs of shoes, and dropped the clothes into the empty washer. She switched on the machine and added soap while the basin filled. After she had dropped the lid down, she returned to the living room moving as quietly as possible.

Gabe was asleep sprawled on the couch. His head was turned toward the back of the couch, one leg almost falling off the narrow seat. Ainsley paused and gently pulled the blanket up over his bare shoulders. He didn't stir, and she resisted the urge to kiss him while he slept. With a little smile, she left him.

She tiptoed into her room and shed her clothes on the floor, pulling back on her nightclothes that she had left on the foot of her bed. The fatigue made her fingers feel clumsy and she dropped her cell phone on the table next to her bed, belatedly remembering to plug it in so that it would be ready for morning.

In seconds, she was asleep too.

*****

She woke to the delicious smell of cinnamon and coffee. It took her just a moment to remember the night before, the bitter smell of smoke, the silent drive, and seeing the exhausted form of Gabe sound asleep on the couch.

She sat up and rubbed her face. She slipped out of bed and went into the bathroom. Wow, she looked rough. But she didn't want to spend any extra time in here. She wanted to rush out, to throw herself into Gabe's arms, to hold him tight for just a little while. She stopped herself. At least she would brush her teeth and hair. She rushed through her quick toiletry and dressed.

Gabe was standing next to the coffee pot. He seemed to be struggling with her slightly more complicated coffee maker, but on the stove was a pan of perfectly browned cinnamon rolls, the buttery spicy scent totally intoxicating. He glanced up when he saw her and grinned.

"It seems to be working," he said gesturing to the pot.

"It smells delicious in here," she said, coming to stand next to him.

He put an arm around her and pulled her closer. "See, I'm clever. Lure you in with my cooking." He bent and kissed her mouth in a quick gesture. "Then I keep you by letting you fall in love with my bird."

She saw then that Dali was perched on the chair back, his usual haunt. The bird had a treat in one claw and was picking it apart, making his usual mess.

"Oh, Dali, are you glad that we're here?" she asked, pulling away from Gabe and reaching for the bird. She scooped up her feathered friend and cuddled him close.

"He was waiting for the cinnamon rolls, but he's not very good at it. He said he needed something to keep him busy in the meantime."

Ainsley smiled. "Not a surprise there." She put the bird back on his makeshift perch.

"Are you ready to eat?"

Ainsley helped him finish setting the table, laying out cream and sugar for the coffee. Gabe had even whipped up some homemade icing for the rolls. When everything was set, they sat down together.

"You didn't have to do this," Ainsley said, fixing her coffee to her liking.

"I know that I didn't have to, but I wanted to. After last night when you came out to rescue me, and I didn't even say thank you, I felt like I owed you one. A big one."

"You know you don't owe me anything," she argued.

"Owed is the wrong word," he said, a half smile tilting his lips engagingly. "I appreciate you for all that you are and what you did last night. Even if I said I didn't act like it, I didn't want you there, I guess I have to admit that I was wrong." He looked at her and sighed. "I didn't want you to come because I was worried about you. But after you were there, I realized that it was nice to have someone, you know, someone who cared about the house too. And I'm a selfish bastard, so I liked it that you were worried about me too."

"I know that," she scolded.

"It has just messed me up. I feel like all of my ideas were backwards. I thought for sure that the painting was there. I thought that we would find it, maybe get it to the law office or some bank vault, let it be known publically that we had it but that it was totally inaccessible, and the problem would just go away. No matter what happens with the painting after the will is read, at least it wouldn't be our problem anymore." He sighed. "But with the fire, that changes things. If the painting was there, then setting the house on fire is the very last thing that someone would do. It could very well have destroyed it. So I guess we were way off base with this one. The painting has either already been found, and whoever it is wants us to stop looking for it, or it was never at Uncle Topper's to begin with. And that I just don't understand. I don't know where else it could be. But it's not in the house."

"How bad was it? The house and the fire?" Ainsley couldn't get it out of her head, the way the house had loomed above them, heavy smoke billowing out like dirty clouds.

"The fire was set. That's for sure. I got a call earlier this morning. It wasn't exactly a professional job. Whoever it was used plain old gasoline, probably taken from the shed on the property. The shed had a padlock on it, always has been kept locked up, but that had been forced. There was gas and oil stored inside for the lawn mower. There wasn't much, but it was enough for whoever did this to start two separate fires."

"Two?"

"The biggest one was in the attic. Just where we were yesterday. And I felt like the biggest ass explaining that I was sure someone had been there while we were in the house, but I had chosen not to call the police."

"We didn't have any proof," Ainsley argued.

"I should have known better. Anyway, I'm going out to the police station to file a formal complaint later on today."

"Do I need to do that too?"

"They'll take our statement. They'll need to get our joint information so that they can look into it further."

Ainsley nodded. "And the other fire? Where was that one?"

"They went into Uncle Topper's bedroom. They started a fire in the middle of his damn mattress. Felt a little personal, don't you think?"

The image had Ainsley's stomach curling. Nothing else that had been done had seemed that personal, that direct, except perhaps the bird in the shower. That had been direct. And with Dali in the picture, it had been intensely personal. But that had been directed at her, and at Gabe she supposed. This, well this one had been directed at Uncle Topper himself. And who would try to communicate with a dead man? But no, that was wrong. Whoever it was may have been angry with Topper, but the fire had been meant for them. She was sure of that fact.

"This is such a disaster," Ainsley said. "And all for that painting. I almost wish they had found the painting and done whatever they wanted with it. It doesn't sound like anyone in your family would have missed it. It wasn't like it was at the top of anyone's list for things that they wanted to see. If it went completely missing, I doubt it would have caused any real concern with anyone. But now, with the fire, and all of this, it's just brought a whole lot of attention to the house and the collections."

"I think this just shows how uncontrolled this guy has gotten." Gabe was looking at her seriously. "It scares me a little. If he's gotten this out of control, in setting a fire without thinking, than who knows what else he might do."

Ainsley nodded. "So what now?"

Gabe ran his hand through his hair. "Now, we go back out to the house. I think we should be fine in the daylight. We'll check around inside as long as it's clear. I want to take some pictures to send to my Uncle. The insurance people will be out sometime during the week. Some of the damage is going to have to be fixed or the house might become even more unstable." He frowned a little. "There won't be any more searching. It's obvious that we don't need to do that anymore. And I'm not about to piss this guy off even more. He's already gone to great lengths to try to tell us something. I'm not messing with any of that anymore."

Ainsley could read his expression easily enough and stood. "Let's go then. Let's get out of here, take care of what we need to do, and then go out somewhere fun for the afternoon. We can shop for some of your family."

"Shopping?" One dark brow lifted, his face relaxing a little, and his lip curled in a half smile. "Only does a woman decide that the fun thing to do would be Christmas shopping."

"Do you have a better idea?" She had taken her plate to the dishwasher and stowed it within. When he approached with his, she took it and placed it in the rack. He was standing close when she stood upright and closed the dishwasher door.

"I have lots of ideas," he said, his smile going a little sultry.

"Like what?" Nothing like playing with fire this early in the morning.

THE COCKATOO CALLED

His mouth covered hers, tasting of coffee and cinnamon. And the man could kiss. She felt it stinging all the way to her toes, which curled on the bare floor. She let out a little sound and felt him smile against her lips. She let herself be pulled into his arms, against that long body, and sighed.

"Bad, bad bird," a gravelly voice interrupted, and she had to pull away with a chuckle. Dali was looking at them from his perch on the chair back, head cocked, dark eye directed at them with a disapproving expression.

"Jealous bird," Gabe responded, but went to rescue the bird.

CHAPTER EIGHTEEN

It was a beautiful day. Although the trees had long ago shed their glorious leaves, the sky was an almost turquoise blue with an occasional cotton candy cloud drifting over the expanse. The wind blew just enough to ruffle Gabe's hair as he climbed out of the car, his long legs eating up the drive, eager to finish what they had started.

The house looked like something out of a bad movie now. There was a sizable hole in the roof and smoke and burning wood had darkened some of the windows in the upper floors like a bruise spreading around blank eyes. What hadn't been burnt had suffered water damage, at least in the attic, the firefighters had told Gabe. He needed to be prepared.

The porch still had puddles of dirty water from the fire department's efforts to put out the blaze overhead. The door was locked. Gabe was a little surprised at that. He couldn't remember if he had locked the door when he left, but he strongly doubted it. Perhaps the housekeepers had been over earlier to check on the place and had locked up after themselves. He knew it didn't matter. The firefighters had had to break open the side door to gain access to the interior of the house anyway, so it wasn't like the place could be secured against vandals or anyone else that wanted to check the building out. And there were plenty of windows upstairs that had been broken out, either by the heat or the rescue attempt.

"Let's go," Gabe said unlocking the door and throwing it wide.

No electricity. For safety, the power had been turned off until the house could be further inspected. But Gabe had thought of that and had brought a couple high powered flashlights along with them.

They stepped inside the front foyer and the first thing that struck Ainsley was the smell. Smoke had more than permeated the air, it had coated it, making her feel like it was clinging to her skin, her lips, inside her mouth, all the way to her lungs.

THE COCKATOO CALLED

"Oh, wow, how do you get rid of that?" She asked, covering her mouth.

"I'm sure the lawyers will want to get in touch with someone about cleaning after the repairs are done. This is probably as bad as it will ever be."

Ainsley shined her flashlight around the room, startled when the light reflected back to her from the eyes of the stuffed animals. She jerked back slightly, and felt Gabe put his arm around her. "Scared myself," she said forcing a smile.

"Yeah, it's easy to do now."

The windows let in some of the natural sunlight, so they used their flashlights only when needed. The downstairs had mercifully remained mostly untouched. Gabe had his cell phone out and was snapping pictures as they went. In the library, he directed the beam to the ceiling, and Ainsley saw what must have been water from the floor above staining the white expanse.

"This must be under Uncle Topper's room. They had to put it out quickly. Looks like we'll need some repairs here." Gabe took a few shots of the ceiling before aiming his light a little lower. But the damage seemed to be limited to the ceiling only.

"Okay, we'll go on up, but we can't go into Uncle Topper's room," Gabe said, leading the way to the staircase. Upstairs, the window's light didn't reach as far as it had in the more open spaces downstairs so Gabe kept his flashlight on, shining a sweeping arc from one side of the hallway to the other.

"Lots of footprints," Ainsley observed. The firefighters had tracked in an abundance of mud and soot that stood out on the dark wood and the hallway runner. All the bedroom doors had been thrown open, and Gabe went from room to room, shining the light, taking a few photos, and closing the door after them.

"I see a few places where the water from upstairs leaked down here, but none look too bad." There was a strong sense of relief in his voice. Then he sobered. "Let's go check out Uncle Topper's room. Just get it over with."

The red doors were ajar, but Gabe pushed them wide. The destruction made Ainsley a little nauseated. The fire had been built on the bed and fed with whatever fuel that the arsonist had been able to lay his hands on. Ainsley felt a wave of gratitude that they had taken the photos with them because whatever may have been left were now curls of charred paper. The flames had engulfed the bed, most of the mattress, and then crept in a clear line across the room. Whatever had been his intent, it looked like the arsonist must have been stopped there. Perhaps the fires that he had set upstairs had started to grow, and he was unable to complete his plan. But whatever the reason, the burnt track stopped abruptly in the center of the room, just feet shy of the pool table. The resulting smoke and soot had stained the rest of the room a dingy gray. The floor was plainly ruined in places, and the paint next to the bed had heated, bubbled and split. The woodwork at the floors and crown molding there was charred, and a wave of blackened ceiling outlined a hole that revealed the upstairs floor joists.

Gabe sighed next to Ainsley and took out his cell phone again. "I'll get some pictures." He was shaking his head as he aimed the lens around the room. "This is such a waste. So stupid! What was that bastard thinking? How did this help anything?"

"I don't know," Ainsley said. She backed out of the room, letting him take the last few photos alone. She was suddenly feeling a wave of dread. She didn't want to see the attic. She had been up there before when the man had broken in. She had felt the cold fear, the terror of exposure. She didn't want to feel that way again, trapped and helpless. But that was ridiculous, she scolded herself. He had done the damage. He had succeeded, finally, to communicate what he wanted. He wanted them to stop, and they were going to do it. No painting was worth all of this. And since he had started the fire here, it was logical to believe that he knew the location of the painting. Perhaps he had it himself. Whatever was going on in his sick mind, he should be done with them. And done with Uncle Topper's house.

"One last stop," Gabe said at her side. "We won't take long. I'll just get a few pictures and send them on. Then we can lock this place back up. Is it too early for a beer, do you think?"

He was teasing, and Ainsley smiled back at him. "You have a beer, I'll have a glass of wine, then we'll shop 'till we drop."

"Or perhaps catch a movie?" he said hopefully. "Or better yet, watch a movie at your house and curl up on the couch?" He drew close and nuzzled her neck, making her cheeks heat before walking on.

"We'll see," she said playfully, following him to the attic door. It was closed as before. When he opened it, the drafty air sucked in some of the tainted warmer air from above and they both had to turn away and cover their mouths. Ainsley hadn't realized how accustomed she had become to the smoke that permeated the air below until she was confronted with this much worse atmosphere.

Gabe muttered a curse and aimed his flashlight at the stairs. They were intact, but very dirty now with the combination of grime from the fire and the footprints of men trying to save the house. "Nice," he said bitterly, and grabbed the narrow railing as he went up the steps. At the top of the stairs, the door that had been propped open before was still held ajar, but now the old stack of books looked like a seamless gray box. The ancient paper had reacted to the intense heat; flaking and burning even though the bulk of the flames hadn't gotten this far. It looked as though the fire had been set closest to the window on the far end of the attic, but as downstairs in Topper's room, the arsonist had created his path of gasoline that meandered over some of the old furniture, through piles and stacks of debris, dipping into the deeper recesses of the space to leave destruction in its wake.

Gabe cursed again. "Looks like he might have enjoyed this," he said grimly. "He managed to get almost every piece that we uncovered, and then went on to target things that we didn't even look at." He was shaking his head. "He took out some of these things just out of spite, I'll bet. There was no reason he needed to do that."

Ainsley had to agree. Among the things that had been burned almost beyond recognition was a full sized baby cradle that looked hand carved, and a giant dollhouse that must have brought some young girl hours of joy in the distant past. "Gabe, just take your pictures," Ainsley said tiredly. They could go no further into the depths of the attic. They were probably farther than the fire department would have liked anyway. Better to take the pictures and escape.

"Yeah, okay," Gabe agreed, taking one halting step forward and pulling his phone out again. "Can you aim your light out there? I want to get some better pictures, but my flash won't reach."

Ainsley obediently held out her light at arm's length, the beam piercing the darkness. Almost simultaneously, she heard a noise behind her, and then a slam, as the door to the stairway was rammed home. She spun, her light still out, and saw a blur of a shape come at them. She heard the sound of something hard hit something soft, and realized with horror that Gabe was falling, dropping to the floor in a strange boneless heap that would never have happened had he been conscious.

"Drop the light." The voice was hard, mean.

"What?" She was trying to turn the light towards the voice when she felt a hard blow to her hand and her fingers went numb just before a white-hot flame of pain raced up her arm.

Then the light was directed at her, sharp in her face, forcing her to close her eyes and stagger back, her hand still a throbbing ball of pain.

"I said drop the light. You're not very smart, are you?"

She was blinking furiously, trying to get her eyes adjusted as the light moved from her face to the middle of her chest. She could see the heap on the floor that was Gabe. He wasn't moving. She found herself staring very hard at his shape. Was he breathing?

"Now we're going to figure something out, you and I." The voice was light now, as though amused. "We need to know where the old man put the painting. Of course, if it's up here, that's all the better. But if it's not, than I must insist that you tell me where it is."

"What?" She was standing so still, blinking, trying to see, trying to think. "I don't know where it is."

"Yes," the voice held the sibilant until it sounded like a hiss. "You do. But let's just see what else you might know." She heard footsteps, and then he was there, close and in the circle of light.

Such an ordinary face. A grown man, somewhere in his late 40s or early 50s, a little bit of gray frosting his brown hair and a heavy slack face that held no humor. But familiar, she realized. She had seen him somewhere before.

"So tell me, what have you learned about the Dali?" he asked suddenly. His face still had an eerie blankness to it.

Her throat felt closed, but she saw with dread the dark shape of the gun and forced herself to talk. She thought for a moment of trying to fake ignorance, but she realized that he might have been standing there a lot longer than they had been aware of his presence. What had he heard of their conversation? How long had he followed them? He must know about their search for the painting, so the lie would only anger him further. "I, well, we know that Uncle Topper bought the painting in Spain and brought it home. He told people that he had it here in the house and was going to get it framed. But then he must have decided not to frame it. That was the last that anyone heard of it, and we know that he never showed it to anyone after that." Her mind seemed to be slowing, shutting down with the fear, because she could see in his hand a gun.

"Oh, surely you know more than that! Have you seen it? This masterpiece?"

"No," Ainsley said quickly. "At least, we thought that we had seen a picture of it. It was a portrait." Her eyes were on the gun. No wonder her hand felt broken. If he had struck her with the gun, and it was a sizable weapon, it had probably crushed some of her bones. But now her hand had started to go numb.

"Yes, a portrait. A woman. A nude," the voice had gone from calm to tense, clipping the words off as though biting the phrases into chunks.

"But we never found it."

"So you say." The voice had gone all soft. She looked back to the man's face and saw that he was again very serene. "And he named his bird Dali. Funny, don't you think? He liked that perverted artist. Flaunted his work."

Ainsley felt a strange disconnection. She didn't want to look away from that plain face, but she wanted to see Gabe. Gabe, whom she loved. Gabe, whom she would not lose.

"Let me show you something," the man went on. "Since you know so much of his side of the story, I think you will find this very interesting." He tucked the flashlight under his arm, and with his free hand rummaged in his pockets until he brought out a paper, very creased, very old, almost greasy from being handled so frequently. "Read it," he said, thrusting it toward Ainsley.

She hesitated. The paper was printed in spidery handwriting with loops and curls, very feminine. There were places that the words had faded to almost invisibility, and other areas where moisture had spread the ink in blotches. But her brain, her mind refused to decode even a single word.

"So you see, this is from my dear mother. And she was so proud. Proud to know this famous man, be his model, be his woman. Proud to be among the wealthy, the famous, the sinners!" Again his sounds had a hiss, and his flat eyes seemed almost empty.

"I, I," her voice was betraying her. Terror had crept up her throat.

"So she believes that she is famous. She thinks that she will live," he took a deep breath, his face contorted, "forever." His hands were shaking, making the paper and the gun tremble. The light, still tucked under his arm, gave a funhouse effect to his features, elongating and distorting him.

"She was the model for the painting." She was staring at his plain face and thinking of the woman in the portrait. So this was her son? And he wanted the painting?

"And she was so happy about that," he said, spittle dotting his lower lip at the last word.

"It was a lovely painting," Ainsley said hesitantly, unsure of what he expected her reaction to be.

"It is blasphemy! My mother, bared to the world, part of that group!" He had turned on her, dropping the letter, fury in his voice.

Then she almost felt the click as she realized the truth. "You came from the theological seminary looking for the painting. You didn't want it because it was valuable. You wanted it because it was a nude of your mother." She could remember the conversation in the antique shop when Topper's friend had told them about the other person searching for the painting. They had known that it didn't have anything to do with the man's religious affiliations. This was no professional interest of his. Instead, he had been on a mission. This man's impetus behind wanting the piece was very different from theirs, or any other collectors. He wanted to hide it, make sure the public never saw it again, destroy it.

"I cannot have that pornography seen any longer," he said darkly, affirming her assumptions. "I have to finish this. I have to save my mother and her reputation. I know that the man that owned this house had the painting, and I thought for sure that it had been given to him," he gestured to Gabe's still form on the floor. "But you both were back here again looking for the painting, so I know now that it never left this house. You've been so very helpful, but always a step behind me. I'd already been to Florida, to the museum, but I have to admit, the boat never entered my mind. If I had known about that, you would have never seen the photograph of the painting." He was frowning, and his voice had taken on a lecturing tone. "But I know now that the painting has to be here. The old man knew that he shouldn't have bought it and smuggled it here. He was hiding it! He knew it was wrong!" He bent and snatched the paper from the floor. "But she never did. Mother never knew what she had done was such blasphemy." He gestured to Ainsley with a quick jerky motion. "Read it! You can see that she had been led down the path." He was holding out the letter again, and Ainsley felt her stomach heave.

"I can't," she said weakly.

"Read. It."

The words were not righting themselves. They refused to be still. With the wavering, uncertain light of the flashlight, the letters seemed to gain movement. "I can't. I just," she didn't see him strike out with the gun, but one of the sharp edges must have caught on her skin, because she saw the red well up and begin to stream down her arm, Oh God, her good arm. And the pain that had burned in her now numb hand seemed to transfer in a moment to that wound. She could see her flesh parting, the bubble of blood, and she felt the darkness coming. She was going to pass out. Of all the damn times, she…

When she lost her balance, she fell forward. She did not intend to hit him, but she was weak anyway, and she distantly felt the cushion of his body as she dropped to the floor. Only at the ragged edges of her dimming vision did she see the other movement in the room, and her last thought was Gabe.

*****

THE COCKATOO CALLED

"Ainsley, Ainsley, come back to me honey. God, I'm sorry. I should have never brought you here. I should have never let you get involved. I love you. God, I love you so much." She felt him holding her tightly, the trembling in his hands as his fingers grazed her cheek, and then the soft dampness of his lips as they touched her forehead, over and over, gentle kisses like one might give a sick child. "I'm so sorry. I love you. I'm such an ass. I should have never brought you. Such an ass."

"You're not an ass," her voice was raw and painful. "You have a cute ass, but you're not an ass."

His lips stilled. "Ainsley?"

She forced her eyes opened and looked into his face. He had a trace of blood coming from his hairline, and she directed her gaze away from that and to his eyes. "Yeah?"

"Oh, God, I thought. I mean, I didn't know what happened."

"The crazy man," she said, interrupting him.

"Managed to fall and knock himself out. At least, I think that's all he did."

"But he's not, he can't," Ainsley couldn't quite get the words out right.

"He looks bad. I'm not exactly sure what he hit. But the police and an ambulance are on their way." Gabe held her a little tighter. "I'm here now," he said.

"The gun?" She felt a little panic bubble in her throat.

"I have that too," Gabe said.

And they heard sirens.

*****

She would have to have surgery to fix her hand. She had also gotten two layers of stitches in her opposite arm, but by then, she had gotten some fine medication that had taken the edge off of her panic.

Gabe had gotten treated for his head wound, and was propped up in a wheelchair at the side of her cot. There was a loud bustle outside and the door swung open. Jack.

"Girl!" he exclaimed.

Ainsley felt a little sheepish. She hadn't expected that Jack would visit her. She wasn't even admitted technically. "Oh, Jack, you didn't have to come," she said.

"Of course I did! I heard about that maniac." He ducked down close to her. "Are you kids okay?"

"We'll be fine," Gabe was holding Ainsley's hand gently.

"Absolutely insane! This whole thing is totally crazy! Did you ever find out who he was?"

"Bruce. Bruce Danburg."

"And who the hell is that?" Jack's face was red, whether from excitement or agitation, she couldn't say.

"He was just a man. But he considered himself to be a very religious man, and when he found out that his mother had been a nude model, especially for an artist like Dali, he just wanted to destroy the painting." Gabe's voice was low. "He was just one crazy bastard."

"I heard he's here too." Jack was standing at the bedside, but looked too big and uncomfortable. Ainsley wondered where Hemingway was, and almost wished that he was there to lighten the mood. But did they allow birds in the hospital? She doubted it.

"He is. He's in surgery. When he fell, he hit his head on the way down, maybe on a piece of furniture. They won't tell us much, but from what I've heard through the grapevine, they have to take some pressure off his brain by drilling a hole," Gabe rubbed his face slowly.

"Fell?" Jack looked at Gabe. "I thought you knocked him flat."

Ainsley smiled faintly. "I think it was my fault. When I saw that I was bleeding, I lost it. As I passed out, I fell and took him with me."

"Well, now," Jack's smile broadened. "Isn't that a great story!"

Gabe was smiling now too. "Yep, if it hadn't been for Ainsley's problem with blood, he might have gotten away with taking us both out," he said. "Never thought it would be useful, did you?" He was looking at Ainsley, gently smoothing a hand over her forehead.

"No," she admitted. "I never did." She hesitated. "But you know, the man looked familiar, and I think I know from where. I saw him at Feeder's when I took Dali there. He must have been hanging around, waiting to see if anyone found the bird. I bet he followed me from there. I thought that someone might have been outside my house a few days ago."

Gabe's face seemed to pale. "I just can't believe how this got so convoluted."

"Boy, it's over now, so you don't need to dwell on it," Jack said heartily, trying to pull Gabe out of his mood. He turned to Ainsley, changing the subject. "They're not going to keep you?" Jack was pacing at the side of the bed now as though the small room could barely hold him.

She felt him pause and turned her head to smile at him. "No. I'll come in for outpatient surgery sometime next week," she responded..

"Well then, that's good I suppose," Jack said uncertainly.

THE COCKATOO CALLED

"Not good for Ainsley. I hate that you have to have surgery." Gabe's voice was a little raw. His face had tightened, frustrated for her. "I'm so sorry," he began, but she shook her head.

"This had nothing to do with you, and nothing to do with me, or any of us. This was some crazy man's attempt to cover up something that he thought his mother had done in her past that was wrong. When she modeled for that painting, I'm sure she was proud of her part in it. It was a beautiful piece. It was her son's misinterpretation of it that turned it so wrong. And that wasn't my fault, or yours, or Uncle Topper's, or the artists."

Gabe nodded, holding her hand to his lips and dropping a kiss on her knuckles. "But he almost cost us our lives."

"But why did he do this now? The son, Bruce, I mean." Jack asked.

"He had been looking for the painting for a long time." Ainsley said, thinking of the man's very ordinary face. "It just took him some time to track it down to Uncle Topper. And when he found out that Uncle Topper had died, and that Dali had been sent to Gabe, he figured that Gabe had the painting. Because he had the bird, he was sure that he had the painting too. I'm guessing that's why he went through your apartment. And I'm guessing he was trying to cause a commotion, so he opened the cage to get Dali. I just assume that Dali escaped at some point. So when he determined that the painting wasn't with you, he figured that it was still in the house. And he didn't want to see it, or own it. He just wanted to destroy it, so it didn't matter to him if it went up with the house in flames, or if he got it some other way."

"I missed a lot of what he said," Gabe said. "So he didn't know where the painting was?"

"No, Ainsley agreed. "He never did. He just knew that your uncle had bought it, maybe a little illegally since he abruptly stopped showing it. Then nothing. And now I wonder if we will ever find out."

"But why tear up old Topper's things?" Jack frowned out the window at the waning light.

"Maybe because he was just angry about it. That Topper had the painting? This guy didn't exactly seem to be firing on all cylinders." Gabe looked toward Jack, shrugging.

"Or maybe Topper knew the man's mother. We took a lot of pictures. I know some of them were missing. It could be that when he came searching for the painting, he saw his mother in some of the photos posted in Topper's room. It would explain why he tore everything up so much."

"It makes sense," Ainsley agreed, and closed her eyes, feeling fatigue weigh her down. She just wanted to go home. She just wanted to see her parents, to feel secure again, to be safe.

By the time they were released to go home, his mother, father, and one of his two sisters surrounded Gabe. Ainsley's parents had taken a little longer to reach the hospital, but were ready to take their girl home. It was a strange introduction for the families, with Jack ducking out before everyone could get there, but Ainsley was unwilling to let Gabe go without meeting her family. He was an important part of her life now, and she wanted everyone to know it.

"Then I'll be out to visit you when I'm cleared to drive," Gabe said, holding Ainsley's hand as she was shifted into a waiting wheelchair. They looked funny, the two of them in their chairs, their clothes and hair stained with ashes and blood. Ainsley was sure she would just throw away her clothes. She never wanted to see them again.

"That's fine," Ainsley said, wincing as her hand was shifted in its heavy wrappings.

"And you call me when you get in," he said gently.

"I will," she said. Then she bent over and beckoned him to do the same. "We still have a movie to watch," she said playfully in his ear, and he grinned.

*****

Ainsley climbed out of her car with Dali in the carrier next to her. She leaned over and grabbed the handle of the crate, leaning over to make kissy noises. Dali returned the compliment, making contented sounds between obnoxious kissing sounds. Ainsley laughed, delighted.

She used her foot to close her car door and balanced the crate gingerly. Her other hand was still in the protective cast. The surgery hadn't been terrible, but she would forever have extra screws just beneath the skin to remind her of the terrible moments in the attic.

Dali was still chattering when she knocked on Gabe's door. He opened it and grinned. Ainsley had to smile back. Gabe had gotten his hair cut short to go with the spot that had been shaved to allow for stitches. The hair was growing back in, but slowly.

"You ready for some work?" he asked, taking the cage from her.

"I am, but you promised to feed me," she agreed.

"The chili will be done in an hour. That should give us enough time to finish." He strolled in the living room. The tree, a five-foot live evergreen that looked like it had seen better days, was already in the stand next to the window. "I'll just set Dali up here while we finish."

THE COCKATOO CALLED

He put the crate on his little coffee table and opened the door. The bird strolled out, confident and at home in the apartment. And he should be, Ainsley thought. This was going to be his part time home. Their agreement to have joint custody had been a joke really, but that was what it most resembled. Gabe would keep the bird for a few days, and then he would go back to Ainsley's house for a while. Gabe put out his hand and told the bird to 'step up'. The bird obeyed, and Gabe took him to the open cage door to sit while they finished decorating the Christmas tree.

"Do you have everything that you need?" Ainsley asked.

"I think so," Gabe said. "I have lights, some ornaments, tinsel, garland, and help to put it all together."

"And Christmas cookies for dessert," Ainsley added. She had gone to Gabe's parents' home the weekend before to enjoy their holiday cookie making. It had been delayed for an additional week so that Ainsley could have her surgery and a few days to recover, but she had enjoyed it thoroughly.

"True," Gabe said. He came close to Ainsley and put his arm around her. "You know, it's not everyone who gets to take home the cherished cookies before Christmas has started."

"My charm," Ainsley said playfully.

Gabe bent and kissed her gently. "I agree," he said with a gentle smile.

"Okay, so let's start," Ainsley said quickly, knowing that the kissing could get distracting, and they wouldn't get anything done.

"Yes, ma'am," Gabe said with a knowing smile.

She gave him a smacking kiss on his cheek and went to the first box, "okay, lights first," she directed.

After the promised hour, they had finished with the tree decorations and were having their spicy chili dinner at the little table. Dali was strutting around on the table, turning his feathers a light shade of orange when he ate the chili beans with relish.

"So are you okay with leaving him here tonight or do you want him to stay with you a little longer?" Gabe was smoothing the bird's feathers as he bent to grab some crackers.

"He can stay here," Ainsley said. "Next week I'll be spending most of the week at my parent's place anyway. And he needs to get used to living here again."

"Part time," Gabe said gently.

"Um, yes."

"About that," Gabe was looking a little hesitant, and it caught Ainsley's attention. "I know that we made up this plan to share the bird, but I think he'd be happier if he was able to be with both of us. You know, all the time, both of us."

Ainsley sat very still, uncertain of what he was saying but afraid to ask.

"So, ah, not that this would be anything official, but say I were to ask you to be his permanent parent, you know, and stay here with us, and maybe, get married, would you say no?"

She stared at him. "Are you proposing to me?" she squeaked.

"No, no, that wouldn't be romantic at all, sitting eating chili with a parrot on the table. Not the atmosphere that would be right at all. Except," he pulled out a box with a strange loop glued to the top. "Dali, fetch," he said, and the bird strutted over to the box and grabbed the loop with his huge black beak. "Okay, give," he commanded. Dali looked between them, and walked over to Ainsley, dropping the box next to her plate and stealing one of her spaghetti noodles before she could catch him.

"For me?" She was talking to the bird, but the question was directed to Gabe where he sat very still and serious across the table.

"Yes."

She carefully picked up the box and opened the lid. Inside was a twist of soft white feathers, and looped around them, was a ring with a single diamond solitaire.

"I know we haven't known each other that long, not long at all, but I felt like, I mean, I feel like…"

"Yes!" Ainsley exclaimed.

"Yes?"

"Yes, I'll marry you! You and your bird!"

*****

Dali helped them clean up. Turns out that soapsuds, propelled by flapping wings, would fly halfway across the room if someone wasn't watching a cockatoo closely enough. After that, they put him on the door so that they could finish up in peace.

"Okay, so we'll get your cage ready now," Gabe said to the bird. He had already put in the water, but now he added food and treats. He added a few new toys that they had found on sale just before the holidays.

"Do you want me to put paper down in the tray?" Ainsley asked.

"If you don't mind."

She grabbed a handful of newspapers, pausing to admire the way the diamond on her ring caught the light, sending out shards of colors. She

THE COCKATOO CALLED

went back over to the cage and looked at the bottom. There was a wire handle to pull out the grating on the floor of the cage, which she ignored, but looked below. "There are two trays here," she said to Gabe.

"Yeah, I don't know why. I just use the top one."

Ainsley pulled out the top tray but then hesitated and pulled out the second one as well. In the bottom of that one, newspapers already lined the metal. "Maybe your Uncle used both, alternating them or something," she said thoughtfully, picking at the newspaper. It was old. The white of the paper had begun to yellow, so it had been there for quite some time. "I guess I'll change it out," she said grimacing.

"Sure," Gabe said. "Hand the old stuff to me, and I'll pitch it." He held out his hand and Ainsley grabbed the shallow stack of papers. A few sheets fluttered to the floor when she pulled them free. She noticed that they felt heavy.

"Wait," she said slowly. She left the other papers and gently began to take off the upper layers. Just beneath the newspaper was a different kind of wrapping, a plain white sheet with a slick texture. "What is this?"

Gabe leaned over and carefully folded back the white paper. He moved slowly, but then more quickly, revealing colors beneath.

"The Dali," he said, looking in awe at the painting now resting in Ainsley's hands. "He hid it in the cage."

"Oh," Ainsley felt speechless, and stood slowly, resting the painting on the coffee table.

"He had gotten the threats. He knew that someone didn't want him to have the painting. So he hid it. I guess he knew that this was one place that no one else would look."

"Do you think that's why he stopped talking about it? Do you think that crazy man was threatening people even then?"

"The theologian? Oh yeah, I'm almost sure he was. And I think that he was serious enough that my Uncle decided not to continue with his plans."

"You think your uncle was afraid?"

Gabe shook his head, looking at the painting before them, intricate and beautiful and slightly disturbing. "He must have been. He stopped talking about it. He basically denied that he had it. And then he hid it."

"And he made sure that when he died, it would not stay in the house, that it would go with the bird to a new home where it would be safe."

"Safe was certainly debatable," Gabe said wryly.

"It's safe now. That sick man will be locked up for a good long time for his crimes. The arson, the terrorizing, the violence."

"All because of his reputation. He was afraid that if people knew that his mother had been the model for this, that his career would be ruined."

"Not exactly the ideal man of God," Ainsley agreed. "But he's put away. And the painting is here. So now what?"

"So tomorrow, we put this in the bank. I have my valuables to take care of now," Gabe said, his half smile easing his features.

Ainsley stood and threw her arms around him. "I do love you," she said, holding him hard.

"Bad, bad bird," Dali scolded.

ACKNOWLEDGEMENTS

I'd again like to thank my publisher, Tony Acree (award winning publisher!), my wonderful editor, Lynn Tincher (and awesome writer), and my beta readers including my mother, Kathleen Lanham and Jeannine Konesko.

I would also like to give my thanks for my wonderful community in Oldham County Kentucky where I was born, raised, and still remain.

And to my readers, thanks for finishing the story with me!

AUTHOR BIO

Rachael Rawlings is a full time mother, wife, writer, pet owner, and Speech Language Pathologist. Her main goal is to tell a good story, dream a little bit, and share her joy about the world we live in.

She lives with her husband, James, a professional architect; her three children, Faith, Nicholas, and Chase; and two dogs. She grew up and lives in the small town of Crestwood, Kentucky and is proud to call it home.

She thrives on good coffee, chocolate, great friends and family. To learn more about Rachael's work and her upcoming releases, visit her on her website: http://rachaelrawlings.wix.com/rachael-rawlings

THE COCKATOO CALLED

CPSIA information can be obtained at www.ICGtesting.com
Printed in the USA
LVOW10s1801060316

478004LV00023B/792/P